Diane Helentjaris's writing celebrates the lives of the overlooked and unsung. She has published multiple magazine articles and a book of poems called *Diaspora*. Her work appears in the bilingual Greek and English anthology *Glimpses of Our World* and the short story international anthology *Strife & Harmony*. She was a 2020 finalist in the Iceland Writers Retreat Alumni Award. She has a BA in Interdisciplinary Humanities, a Medical Doctor degree, and a Master's in Public Health. She lives in Leesburg, Virginia with her husband, son, and spaniel.

The Indenture of Ivy O'Neill

Diane Helentjaris

AIA PUBLISHING

The Indenture of Ivy O'Neill
Diane Helentjaris

Published by AIA Publishing, Australia
ABN: 32736122056
http://www.aiapublishing.com

-

All characters in this publication are fictitious and any resemblance to real persons, living or dead, is purely coincidental.

Paperback ISBN: 978-1-922329-29-5
Hardback ISBN: 978-1-922329-31-8

Dedication

To my brother Greg,
who opened the path to this world for me.

IRELAND

Chapter 1

Aird Mhór, Contae Phort Láirge, Éire
(Ardmore, County Waterford, Ireland)

July 1690

The sun came up as always on the day Ivy O'Neill learned to hate. Eight years old, she gamboled down the Cliff Walk toward the headland. Her sister, Honora, at three years of age, scrambled to keep up. Wind laden with the sea's tang buffeted the girls. Their mother needed berries.

A faint footpath off the Cliff Walk pointed Ivy and Honora to the berry patch. A few hundred yards from the O'Neills' cottage, hillocks and arching canes created a secluded and secret world for the sisters. Overhead the sea wind snarled, its chilly fingers unable to reach the girls in their sheltered nook. The sun warmed Ivy's shoulders through her cotton dress. Golden highlights glinted among her red curls.

"Ouch!" Ivy stuck her finger as she probed the raspberry canes. She peeked into Honora's willow basket. Five berries.

Honora stopped chewing and looked up at her sister. Her eyes flashed blue and green through copper lashes. Like her father, sister, and two older brothers, Honora's right eye was blue and her left eye green. Even though Baby Aiden's eyes had yet to change from the hazy gray of the newborn, everyone knew his eyes would not be a matched set.

Taunted as "spawn of the devil" by a town boy when she was five, Ivy had run to her father. He hugged her and pulled her onto his lap. "Ivy, darling, everyone's different. Your brother Sean has black hair. Father Declan has the hugest, longest nose I've ever seen. His nose doesn't stop him from sharing the Word. That boy in town, I'll wager, has something that sets him aside from everyone else, too. Our differences add salt to our lives."

Ivy had snuffled, jumped off Patrick O'Neill's knee, and never again regretted anything about herself.

She looked down at her sister. "Don't fret, Honora. You can eat them. We just need to be sure to take a few home to Ma. She wants enough for a pie. Remember, Father Declan's coming by to baptize Aiden tomorrow, and Ma wants him to stay for supper. Daddy says babies need to be baptized for the good of their souls, else they go to limbo. Don't want Aiden to go there. We can't go to church, so Father Declan's coming to our house."

"Church?"

"No church. Daddy says it's not safe right now. Don't worry. We'll have mass at home for a while, just until the English soldiers move on. They're not true believers and just don't understand."

Honora nodded and went back to chewing berries. Red juice dribbled down her chin and dripped onto her bare feet.

The girls, their backs to the sun and their faces shadowed, resumed picking in a companionable silence. Identical to Ivy in coloring, gracefulness, and leggy build, Honora appeared to be a miniaturized version of her older sister.

With soft rustles, the brambles gave up their fruit.

Ivy daydreamed. She relived the previous day's outing. The O'Neill girls had gone on a morning wander with their mother after chores. Ivy helped wash the dishes. Though asked to sweep up the sand left by their fishermen father and older brothers, Honora mostly poked at the tabby cat with her broken-off broom and giggled when he hissed.

Their mother often took Ivy and Honora outdoors on fine days while their brothers Rory and Sean fished with their father. She said the exercise helped them grow strong and "cleared their heads of cobwebs" as well. Ivy worried at first about the cobwebs. Were there really any inside her? Her mother laughed and explained it was just a saying, words, and not real.

Yesterday they had rambled down the Cliff Walk to the Round Tower. The ancient stone turret overlooked their village of Ardmore and pointed its narrow finger to heaven, silently and faithfully guarding a necklace of ruins and graves.

From the heights of the Cliff Walk, the girls had seen fishing boats bobbing in the cove. They wended their way through the tilted gravestones. Like ducklings, they trailed their mother to the ruined cathedral. Although the slate roof had clattered away years earlier, its ornately carved walls still stood firm on the stone floor. Time had erased many details in the carvings. Only ghostly figures remained to carry the rhythm and beauty of the religious messages. Adam and Eve stood naked, separated by the Tree of Knowledge. A harp spoke of the music of life. King Solomon sat forever in judgment and pondered the fate of the baby held out to him.

Ivy never tired of hearing the tale. Her mother's melodious voice, low-pitched and rich, rose and fell dramatically. Ivy always held her breath at the king's admonition to cut the baby in two. She'd let out a relieved sigh as her mother described the child's rescue. The girls had no trouble falling asleep for their afternoon nap after a trip to the Round Tower's ruins.

Ivy paused in her berry picking. "Honora, maybe Ma will

take us on a ramble today. We must hurry, though. You need to pick more berries than you eat. Come on. What do you say?"

"But I like to eat berries. I'm hungry."

"All right, all right. I'll pick as fast as I can. You go on and eat. I'll put some of mine in your basket before we get home."

Honora giggled, her lips rimmed in juice and her chin stained.

"You're right, Honora. Gathering berries is the best chore yet. All by ourselves. And we can even eat them if we want. Look." Ivy tossed a raspberry up into the air and expertly caught it in her mouth.

Honora nodded, unable to speak. She'd stuffed her bulging cheeks chock-full of raspberries.

"Ma might be done hanging the clothes. Aiden's asleep for sure. That's all he does now, all swaddled in his cradle. I can't wait till he's big enough to play. I like to hold him, don't you?"

"I like to rock."

"Yes. Me too. He's the sweetest baby ever."

Ivy knew her mother was probably watching the path for the girls' return, anxious to get started baking the highly anticipated fruit pastry. She quickened her plucking and pulled several berries at a time off the canes.

A breeze ruffled the tattered hem of Ivy's dress and brought with it the smell of burning peat.

"Ma must be baking the bread already, Honora," said Ivy. "I can smell the peat burning."

Bread fresh from the hearth held a place of honor in Ivy's life. She would hover by the table as her mother cut a thick slice from the warm loaf, slathered it with golden butter, and split it between her daughters. Ivy would take her bread and sit on the stoop, eyes closed. She would savor each bite, rolling the warm, buttery morsels in her mouth. Finished, the sparrows would hop in for her crumbs. The thought of a new loaf spurred

Ivy into action.

"Let's go, Honora. You've et enough berries. Time to go home and get some bread."

The breeze picked up as the girls emerged onto the Cliff Walk. Gusts of wind carried a pungent odor and a woman's screams.

Ivy's heart jumped in her chest—the horrible noises were from her mother.

"Come on, Honora." Ivy grabbed her sister's hand. "Something's wrong. We have to help."

The berry baskets fell to the ground. Out spilled the crimson harvest. Honora's head swiveled back. She began to blubber.

"Shh. Stop it, Honora. We'll be back."

Ivy dragged and coaxed Honora along the Cliff Walk. Reaching the final rise before their home, she scooped her sister up in her arms. Smoke rose skyward ahead. She heard men with harsh foreign voices and the drumming of horses' hooves intermingled with her mother's wailing.

Ivy's sweaty hands slipped as Honora squirmed in her arms.

"Honora," she whispered, "shush. Be very, very quiet."

Honora, her lips pressed together tightly, gave a nod. Her berry-stained chin quivered.

The two crawled up to their home's privet hedge. Ivy peered through a thin patch in the shrubbery and quickly turned Honora's head away from the sight.

"Don't look, Honora. Look at me instead."

Orange, red, and yellow tongues of fire licked and roared up the walls of the O'Neills' cottage. Acrid black smoke billowed through the beams as the final sheaves of thatch disintegrated into ash and drifted away.

Wearing coats as scarlet as the flames, three mounted soldiers, upwind of the fire, watched the house burn. The wild-eyed war horses tossed their heads and stamped their hooves, nostrils flared. Ivy had never seen anyone in such bright clothing or atop such finely outfitted horses.

Ann O'Neill sat sprawled on the ground by the well, holding a bundle of laundry in her arms. The right side of her face glistened bright red as she wailed and keened.

The tallest of the English soldiers, his face contorted with rage, yelled at her mother in words Ivy didn't understand.

A stout soldier chimed in from atop his chestnut horse, his gestures threatening.

The third soldier, who looked about Rory's age, sat silent. Three of the O'Neills' chickens hung limply from his hand, their heads flopping on wrung necks.

"Stay here, Honora."

Honora gaped as Ivy burst from the hedge and ran out. Ivy stopped a few yards from the men, planted her feet on the ground, and screamed at them.

"Stop it! Help her! Stop the fire! What are you doing?" Ivy shook her clenched fist.

The soldier with the chickens spoke to her in the language she did not know.

The tall soldier and the stout soldier laughed aloud. The tall man barked at the soldier with the chickens. After a mocking whinny from the chestnut, the three foreigners trotted off toward Ardmore.

Ivy flew to her mother. Honora howled behind the hedge.

"Ma, Ma!" Ivy cried. "What happened? Where's the baby? Did the soldiers take him?" She stopped.

A bit of lace clung to the soot-darkened bundle in her mother's arms. Ivy had held the yarn as her mother wound the ball. She had watched her knit that lace for the new baby's blanket. Ivy stared, realizing what her mother clutched to her bosom.

Her brother Aiden lay dead in his mother's arms.

Ivy's soul fluttered, heaved, then floated back into place. As if from a great distance, her mother's voice croaked a warning.

"Ivy, run. Hide. Take Honora. Go, girl—now. Take Honora back to the berry patch. I'll be fine."

Ivy stared at the raw, red wound. Its blackened borders engulfed the right side of her mother's forehead and scalp. A sickening new smell filled her nostrils.

"No, Ma, no. You have to come, too. And Aiden." Uncertain where to touch her damaged mother, Ivy tugged at the bottom of her mother's singed skirt. "Come. Please."

Honora left the hedge. She screeched like an owl, hands to the sides of her face and her eyes enormous.

Ivy yanked Honora's hand.

"Stop the noise, Honora. Stop it this minute. The soldiers will hear you and come back. Come on. We have to hide in the berry bushes. Ma says so."

Ivy led Honora into the scrubland behind the smoldering ruins of the O'Neill home. The girls' mother trailed after, her dead baby tight to her breast.

Ivy swooped down and collected Honora's berries and basket as they fled. Reaching the shelter of a gorse thicket, Ann collapsed under the bushes. She lay on the ground, her blackened bundle beside her.

Ivy heard her mother's harsh breathing and the whimpers escaping from her pursed lips. With Ivy's encouragement, Honora ate a few bruised berries, then fell asleep huddled on her mother's skirt.

Ivy kept guard. She remembered Father Declan's warning of the fate of unbaptized infants. They went to hell, to limbo. She cried at the thought of her baby brother lost in limbo.

The summer sun cartwheeled across the blue sky and passed its midmark, untouched by the O'Neills' plight. Her mother slumbered, deafened by losses and injuries. Her chest rattled with each breath as if even her insides were burned. Honora whimpered and stirred in her sleep. The shadows lengthened. A meadow pipit flew up and startled Ivy.

Ivy heard a soft short whistle from the direction of the cottage. She gave the answering whistle as she'd been taught. Within minutes, her father, Rory, and Sean silently materialized, perfumed by the scent of the ocean with an undertone of fish guts.

Flinty-eyed Patrick O'Neill stood before the remnants of his family.

"Damn. Damn. Damn," he whispered. "Oh, God. I should have taken them away. Oh, God."

"Daddy," said Ivy. She and Honora began to cry.

His voice steeled.

"Ivy, be quiet. We've no time to weep. The soldiers are likely still about. Rory, you carry Honora. Sean, walk with Ivy. I'll take care of your mother and Aiden. We need to get to the boat."

He knelt over his wife, lifted the cloth from Aiden's face, then put it back.

"I'm so sorry, Pat. I'm so sorry. I left him. I left Aiden to go to the well. I thought he'd be fine. Oh, Patrick . . ." Ann gasped from the effort of talking. A string of coughs erupted.

"Ann, be still. Did the soldiers hurt you? Did they interfere with you? What about the girls? Did they harm the girls?"

"No, Patrick. No. They burned the house. I was at the well, I was. I smelled the smoke, then rushed in for Aiden. He won't wake up."

"Shh, Ann. Let's just get out of here. Be as quiet as you can, love."

"What about the house? What about dinner? I'm hungry," said ten-year-old Sean. Tears flowed down his cheeks. He swiped at them with the back of a grimy hand.

"Everything's gone here, Sean. You'll eat later. The English Protestants want this land, and we can't win. We're fishermen, not soldiers. We've already lost Aiden. I'm not giving up any more of you. Now get going. We've no time to stand around palavering. We're done with Ardmore. Let's get to the boat."

Sean pushed his forelock of black curls from his forehead and reached out for Ivy's hand.

"Come on, Sis. Everything'll be fine. Let's get to the *Phelim*."

Sean was lying, trying to act grown-up, hoping to make her do what he wanted. She was too stunned and too tired to protest.

Rory, a muscular man-sized teenager, picked up Honora. Patrick gently but hurriedly led his wife. There was no time to stop at the ruins of their home. The pervasive smell of smoke irritated their noses.

Ivy, terrified the English still lurked, struggled to stifle any cough. The family sped to the beach. At one point, Ivy heard their cow moo off in the distance, bewildered and begging to be milked. She shot her father a questioning look.

He shook his head. There was no time for anything except the family's escape.

When they reached the shore, only a smudge of light lingered in the west. A second, brighter artificial sunset glowed in the north, created by the reflection on low clouds of Ardmore aflame. The conflagration, rooted in a royal dispute across the Celtic Sea, consumed Ivy's entire sphere of life.

"Daddy, we won't all fit," she said with a glance at the *Phelim*, the wooden fishing boat her father had named for a children's song. With no mast and no sail, the weathered red vessel demanded a skilled master.

"Hush." Rory shot Ivy a scowl from under his mop of red hair.

Patrick put a gentle hand on Ivy's shoulder. "We'll be fine, love. Keep silent. Sound carries far over the water. Rory and I will have you away from all this in the shake of a lamb's tail. Just don't move about."

The O'Neills then did what they knew best; they took to the water. They fled Ardmore with the remainders of their life—the clothes on their backs, the *Phelim*, and Aiden's soulless body. Ivy and Sean collapsed against a coil of rope. Honora clung to her mother and Ann clung to Aiden's body as if he were alive.

Rory and Patrick slipped the oars noiselessly into the water and rowed. Their ropey arms oared in unison; their faces settled into matching profiles of determination.

The man in the fat rising moon smiled down, oblivious to their plight.

The *Phelim* abandoned the shoreline, holding the O'Neills like berries in a cupped hand. They headed east toward a narrow spit of land jutting out into the Celtic Sea. Mist shrouded the peninsula, a place so lonely, with land so worthless, the English wouldn't bother with the Irish there for generations to come.

Chapter 2

An Rinn, Contae Phort Láirge, Éire
(Ringville, County Waterford, Ireland)

August 1690

"Ivy. Ivy! Honora needs you," said Sean.

Honora stood motionless by the pallet she shared with Ivy, her head hanging. Tears glittered on her cheeks. A urine-splotched shift covered her nakedness.

Ivy put down the tin porridge bowl and spoon.

"You feed Ma, Sean. I'll get Honora a dry shift."

Ann's hands, burned in her attempt to rescue Aiden, were scabbed with open raw spots. Her porcelain-white oval face and glossy brown hair were beautiful as ever, so long as Ivy approached her mother from the left. Seen straight on, black scabs immobilized the right side of her face. A portion of her scalp lay denuded of hair.

"Sorry," said Honora. "Sorry." Her chin quivered.

"Don't worry, Honora. Everyone wets the bed one time or another. I love you. You are my favorite girl. Let's just get you another shift, eh?" said Ivy, her voice low and warm. "We don't want to put your dress over a wet shift, do we? I'll help you."

After Ivy had fixed her up, Honora skipped off to play.

Honora wet the bed nearly every night. Dark hatred of the British soldiers and blame for Honora's regression rose in Ivy's throat. She took the spoon from Sean and resumed feeding her mother, cooing at her mother while she planned the murder of the three soldiers. Killing them was the only future Ivy could imagine for herself. Nothing else mattered.

Her eyes roamed around the derelict cottage. She wondered about the family who had built it. How many children had lived here? Where had they gone? Were they happy living somewhere else, or had they met a sadder fate?

A single room like their home in Ardmore, the house boasted a hearth and chimney but otherwise could only be described as shabby. Sean and Rory had helped Ivy clear out the debris that cluttered the abandoned house. A small portion of the thatch roof remained as partial protection from the frequent rains. Her father promised to put on a new roof before the weather became much colder.

An Rinn was no town and was barely a village. Fewer people lived here than in Ardmore. Even with the refugees from the renewed English aggression, fewer than five hundred souls called An Rinn home. It was no Ardmore.

Ardmore's beguiling landscape rolled above sea cliffs with lines of trees edging green fields. Its ancient ruins evoked the days when St. Declan established one of the oldest enclaves of Catholicism in Ireland.

An Rinn, in comparison, lacked the texture, history, and richness of Ardmore. It was flat. Few trees broke the power of the wind coming off the Celtic Sea. The peninsula resembled a featureless green layer cake surrounded by water on three sides—and a single layer, at that. An Rinn looked like the aftermath of a green worm almost, but not totally, smashed by a giant.

"When do you think we'll go, Sean?" Ivy said one evening as they carried buckets of water.

"Go? Go where?"

"Home, silly. Ma's getting better. When do you think we'll leave here?"

"Ivy, I don't know. Ma might not want to leave Aiden. She prays over him in the graveyard every day."

Ivy's face fell and she sniffled.

Sean's eyes stayed stuck to the dirt path. "I think Daddy plans on staying. He says the English have filled Ardmore and they have no intention to give back our land or anyone else's. I like Ardmore, but I think Daddy's right. He usually is."

Ivy stopped walking. Water sloshed over the brim of her bucket. "Well, I don't." She ran barefoot down toward the sea.

The next morning, after her father and the boys left to fish and while her mother dozed, Ivy led Honora outside.

"Shh, be very quiet, Honora. We're going on a ramble." The sisters traipsed off, following the sun's course.

"Home is this way, Honora. West. We'll go visit and be home for supper. What do you say?"

"Home?" Honora pointed back toward the wreckage housing the O'Neills.

"No, not there. Our old place. Ardmore."

Honora smiled sweetly and slipped her hand into her sister's.

"Home."

Heading up the dirt lane, the first leg of their journey passed with misleading ease. At the edge of the settlement, a spotted dog rushed out to bark. Short-haired with ribs rippling her sides, her distended teats explained her protectiveness.

Honora's fingers tightened on Ivy's. Ivy looked the pitiful dog in the eyes and gave a firm, "Go away."

The starving animal slunk back to her mongrel litter.

On and on, the girls trudged, until Honora fretted and complained, "I'm hungry, Ivy."

"Don't worry. I brought us a bannock to share. We can have it now." She led Honora over a low stone wall into a pasture dotted with sheep. They settled down to eat under a tree. Ivy broke the crumbly round bread in half.

Honora hummed "mmm mmm" with each bite. Ivy didn't waste the time and devoured her half. Stomachs full and lulled by the buzzing of bees in the clumps of wild flowers, they fell into a sleep deepened and sweetened by the belief they'd soon see their true home.

Ivy woke with a nudge to her foot. Thinking it a nosy sheep, she muttered, "Go away. Go away."

"I'm not going away, Ivy," answered Rory. "Come on. You're in trouble now, girl. Letting mother be all alone and missing dinner. Taking Honora, too. Now, come along home."

Rory's shadowed expression mixed relief, anger, and amusement. The sun, low in the sky, lit his hair like tongues of fire, and Ivy flinched at the sight of it. Honora blinked groggily. She turned to Ivy for an opinion.

"Oh, Rory, we just wanted to see Ardmore again. Can't you take us? It's not too late, is it?" said Ivy.

"Silly ninny. Ardmore's more than a day's walk away for a man. We can't go there. An Rinn is our home now. You need to get used to it."

The walk back to An Rinn lacked the joyous anticipation of the trip out. As they entered the village, the spotted dog crept out, head down in submission. She wagged her tail in a hesitant welcome.

An Rinn sheltered other refugees, drawn to a sense of security in the village's isolation. Every evening, while their dogs twitched their legs, whimpered, and dreamed of catching rabbits, the exiles dreamed of returning home to the land that was stolen by the English. Many had fled overland. Pushed and shoved across Waterford County by the English, they had not stopped until their backs were to the sea and they could go no farther.

Others, like the O'Neills, had come to An Rinn by sea. All were refugees in their own homeland. They found a precarious safety in the peninsula's austere landscape. No Englishman coveted their life or their pitiful belongings. Few outsiders traveled the road that led to the village, perched on its spike poking into the sea. The Irish of An Rinn were left to glean a living from the waters, speak Gaelic, and practice their outlawed Roman Catholic religion in peace.

Here, the O'Neills no longer needed to hide their faith. Everyone in their small world shared the same beliefs. Each Sunday Ivy joined her family in worship at the village church. After the Sunday services the family always stopped to pray for Aiden. Their tears fell and voices thickened among the tombstones behind the church, where a simple cross marked his grave. In a sin of omission, Patrick had failed to mention Aiden's unbaptized state to the priest. The priest did not ask, and Aiden had been buried as if he weren't lost in limbo. Ivy knew enough to keep her mouth shut, though she'd never known her father to sin before her baby brother died.

Ivy's heart burned with blackness as her thoughts returned to her final day in Ardmore. All the sadness and turmoil coalesced into one picture: three men in red on horseback watching her mother cry. The image came unbidden and filled her with bitterness. Though she heard nothing but Gaelic in An Rinn, a glimpse of scarlet or a jumping flame in the hearth would be enough to bring on the painful vision. While Honora often woke up crying, Ivy's nightmares were stealthy, though no less terrifying. They took her breath away.

Chapter 3

An Rinn, Contae Phort Láirge, Éire
(Ringville, County Waterford, Ireland)

September 1693

"Bam. Bam. Bam! You evil devil, die!" she screamed, lost in her imaginary fight. "Die, you English bastard. You're dead." Ivy held the broomstick to her shoulder and aimed it at Sean's chest. At eleven, Ivy towered over her thirteen-year-old brother.

Sean brandished a small branch. He'd tied a red rag around his neck.

"No, you're dead," said Sean, glaring at his sister. "I've shot you three times, Ivy."

The two stood toe to toe in the roadway fronting their cottage. Patrick and Rory would be coming up the road any minute, back from a day hauling fish out of the sea. They had left Sean home with instructions to help Ma and Ivy carry the laundry tubs. The laundry hung over bushes in back of the house now, drying in the warm autumn sun as their mother warped her loom and their little brother Joey napped. At two, the chubby boy slept most afternoons. Chores all caught up,

Sean and Ivy played in the golden light.

"No, you missed, Sean. You're an English loser. You are."

"Children," said Ann, her musical voice coming from the doorway. "Stop that fighting. What are you two up to?"

"We're just playing, Ma. I'm pretending to be the soldiers and Ivy's a-killin' me."

"Stop that right now and come in."

Pouting, the two dropped their weapons, hung their heads, and followed their mother inside. Ann gestured for them to sit at her feet. She perched on the stool by the hearth.

"I don't want to hear or see you playing at killing anyone again." She waggled her long forefinger at the two. "Killing's a sin. You both know that."

"I'm sorry, Ma," said Sean. His even features crumpled, and tears welled. Ivy pulled a face at her brother.

"Ivy," her mother warned.

"Well, I'm not, Ma. Not sorry at all." Ivy's brows furrowed. "I want all the English to be dead, dead, dead. They are evil and evil people should die. Those soldiers killed Aiden and hurt you." Ivy crossed her arms in Old Testament-worthy righteousness.

"Oh, Ivy. You must forgive those poor miserable soldiers, like Jesus says. You must. I have and so has your father. Hating others hurts you more than anyone else. Holding a grudge rots your soul. Can you try to forgive them just a little, maybe?" Ann's blue eyes looked directly into her daughter's blue and green ones.

Ivy gave the tiniest nod and promised to try. Maybe. Sean raced outside as if he couldn't leave the cottage quickly enough.

"Here, dear, why don't you help me with Joey?" Ann picked up her baby, drowsy from his nap, and handed him to Ivy.

Ivy snuggled him in her arms. A sunny child, Joey always cheered her up. Unlike black-haired Aiden, Joseph O'Neill's hair gleamed bright red. He bore the one blue and one green eye of all the O'Neill children. Ivy often ran her thumb over his cheeks.

"Pity the poor woman unable to nurse her child," said her mother. "Cow's milk lets the little ones survive, but their skin is never as soft as a baby fed at its mother's breast. It's truth."

Joey looked up at Ivy. "Strooth."

Ivy giggled. Joey was so much fun. He rarely cried or grumbled but toddled cheerfully through his day. Ma said they should enjoy him as he was likely to be their last. She was getting too old to bear children.

"The next baby will probably be a grandbaby," said Ann.

Ivy turned that thought over in her mind. She pondered her future. Who would she marry? How many children would she bear? When would Rory marry? Or her other brothers and sister? The future glimmered with uncertainty.

That night she returned to Ardmore in her dreams, as she often did when important rumblings roiled her mind. A fresh mossy scent with hints of peat filled her nose and lungs. Cool white mist mingled with the green grounds surrounding the ruins overlooking Ardmore. A skylark warbled. She sank deep into peacefulness. Ardmore was beautiful.

Chapter 4

An Rinn, Contae Phort Láirge, Éire
(Ringville, County Waterford, Ireland)

February 1694

The clacking of the rickety loom stopped. Ivy looked up from her spinning. Light tiptoed through the window and gleamed on her mother's ruined face. Disfigured by the fire, her mother rarely ventured beyond An Rinn. Even in An Rinn, she kept her head covered with her shawl and swept her hair over as much of her melted cheek as she could.

By the grace of God, her mother's eyes had been spared and her hands had healed. She could weave. And the family needed every coin they could make.

Ivy's thoughts drifted as she spun the spindle. She'd carried three lengths of cloth about An Rinn earlier in the week and had done her best to sell it.

"Did you help your mother make this, Ivy?" Mrs. Sheehan, their neighbor, had asked her. Ivy beamed.

"Oh, yes, ma'am. Feel it. Honora and I helped with the wool. Honora picks the wool. We both card it and I spin it on the spindle. Ma did all the weaving. What do you think?"

"I think your mother is lucky to have such fine daughters. This brown piece is so soft and such a wondrous color. Does your mother make her dyes, too?"

"Of course, ma'am. We pick the plants and lichen and help brew it. Like making tea, it is."

Mrs. Sheehan ran her freckled hand over the length of brown wool in Ivy's basket.

"It is so soft. I'll buy it. Do you know if your mother plans on weaving any purple this year? I know I must wait till the summer for purple."

"I believe so. I'll tell mother to hold a length of purple aside until you see it. Will that do?"

"Yes, thanks, Ivy. You're a good girl and so is Honora."

Her basket lighter, Ivy had strolled home. Most of her mother's weavings were undyed and precisely echoed the white, gray, and black sheep out in the meadows. She made the dye by steeping natural materials, often gathered by Ivy and Honora. The colors mimicked those found in nature—brown, ocher, yellow, orange, dark red.

Purple, however, was another matter. There were no purple sheep, vegetables, lichen, or fruit. The origins of purple dye hid from sight and did not readily come forth. Creating purple, the most prized dye, demanded a harvester and dyer of finicky patience.

And Ivy fit the bill. As Ivy grew older, she began to gravitate toward tasks with intricate steps, complexity. She found pleasure in sinking deep into activities, blocking out her surroundings, and concentrating on small successes. Baking and sewing filled this appetite, as did the creation of purple dye.

Purple dye was made during the summer, after the Dog Star became visible in the sky. Ann O'Neill and her daughters would clamber down the rock's shore until they reached the ancient, primeval strip of beach revealed by the low tide. It was here the white sea snails awaited harvesting.

The girls and their mother would pile their bounty of dog whelks above the tidal reach and set to work. They crushed the littlest whelks to release the dye. The larger snails were poked on their pointy end with awls to release the dye from their tiny sacs. The liquid flowed into their pot. At first, the color was green, but it quickly turned to a lovely violet, a reddish purple. This prized purple dye was colorfast as well as beautiful. Dyeing cloth was considered women's work, which was fine with Ivy. She thrilled to be learning her mother's secrets.

Ivy looked up from her reverie to watch her mother weave. Ann's hands gracefully handled the shuttle. She was a woman of constant motion. If not cooking, she was sewing; if not patting her baby, then sweeping. She only stopped to sleep and even then, not for long. She filled her daughters' days as she taught them the tasks of womanhood.

At first, she'd started them off weaving *crios*. *Crios* were sashes fishermen wore to belt their pants. No loom was needed. A gentle teacher, Ann explained even the most complex technique in a clear manner. She showed Ivy and Honora how to loop the yarn around their big toe and how to weave the strip up from there.

"You can make the center of the *crios* any colors you wish, but the outside must be white, girls."

"Why, Ma? I want mine to be purple," said Honora.

"Because that's the way it is done, Honora dear. Always has been and always is."

"But what if we run out of white yarn?" said Ivy.

"Then we'll not be making a *crios* till we get some spun. Pay attention to this bit. Have you thought who you'll give yours to?"

"Sean," said Ivy.

"Daddy," said Honora.

"I'll make one for Rory, then," said their mother. "Everyone will have a new *crios*. Later I'll teach you how to use the wooden loom."

From there, she had coached her girls' skills to a high level.

Today, Ivy could hear rain softly falling outside. She worked hard to keep up with her mother's ravenous loom.

"We've nothing for supper, Ivy dear, but a bit of bread," said her mother. "We finished the last of the pork. Maybe Mrs. Flinn can loan us a few eggs."

Loan was a euphemism. The O'Neills had no chickens here in An Rinn. No pigs, no cow, no land, no farm, no garden. The English had taken it all. The O'Neills lived on a razor's edge, teetering and threatening to fall into the abyss. They made do in this thatched room, living off their weaving and the vagaries of the fish in the Celtic Sea.

"Yes, Ma. I'll go see to it." said Ivy. Honora looked up hopefully from her carding paddles. "Honora, you stay here. Ma needs your help."

"Hmph," grumbled the seven-year-old. She stuck out her tongue at Ivy.

Ivy covered her coppery curls with a shawl and grabbed the egg basket. Outside, smudgy clouds hovered low to the ground and emptied misty rain down on the village. She kept close to the line of shabby houses, her long legs making short work of the walk out to the Flinns' place.

Drawing near the whitewashed chicken coop, Ivy saw the door was ajar. She picked up her skirt and ran toward it for shelter from the rain. Without a word or a knock, she shoved the door open. Inside, Kevin Flinn tended the birds. A year older than Ivy, the red-cheeked and black-haired fellow was one of the few boys in town taller than she. That alone would have been enough for her to like him. Even better, he never teased her.

"Ivy, what are you doing out in this rain? Come on over here," he said.

"We were wondering if we could borrow a few eggs, Kevin. You know, in trade," she stammered. "Ma is finishing up a length of wool you can have. It's quite fine." Ivy breathed in the familiar scent of straw and chickens and remembered the red hen she'd raised back in Ardmore.

"Plenty of eggs to spare, Ivy. Don't worry about the cloth. These girls have been outdoing themselves." Whistling, Kevin rummaged through the hen house. He carefully slid his big hand into one nest, then another, managing not to over-annoy the chickens huddled in the straw, though he did have their attention. The rooster alone appeared indignant, cocking his head threateningly and fixing a shiny black eye on the boy. Kevin gently cradled the eggs, then placed them one by one in Ivy's basket. The two broad points of the basket's base kept the eggs from rolling about.

"There you are, my Ivy. Happy to share." Kevin winked.

Blushing, Ivy murmured her thanks and trotted home in the rain. The O'Neills would have a little supper tonight. Who knew about tomorrow?

Chapter 5

An Rinn, Contae Phort Láirge, Éire
(Ringville, County Waterford, Ireland)

May 1700

"Come in," said Ann O'Neill, calling from her loom. Ivy sat spinning by the hearth, absorbed in her work.

Kevin Flinn ducked his head and entered the O'Neills' cottage. Kevin commanded more space than most men, filling their home with his pleasantness, long arms, and even longer legs.

"Good afternoon to you both, Mrs. O'Neill, Ivy. How are you this lovely morning?"

"Fine, Kevin. How's your ma? And your daddy, of course?" said Ann.

"They're well, thanks. We need a few sundries from town, so I came to buy them. I was wondering if you need anything?"

"Well, we could use a spool of cotton thread, couldn't we, Ivy? It never seems to last. But I don't want to trouble you, Kevin. Ivy can fetch it later."

"Are you sure? I'm happy to get it."

Ann glanced at Ivy. Ivy's face pleaded, much like a spaniel begging for a bone.

“Well, I’d be grateful, Kevin, if you could fetch it. Now that I think, maybe Ivy could go, too, and pick out the thread and—”

“Oh, that would be grand, ma’am,” blurted Kevin.

“Then go along, Ivy. Be home for supper, please,” said Ann. She went back to her loom, singing softly, her shuttle flying between the warp threads. The clunky wooden loom sang along with her.

Kevin often discovered reasons, errands, excuses, and ploys to come to the O’Neill home and spend time with Ivy. A strapping fellow known for his hard work and cheerfulness, he owed no one any debt and in a few years expected to take over the family farm. He was also a talented dancer and raconteur, and sang with a mellow baritone which made him very popular at local weddings, christenings, and wakes.

Old Widow Whelan, a notorious gossip, spent most days in a rickety chair by her stoop. She smiled as Ivy and Kevin passed by on their way to buy thread and whispered secrets to the decrepit cat in her lap. Ivy straightened her shoulders and walked even taller under Mrs. Whelan’s black gaze. Ivy believed she and Kevin made a fine couple and besides, who else within sixty miles was taller than Ivy?

Chapter 6

An Rinn, Contae Phort Láirge, Éire
(Ringville, County Waterford, Ireland)

June 30, 1700

"Be careful tomorrow, Ivy. Dungarvan is a harbor town. Not like here. All kinds of riffraff show up there." Kevin stopped shelling peas long enough to give Ivy a side hug. They sat at Ivy's hearth. The inviting smell of roasting pork filled the cottage. Kevin always looked forward to supper with the O'Neills.

"Oh, Kevin, don't worry. I'll be with Sean. We'll be fine." She tucked a lock of hair behind her ear. "These are the last green peas of the season. Sad to see them end."

"Well, I want you back safe and sound. Tomorrow I'm going out on the *Phelim* to help your father. There's a question I need to ask him. Figure his boat's the best place. He's always on the move. But he can't get away from me on the *Phelim*."

Ivy flushed with embarrassment and joy, certain Kevin intended to ask for permission to marry her.

Burning peat gave off a dim light from the fireplace, barely enough for Ivy to see her task. She wrapped the square of linen around a piece of bread and placed it atop the salted herring in her basket. The dried fish, lined up like soldiers, swam on a cushion of clean straw. A sudden draft of air wrapped tendrils of coolness around her ankles and neck. Her brother Sean poked his head into the cottage.

"Aren't you ready yet? It doesn't always have to be perfect, Ivy," Sean whispered.

Hastening, Ivy sloppily wrapped the next bit of bread, but then stopped. With a huff, she removed the bread and straightened the linen. She put it back in the basket, edges matching the first package of bread.

Hearing a rustle from her parents' bed by the hearth, she looked up. Ma, curled against Daddy, stirred again. Honora slept open-mouthed on her back in her cot in the corner. Rory's snores drifted down from the loft. A whiff of pork from the evening meal hung in the air. Everything was as it should be or, at least, as it usually was.

"All set, Sean," said Ivy. She closed the door behind her and tightened her green shawl. The briny breeze ruffled her hair. Ivy didn't need a mirror to know the mist was frizzing her tresses into tight ringlets.

The full moon lent a milky luminescence to the night, giving Ivy the barest outline of her brother holding the reins of their swayback pony. Behind the horse, a rough two-wheeled cart held lumpy bundles. Ivy nestled her basket among the cargo. With a leg up from Sean, she hopped onto the bench seat.

"Hee up," said Sean and off they shambled. His milk-white

face shone in the moonlight.

Today Sean wouldn't be fishing with Rory and their father as he usually was. Instead, Kevin would be on the boat. A thrill of joy filled her. Surely her father would approve a marriage with a good man like Kevin.

While Ivy's mother rarely left the cottage, the men were always on the go. Outside in the open air, they fished and tended to their boat. In the warm months, they came in only for meals and to sleep. Ivy smiled in the darkness at Sean.

"Glad it's you and me today, Sean."

Maybe Sean wasn't the greatest fisherman, but he was her favorite brother. Even adorable Joey could not displace Sean in her heart. Time spent with Sean sailed by as smoothly as a paper boat on a pond and left not a ripple of discord.

"What you mean is, you're glad Daddy didn't send you and Rory. You two should try to get along, Ivy. Being always at loggerheads is no good. I know he can be a pompous ass, but still. You need to learn to get along better, my girl. At least you and Honora don't argue."

Embarrassed by Sean's chastisement, Ivy said nothing. Thoughts of her family and her likely upcoming marriage consumed her attention as the cart creaked and lumbered through the darkness.

Up ahead, Lily snuffled and bobbed her head in rhythm with her hoofbeats. The pony's harlequin black-and-white coat stood out in the low light. If Ivy squinted, the black disappeared, leaving ghostly white disembodied shapes moving to the beat of Lily's gait.

"It's certainly hours to the harbor. Sean, how'd you find out about the ship? Did Daddy tell you?"

"No. Don't worry, Ivy. I found out on my own, from my friend Kieran. He heard it from a man he knows on the coast.

Kieran knows everything and everybody. The ship hails from Bristol, on its way to America. If we get there early, maybe we can sell them all of Ma's weavings and such. Kieran says those trading ships pay a decent penny."

"Hope the fellow on the coast knows what he's talking about. Hope you're right." Remembrances of past peccadilloes in which Sean's friends talked him into foolishness fluttered through Ivy's mind.

"Ma said she thought it was a bad idea."

"Oh, Ivy. You know how Ma is. She's a little scared. Daddy thinks it's a good way to bring in some money. Plus, he thinks you need to learn more about selling in Dungarvan before us boys marry up and leave home."

"Kevin was a bit worried too."

"Oh, well. Kevin. He's so sweet on you. He worries when he doesn't need to."

Ivy's thoughts flew to the *Phelim.* Had Kevin had his conversation with Daddy? She wondered about the outcome. Her mind turned again to marriage.

Babies floated through her thoughts. Newborn fingers wrapped around her pointer. A nursing babe falling asleep at her breast. A toddler with Kevin's hair.

Maybe she could talk Kevin into setting up a home in Ardmore. She would hold her children's hands as they wandered up to the cathedral ruins. With the vividness of reality, Ivy could hear her own voice recounting her mother's stories of King Solomon.

Lily interrupted her daydreams with another snuffle.

"So who's your future wife, Sean? Siobhan? Or maybe Helen? Helen's a lovely girl."

"You'll know when I know, Ivy." Sean grinned and poked her side with his elbow.

The cart rumbled along over softly rolling open terrain. From the right came the rustle and smell of open water. The rutted road gave the only testimony to the presence of people living in the area.

"But will there be soldiers in Dungarvan, Sean? I don't want to see any soldiers. Or any kind of English. I hate the English. I hope they all burn in hell."

"Ivy, of course there will be English there. Who do you think sails English ships? But I don't usually see but one or two in town." Sean shot Ivy a sharp look. "I wish you'd remember what Father Declan says about forgiveness. Where you're born doesn't make you good or bad. It's who you are inside and what you do that counts. Right?"

"Whatever you say, Sean," muttered Ivy. She didn't agree with her brother's compassionate ideas. He hadn't watched their home burn while their mother wailed. She would never forget.

"Don't worry, Ivy. You'll be fine. Stay with me, and don't talk to anyone. You can help me answer questions about Ma's weaving, if anyone asks, and mind the horse if I have to step aside for a minute or two. That's all you have to do. Don't tell Dad, but I do hope to have at least one pint," said Sean.

"Fine with me," said Ivy. "Maybe I can buy a packet of needles or even a bit of calico."

Rocked by the rhythm of the pony's hooves, Ivy leaned against her brother and dozed. His broad shoulders and chest shielded her from the worst of the wind as she snuggled against his wool jacket.

Visions of calico dresses in green and blue filled her mind. Green would make her hair shine. Kevin liked green. Kevin spoke to her so tenderly. Even though he farmed for a living, he'd managed to do well where others failed. Kevin seemed the sort to truly care about people. Always. But blue could be handsome as well. Blue was Ivy's favorite color. Either would do. A new dress. She imagined herself standing in front of Father Declan, spring flowers in her hair, vowing to love Kevin for the rest of her life. Kevin's black hair against his fair skin and ruddy cheeks melted her.

Truth was, though, Ivy had little time for dreaming most days. Her days in An Rinn filled quickly with cooking, washing, spinning, tidying up, helping with Joey, and minding the chickens and the geese. She expected things wouldn't change much if she married Kevin, except she'd be in a different home and wiping her own children's noses.

Ma had little time—and even less interest—in housework. She spoke to few people outside her family except for Father Declan, who'd also fled to An Rinn. Ivy thanked God her mother still lived and managed to weave and spin and knit. Somehow the family scraped up enough to eat and keep from freezing. They were blessed. Though a length of calico would be such a pleasure.

Chapter 7

Dún Garbhán, Contae Phort Láirge, Éire
(Dungarvan, County Waterford, Ireland)

July 1, 1700

Ivy's calico dreams halted with a crash. Startled awake, she found they were on the outskirts of Dungarvan. Cottages and shops lined the street cheek by jowl as if shoved together by a giant hand.

Beside a cart of barrels, a small drama was playing out. A burly bearded man shook his fist in a boy's face. The scrawny lad cowered and held a ragged cap in his hands. At their feet, liquor bubbled from a shattered wooden cask.

Sean urged Lily on past the excitement. Not long afterward their wagon stopped with a lurch.

"We're here," Sean announced. He patted Ivy's shoulder.

An apron of cobblestone separated two- and three-story stone buildings from the water. A tall wooden ship dominated the harbor. The skeletal remains of an abandoned fishing boat bobbed and poked the ship's side. Aloft, sailors crawled and dangled from its three masts. Out near the horizon, the fishing fleet dotted the water like cows grazing in a hilly pasture. Ivy picked out one or two English words among the babble. Odors of sundry rotten items, pieces of cargo left on the dock, wafted about. Dirty water puddled between the cobblestones.

A fat rat scurried up the gangplank onto the tall sloop as if anxious not to miss the trip. The minute the rat dove into the dark recesses of the ship, a man clad in a purple coat reaching his knees and spangled with shiny buttons appeared at the top of the gangway. His eyes roved the harbor and glanced briefly toward Ivy and Sean.

An icy, narrow chill tingled along Ivy's spine. She knew she shouldn't be there. Things did not feel right.

"Sean, we've got to go. Let's go home. Now. Please, Sean. We can sell our goods in An Rinn. It might take a while, but we need to leave. This feels wrong."

Sean gaped at her.

"Wake up, Ivy. You must be dreaming. Wake up. We've got work to do."

"I am awake. Let's go home, now. Please." Tears gathered, ready to burst forth.

"No, silly girl. You always worry too much. Everything's roses and sunshine. Wait here while I go find the captain. And don't talk to anyone. You'll be fine."

Sean jumped off the cart and walked toward a cluster of men on the quay. The man in the purple coat strode down the ramp and joined them, a smirk on his face.

With a sigh and a hiccup, Ivy settled onto the bench seat. She scooted to the middle to get as far away as possible from the ragamuffin crowd wandering the wharf. Even with her eyes down, she could feel the stares of the rough men and boys. Her right hand slid toward the pocket tied underneath her skirt, then thought better of it. Although her rosary was only ten beads, created specifically to be used in secret, she didn't want to take any risks. She'd pray the rosary later.

"Psst. Psst," she heard from a few feet away. Ivy kept her eyes on her lap. Her hands tightened on the ends of her shawl. Suddenly a brown, wrinkled visage appeared at her elbow. Ivy nearly fell off the seat, and she slid as far away as she could.

"Hey, girly," said the old man with a wink. "Wanna see—"

"Stop troubling my sister, you old fool," yelled Sean as he ran over. "Leave her alone."

The old codger scuttled away like a hermit crab in a shell. He looked over his shoulder and muttered what sounded like "devil-eyed witch."

Sean said, "Hold on, Ivy. We're almost done." He rejoined the other men.

Ivy, picking him out by his head of black curly hair, saw him turn frequently in her direction. He looked nervous to her. A few minutes later, a team of sailors unloaded the cart, carrying Ma's carefully wrapped packets of cloth up the gangplank. Sean and Ivy stayed by their pony and oversaw the work.

"Halloo," shouted the man in the coat, leaning over the side of the ship. "Come on aboard both of you and you'll be paid. I wouldn't leave your lady down on the wharf unattended, Mr. O'Neill. Little Rhys will watch your pony."

"He's the captain, Mr. Smythe," said Sean. "Come with me, Ivy. We'll get our payment and head straight home. You're right. This is no place to linger."

Hand in hand, the two walked up the gangplank to the ship's deck. A sailor chin-nodded for them to go below. Sean ventured first down the wooden ladder, then turned to help Ivy.

Later, Ivy would clearly recall Sean's hand reaching out for hers, then his eyes rounding with surprise. The rest swirled in her memory in a storm of shouts, flying fists, and thuds overlaid with a woman's screams. She knew the screams came from her own lungs but didn't have a sense of making them.

Sean's brown jacket and striped pants flashed into and out of view. Calloused hands pulled her from the ladder as she turned to escape the melee. Long fingernails bit into her wrist and waist. All became darkness.

Chapter 8

Aboard the Prometheus
Under sail on the Celtic Sea

July 2, 1700

Ivy awoke, hot and thirsty. She had a headache the likes of which she'd never experienced. She kept still, afraid to open her eyes. Something warm lay against her back. Her nostrils stung with the odor of vomit and full chamber pots.

The ground rolled underneath her.

Confused and terrified, Ivy pretended she was still unconscious, listening with her eyes closed. She heard the chatter of men interrupted by an occasional shout. Each noisy outburst skewered a spike of fresh pain into her head.

She drifted off for what might have been a minute or a day. Her head pounded and she needed to use the pot. She opened her right eye a slit. It was nearest the floor. Blue flowered calico filled her view. Opening both eyes did not clarify her situation. All she could see in the dim light were sprigs of blue flowers on a dingy white background. The calico shifted, releasing the smell of an unwashed body, of a woman. The floor rose under Ivy, provoking another wave of nausea.

"Ah, you're awake," trilled a woman's voice in Gaelic. "Don't worry, dear. Can you sit up? I'm Fiona."

Ivy pulled herself up and looked around. She willed her queasy stomach not to betray her. Fiona, a delicate brunette, looked every bit a healthy girl. Her homespun dress, though undecorated, was clean and had not a single straggle or rip. Not a speck of dirt could be seen, even on her hands. Her brown eyes shone with confidence and the promise of competence. In contrast, the five other women arrayed behind her looked as if their clothing as well as their faces all needed a good washup.

Ivy fell back on her manners. "Hi, I'm Ivy. Ivy O'Neill."

The bedraggled women stared, then slid their eyes toward Fiona.

"They don't speak Gaelic, Ivy. Only English. I'll tell them. Try to use English, if you know any," said Fiona.

"English! Why would I want to speak English?" Ivy's heartbeat quickened.

"Because they are English, Ivy. We're on an English ship."

Fiona turned back to the others and spoke fluidly to them in their own language.

Ivy abruptly felt herself leave her body and hover in the air, as if an angel had plucked her soul up into the ether. She saw herself, Fiona, and the English girls from a far, far away place. Their voices echoed below her in the dark belly of the ship. As quickly as it began, the episode ended. Ivy's body and spirit reunited. Her heart beat unhurriedly. Her breath came easily. She was back in the moment.

Ivy looked at each of the five English women one by one. A bony girl in a green skirt punctuated the passing time with a rattling cough. Not one of the women appeared to be past her midtwenties and not one appeared to be younger than eighteen.

The tall blonde asked Fiona a question.

"They want to know about your eyes."

"Well, simply tell the silly cows that every person where I come from has eyes like mine. Nothing wrong with them at all."

Fiona repeated this in English. The women chattered together for a moment, then quieted.

"Well, my sister and I have webbed toes and we're all right. Must be one of those variations God offers. I guess this girl's human," said the tall blonde. "I'll not worry myself about her eyes. I think we have bigger problems than her eyes."

Fiona translated.

Looking past the women, Ivy's gaze landed on a partially filled chamber pot in one corner. A stained petticoat tied to a wall served as a privacy curtain. Fiona caught Ivy's eye.

"Go ahead and relieve yourself, dear," she said.

Ivy's head swam when she stood, and she stumbled as the ground shifted under her. To her consternation, the tall girl grabbed her arm. She gently guided Ivy to the pot.

"I'm Sally. I'll help you."

Ivy retrieved an English phrase. "Thank you."

As she squatted on the clay pot, Ivy spied iron bars behind the petticoat curtain. Her eyes traced it. An involuntary gasp marked her realization: the women were caged like beasts. All of them, including Ivy, were imprisoned in the ship's hold. The ship's wooden wall served as the back of the cage. Heavy iron bars delineated the other three sides. The seven women's world measured ten feet along the ship's inner wall and six feet out from this wall. Ivy doubted there was room enough for them to all lie on the floor at the same time. Two canvas hammocks suspended from above confirmed this suspicion. Each of the creaking and swinging hammocks held a pair of women, their feet dangling in the air.

She rejoined the others and tried to keep the panic out of

her voice. "Do you know where my brother Sean is?"

Fiona pointed down toward the far end of the ship. "There're men down there—captive the same as us. He's probably there. You can see part of their cell if you stand over in that far corner."

Ivy darted to the corner. "Sean, Sean," she hollered.

"Hush, girl," said Fiona. "You don't want to bring the captain down here. Be quiet. We'll find out from the cabin boy about your brother." Ivy wiped the tears from her eyes with her skirt.

"I don't understand. Why are we here? We didn't do anything wrong."

Fiona explained what she knew about their situation. The seven women and the ten or so men were captives, prisoners of Captain Smythe and his crew. No one knew where they were going or what would happen to them.

As she spoke, the English women watched for a few minutes, then huddled together and talked. Ivy knew they were speaking about her from the frequent glances sent her way. The girl in the blue-and-white floral dress frowned, lifted a hand, and gestured toward Ivy. Her long fingers arrowed straight at Ivy's eyes. Sally gently pushed the girl's hand down and spoke to her, a pleasant but serious look on her face. One woman in particular clearly disagreed with Sally. She, too, was blonde, but shorter and bosomy.

Ivy turned her attention back to Fiona. Her headache made it difficult to follow everything Fiona said.

"You and I were picked up yesterday in Dungarvan, Ivy. You got a bit scuffed up before you were put with us, by the looks of that bump and bruise on your forehead. We thought it best to let you sleep. How do you feel, dear? Better?"

"I think so, thanks. I just have a headache and feel a little sick to my stomach."

"Well, good. I think you'll be fine. As I was saying, my

father's a ship chandler in Dungarvan. The English women are all from around Bristol. Four say the court sentenced them to serve as servants in the colonies and turned them over to Captain Smythe for transport. A bunch of thieves, or even worse, they were. The plump one with the golden hair—she calls herself Betty—claims she was tricked by a pair of ne'er-do-wells. A man and a woman working together spirited her away. They tossed her into a shopman's garret and kept her there, they did, for days. Then rogues carried her onto this ship in the dark of the night."

"Do you believe such a tall tale, Fiona?"

"Well, there is evil in the world, for a certainty."

"But why me, Fiona? I'm no thief. And you—what happened?"

"The story is there were two other women on the ship. They were sickly and died on the trip from Bristol to Dungarvan. So the pirates grabbed us as a replacement. They like to keep a full hold of cargo."

"Pirates? What do you mean pirates? I thought this was a trading ship."

"Well, what else do you call it when bad people steal men and women to sell to others?"

"Sell? Pirates?" Ivy began to weep.

"Be careful, Ivy. Don't ever call them pirates to their face. Especially the captain—he's a mean devil. Look, I don't want to scare you, but you must understand things. We need to get through this if we can and prayer is not enough. We have to do things for ourselves and the other women. Work together. God helps them who helps themselves."

Fiona gave Ivy an encouraging smile.

"The English girls say Captain Smythe plans to sell our labor to colonists, whether we want him to or not. Either in the Caribbean or North America. I've heard tales in Dungarvan about people being kidnapped and sold into servitude. Didn't believe it till now. I certainly have seen many men, and even some women, sign on to serve as servants in the colonies. They trade a number of years' labor for their passage. Even my cousin James did so. Kidnapping is another thing entirely."

"What can we do?"

"I don't know yet, but we need to work together. You, me, and the other women. I believe it's the best way to come to good."

Ivy shot a dubious look at the English women. After all her and her family's suffering under the English, it didn't sound right to trust anyone from England. She did believe she should learn as much as possible about her situation. Maybe Fiona had a point. Ivy sat quietly for a few moments and turned options over in her mind.

"Fiona, could you introduce me to the others?" Learning their names should be harmless and possibly helpful.

"Of course, Ivy." Fiona proceeded to do so. Each, with prompting, shared their name, then Fiona told Ivy what little she knew about them. These were the first English women Ivy had ever met. She camouflaged her terror with a thin smile.

Sally, along with Eleanor, Anne, and Mary, said they had been scooped up from the streets of Bristol, charged with vagrancy, and tossed into jail.

Mary cleared her throat. "Yeah, I sat in jail for weeks, I did. Starved, dirty, with the worst sort of people—no offense to any of you girls. Then one day, the bailiff came and hauled me into court. In one minute, the judge decided my fate. 'Transport the wench.' The next thing I knew I was hauled away in a cart to this godforsaken ship, only to be crammed into a cell even smaller and with worse food than the one in Bristol. That is my story and pretty much the one we all tell, girl." Appearing exhausted from the speech, the thin girl collapsed against the wall in a string of quiet coughs.

Ivy thought Mary looked feverish and found herself drawing back from her.

Eleanor, a dainty girl with black hair and red cheeks, sat quietly. She gave Ivy a warm smile.

Anne wore the blue-and-white floral dress Ivy had awakened to and said nothing. Dimples punctuated her mobile, heart-shaped face.

Betty, the plump blonde, spoke up. "I went out to buy a packet of needles on the high street in Bristol, I did. That's all. Abducted by spiriters. I never went to jail. Just to this horrible vessel."

Beyond the cell, Ivy saw coils of hemp rope and stacks of folded canvas. A dozen wooden barrels lined the opposite side of the ship. Ivy wondered what possible use the four-foot-high barrels might have. At the far end of the ship, trade goods filled the hold.

Ivy spotted a bundle of her mother's weaving amid the piles. Desolation washed over her with the suddenness of a thunderclap. In shudders and gasps, she wept. Fiona rocked her and patted her shoulder till Ivy stilled.

Like smoldering peat in a hearth, anger burned inside Ivy. She and Sean had done nothing wrong, yet here they were. These scoundrels had even stolen her mother's cloth. Fury rose up in Ivy. What monster kept people in cages? What about the sailors on this ship? Certainly, they knew the women languished behind bars. Why would the sailors go along with such an atrocity? What breed of humans were they?

For a few seconds, or perhaps a minute or two, Ivy feasted on the relief offered by cruel thoughts. She craved the joy of murdering her captors. Of cutting their throats, running a blade through their guts, feeding them poisoned stew. She wanted the release of hurting those who had hurt her. She savored the idea as it rolled around in her mind and overtook her morality.

Shame then flooded Ivy—shame for her bloodlust. The desire to harm left her as quickly as it had come. Ivy was relieved. She did not want to risk her soul.

Fiona turned to Ivy with a smile and patted her hand.

Ivy sent up a brief prayer of thanks—thanks she no longer wanted to kill anyone, and thanks Fiona could not read her mind.

A lamb bleated somewhere in the bowels of the ship. Chickens clucked. Ivy knew the caged animals awaited certain slaughter.

The day wore on. She cushioned her aching head with her shawl to doze on the floor, up against the ship wall. Overhead, Eleanor and Anne slowly swayed in the hammock. Their skirts created an alcove for her. Little sunshine made it all the way down from the deck to the women. At the far ends of the ship, skylights dimly illuminated the hold.

She blessed the darkness, retreating into her pain and heartbreak. Muffled noise from the sailors working above filtered down, punctuated by an occasional shout. Rhythmic chant-like singing and stomping of feet erupted. The ship's wooden sides vibrated with the commotion. Ivy's chest tightened in fear.

Fiona leaned over and whispered. "They're singing while they labor, keeping time. Helps them work. Don't fret, sweetie." She patted Ivy's hand.

Ivy smelled the food before she heard the boy sing out.

"Supper. Suppertime. Wake up, my lovelies."

Sally greeted the boy, an even-featured child of about ten years of age.

"Rhys, my love, my favorite rapscallion, what did you bring us tonight?" Her voice sounded as mellow as a church bell.

"Well, Sally," said Rhys with the smile of a born charmer, "a feast for sure. Fit for royalty."

A shiny black curl flopped into his face as he bent over the cell's padlock. The door creaked open. The captives made no move to leave the cell.

Ivy realized the iron bars not only kept the women in—they kept the sailors out and offered safety of a sort.

Rhys lugged a bucket of pork and vegetable stew, bread with butter, cheese, and a bucket of water into the cell. Ivy recognized the cheese as from Waterford. The crumbly white cheddar sold well on market day in An Rinn. The boy scampered away on bare feet and quickly returned with metal cups, plates, and spoons for the women. He took the chamber pot to empty.

"I'm not hungry," said Ivy. "Someone else can eat my dinner."

"Oh, no, missy," said Fiona as she ladled stew from the bucket. "You have to eat and drink every scrap, every meal, or you'll not make it. The fresh food they bought in Dungarvan won't last but a few days and you need the nourishment. Eat."

Ivy did eat and drink her share and felt better for it. Her headache waned with the nourishment and, after her supper, cleared entirely.

Chapter 9

Aboard the Prometheus
Under sail on the Celtic Sea

July 3, 1700

Cutting like a rusty knife into Ivy's formless dreams, the metallic screech from the men's cell door startled her awake. Her thoughts coalesced as the shuffle of the male prisoners' feet grew louder. She remembered. She was locked in a cage with six other women.

She turned and watched through the bars as disheveled men climbed the ladder to the upper deck. Spying Sean's unmistakable thatch of black curls brought a grin to her face, though she was afraid to call out to him.

The women talked it over.

"Captain Smythe's putting them to work, I'll wager. Why feed them and let them loiter about in the hold?" said Sally.

The following morning Ivy was ready. She pressed herself against the bars, as close to the ladder as she could. Her ploy worked. Sean, trudging with a hangdog expression, looked up when she cleared her throat. His sad look evaporated. He wiggled a finger in a secret greeting. The small gesture grew to be the highlight of Ivy's day.

Each morning, the men went atop and labored while the women languished below. Ivy imagined even the freckles on her arms were fading from lack of sunlight, disappearing one by one in the gloomy cell, like stars fading with the morning light. If she stayed down in the hold long enough, she'd be white and transparent as a ghost.

The sea was calm for the first days of Ivy's imprisonment. Afraid of the English girls, she clung to Fiona. She jumped at the smallest sound—the scamper of a mouse or a sneeze from one of the other women. Every rustle during the night reminded her of the rat she saw running up the gangplank. Each thump on the deck above spurred her heart to a faster rhythm.

She held her breath and strained to hear her father's whistle signal. Surely, her father and the men of An Rinn were coming to rescue her and Sean. Her father must have come to Dungarvan to seek them. Maybe Kevin had joined with her father and they were sailing to find them right this minute. She listened, and strained her ears, and yearned.

She missed Joey and Honora. She even missed sparring words with Rory. Ivy prayed often, hiding her short rosary in the folds of her skirt. She begged God to send a message to her family, to tell them she and Sean still lived, to command Daddy to come and take his children home. She prayed Kevin would forgive her for going to Dungarvan. Most nights she dreamed of An Rinn as she fell into her restless, irritable sleep. She counted herself lucky on the nights she dreamed of Ardmore.

Ivy scratched the seventh mark on the plank behind one of the hammocks. Hearing steps on the ladder, she stashed the nail in its knothole berth. She turned in time to see Captain Smythe's white stockings and purple coat tails emerge from the top deck. She had not seen the man with the purple coat since her capture. Ivy stared at the filthy floor until buckled shoes appeared opposite her, outside the bars. She glanced up.

"Ah, there they are. Those eyes. One blue and one green. On my life, I've never seen the like in a woman. Of course, your brother has them too. His are not nearly as lovely a pair as yours."

He surveyed the females and cleared his throat, tugged at his cravat. Fiona shot a warning glance at Ivy. Ivy wasn't sure what she was being warned to do or not do.

"Ladies," he said, "Rhys and Mr. Neville, my quartermaster, will be taking you up top today to exercise. Don't be frightened. The sailors know not to harm or distress you. You'll have the chance to breathe fresh air. We need you to stay strong and healthy for your new lives in Maryland, in America."

Fear like a prick of an icicle shuddered through Ivy, then melted away. Knowing her destination dropped a piece of the puzzle of her future into place.

Circling the deck with her cellmates invigorated Ivy. A cool breeze lifted tendrils of hair from her forehead. As she gazed at the watery horizon, she hummed the song about Phelim's boat.

Back down below, the women agreed to take turns pacing back and forth in the cell. They believed the additional exercise would be a benefit.

"America must be a good distance away," said Sally. "We must stay strong. Besides, I always am more cheerful after a stroll."

"I'll go first," said Betty.

Mary murmured. "I'll do my best." She appeared even bonier than she had the week before, if that were possible. After three lengths of the cell, she sat down. Her chest heaved in recovery.

The next day the women went up top and, chaperoned by Rhys, again circled the deck. Mary's green dress hung from her shoulders as she slowly made her way around the ship. Her shuffling feet barely lifted from the deck. Every so often, she brought a soiled handkerchief to her lips and coughed.

Ivy noticed dribbles of blood on Mary's bodice. Captain Smythe's eyes followed the sick woman like a predator follows prey, then moved on to boldly stare at Ivy. Ivy hurriedly looked down and sped up her walk.

When night came, Rhys brought them their food as usual and emptied the slops. He smiled as if he enjoyed the work.

Fiona whispered to Ivy, "The girls all feel safe with Rhys. He's too small to do us any real harm, though he does swear as well as the sailors. I rather like him. He reminds me of my brother."

"You'll have a wonderful life in the colonies," announced Rhys when he returned for the empty food buckets and tinware. "Every man in America is rich, indeed. Fruits hang ripe all year round. I even hear the animals in Maryland can talk."

"Oh, Rhys. How do you know? Have you been?" said Eleanor.

"I heard the quartermaster telling the men prisoners," said the cabin boy. With that, the youngster left.

A quarter hour later, Captain Smythe appeared beyond the bars like an apparition of doom. The women's postures relaxed as he walked over to the men's pen, only to stiffen when he circled back their way.

"You," he barked, pointing a long finger, its nail rimmed in black, at Ivy.

She froze. A strong hand squeezed her shoulder and she began to step forward.

"Captain, surely you'd prefer an English girl to a cheap Irish one," purred Betty, in an ingratiating tone new to the others.

"Nothing like an English rose." She ran the tip of her tongue over her plump upper lip to emphasize her case.

The captain's face transformed to a mask of carnality. With a fleeting flash at Ivy, he drew his lips back into a sneer.

"Too right. Come with me, darling."

Without a backward glance, Betty flounced out through the opened bars and with false gaiety led the leering man up the ladder.

The others gaped at Ivy.

"Well, I hope you understand what you owe Betty, Irish girl," said Sally. "She saved you, you know. The captain is not who you want to lose your virtue to. Once he comes to his senses, he'll realize you're worth more to him as a virgin. I'm sure Betty will remind him."

Fiona put her arm over Ivy's shoulders and gave her a hug. "Don't worry, Ivy. Betty's been with worse. But you do owe her a debt. That is for certain."

A few hours later, one of the older sailors brought Betty back to the cell. Ivy, roused from fitful sleep, tried to whisper a thank you. Betty pretended she didn't hear.

After that, Betty became a frequent visitor to the captain's cabin and a source of information to the others as to the status of things on the ship, its progress, and the mood of the pirates. Of almost more import to the others, she smuggled food back from the captain's private stock. A handful of raisins, a crust of bread, or a chicken leg painstakingly divided raised everyone's spirits. Even poker-faced Betty managed a smile when she saw the others' excitement.

When Ivy innocently asked how she spent her time with Captain Smythe, Betty replied:

"Discussing the Restoration."

The English girls howled. Even Fiona and Ivy giggled.

Ivy discovered Fiona was correct about many things. The fresh food soon disappeared. The Irish meat was the first to run out, followed quickly by the vegetables. Scraps of salted pork with stewed peas three days a week and salted beef the other four became supper. Breakfast was a watery gruel that Rhys called "porridge." They drank barreled water and small beer. Fiona assured Ivy she was better off with the beer than the water. The closer to the bottom of the barrel, the cloudier and more disgusting the water became. Fiona drank the beer and used the water to keep her hands and face clean. No one else bothered. The girls all prayed for rain to replenish their drinking water.

Time and heat intertwined with deleterious effect on the food and drink. Portions were small to start and became even smaller. An underlayer of hunger haunted them. With it, they sank into lassitude and passivity.

One afternoon, Ivy watched Sally eat her supper. Hardtack had replaced the fresh bread of the first days at sea. Ivy thought the name, after Fiona explained it, was apt. She wondered what magic curse transformed water and flour into rock-hard biscuits as big as her palm. Before every bite of her hardtack biscuit, Sally carefully rapped the dimpled disk on the floor. Remarkably, it did not break.

Ivy's curiosity outstripped any shyness at speaking the foreign language. She said in slow, but clear English, "Why do you beat your bread on the floor, Sally?"

"It knocks the little weevils out, girl. Haven't you noticed the nasty critters? Otherwise, they get caught and wriggle between my teeth."

The other women laughed at the open-mouthed expression on Ivy's face.

"Well, I don't rap my hardtack. Never," said Betty, the plump blonde. "I like the extra bit of meat the little creatures add. I need the food."

Neither meat nor eggs from the noisy and smelly clutch of chickens in the hold ever appeared in the women's cell. As the weeks rolled by, the clucking grew quieter and finally ceased altogether. Rhys said the sailors, or maybe Captain Smythe and his closest cronies, had consumed all the chickens once they ran out of chicken feed.

The girls talked to pass the time. English became their common tongue. Ivy had learned a few words in the language growing up. She began to listen intently and to string words together. Fiona encouraged her to keep her knowledge of English secret from the captain and crew. Unsure why but trusting Fiona, Ivy did so. She practiced keeping her face blank in front of the pirates when English was spoken.

"You're really good at hiding your understanding, Ivy," said Fiona.

The young women took turns telling stories from their childhood. The tales, Irish and English alike, featured wolves, elves, witches, and demons in counterpoint to princes and princesses. Sharing terrifying supernatural events shifted their focus and blunted the women's anxiety about their predicament. They rarely spoke of their friends left behind or their families. They dodged that pain. Except their mothers. They loved to speak of what their mothers did for them and what they taught them.

One morning Betty scraped the last morsel from her tin bowl and set it down with a clatter.

"What do you suppose they really want with us in America? They say they need servants, but why steal us away? I'm a seamstress and don't know a whit about serving. I don't think any of you do either. Shouldn't they have stolen servant women?"

A look passed between Sally and Fiona.

"What? Tell me," demanded Betty. The others offered their

full attention, quietly awaiting an answer.

Fiona, ever the storyteller, fluffed her filthy skirt and settled in to explain.

"I hear things from working in my father's chandlery. Apparently, there's more work in the colonies than laborers to do it. The landowners sorely need workers, so they offer free passage in exchange for a promise to work."

"All well and good," said Eleanor, "but I didn't ask to go. I had no choice. And calling me a vagrant was a nasty lie. I was merely walking down High Street, looking at the goods for sale, minding my own business."

Sally broke in, "The need is too great, and the colonies are desperate. So, to keep the colonies afloat and churning out money, things have grown ugly. There's wealth to be gained by those who can bring in workers. Or wives."

"Wives?" said Betty. "Wives! It's one thing to be dragged away to work, but quite another to be stolen to become someone's wife. We'll see about that."

"I don't want to go to America. I want to go home," said Ivy. "I've a sweetheart at home. I can't marry anyone else."

"Yes, we know, dear," said Fiona.

Hot tears wet Ivy's cheeks. She sniffled. "So I'll be a house servant? Or even worse, married off? Against my will? For how long? Will they bring me back? What can I do?" She snorted and wiped her nose with her hem. "I'll not have it. No one is going to force me into marriage. You wait and see."

"We don't know what's going to happen for a certainty," said Sally. "We've heard bits and pieces from the cabin boy and Fiona's heard from her pa's customers. We know we're going to America and our labor is to be sold to the colonists. The cabin boy swears some of us are being taken over to serve as wives to the Americans. I don't know. He says we can become free after serving for a few years. Of course, Rhys also claims the animals in America talk. All we can do is try our best to survive this crossing and take care of each other here on the ship and once we land as well."

That night, it was Ivy's turn to sleep in a hammock. Her predicament stunned her. She indulged herself with a short bout of quiet weeping, yet soon roused. She began to plan in earnest. Ireland was now behind her and America ahead. She must take care of herself if she were to ever return home to her family and Kevin. Ivy decided to go along with the men's plans when they docked, while keeping a lookout for a chance to escape—hopefully with Sean. They'd make their way back to Ireland on another ship. Yes, they would. Having a plan, Ivy rolled over and slept.

Chapter 10

Aboard the Prometheus
Under sail on the Atlantic Ocean

July 22, 1700

Supper, such as it was, ended. Sally watched Rhys make his final ascent up the ladder. She leaned against the wall and gathered the other women's attention with a sweeping glance. Her sharp eyes settled on Eleanor.

Eleanor's belly had become bigger despite the poor rations given the prisoners. The women all noticed. No one had said a word. In recent days, even the eyes of one or two of the pirates followed Eleanor with silent pity when she dragged herself around the deck. Ivy understood it was time to acknowledge the obvious and make plans.

"Eleanor, dear," said Sally. "It's clear to anyone with eyes to see. Something, or rather, someone is growing in you. You're with child, aren't you?"

Eleanor's cheeks flushed. Her hand went to her belly.

"Well, who's the father?" said Betty.

"I don't know his name. He grabbed me one night as I walked by a tavern on my way home. A drunk. Forced himself on me." She began to sob.

Ivy didn't know if she should say or do something, but Anne did. Without hesitating, she hugged Eleanor.

"Don't worry, Eleanor. We'll all help," said Anne. She turned to the others. "We all must give Eleanor a portion of our food. She needs the extra for the child she's carrying." Anne gave Ivy a sharp look.

Ivy pressed her lips together firmly then nodded in assent. Even an English bastard baby deserved a chance at life. Thereafter, the women gave their best portions to Eleanor.

Ivy warmed with a soft, private pride as she watched Eleanor rally and her belly grow.

Chapter 11

Aboard the Prometheus
Under sail on the Atlantic Ocean

August 1, 1700

On the first of August, Ivy heard the lamb bleat for the last time.

That afternoon, the women half-heartedly reminisced. Fiona began to sing with a pleasing timbre, her voice richly rendering the children's song about Phelim and his little boat. The English girls hummed along to the Gaelic.

Anne, a clear soprano, came next with a rollicking rendition of "The Old Maid in the Garrett."

There's nothing in this whole world
would make me half so cheery,
As a wee fat man to call me his dearie . . .

Everyone knew this one. They clapped to the quick beat.

Ivy's thoughts turned to Kevin Flinn. Would he still be single when she made it back to Ireland? Or would she end up an old maid and a burden to her family?

Amid the gaiety, Mary began to cough. The girls had grown accustomed to seeing her spit red into the rag she always carried. They weren't surprised when she coughed. The fit crescendoed, and then a flood of bright red blood erupted from Mary's mouth. She choked and gasped.

Betty screamed. The others joined in, yelling for help.

Ivy held Mary in her arms as the blood flowed. Within minutes, the girl lay dead, the front of her dress soaked with blood.

A cacophony of wailing and cries burst from the six women. Ivy sat stunned, Mary's limp body in her lap. Betty cringed in a corner. Sally spoke soothingly to Mary's corpse. Tears flowed all around.

Eventually Mr. Proctor, the ship's surgeon, made his way down the ladder with Rhys and the quartermaster, Mr. Neville. Tall and serious as a priest, without one ounce of extra fat on him, Proctor had soft, clean hands and long mobile fingers which promised skill. Unlike the sailors, his clothing was immaculate and without any unnecessary decoration. His demeanor inspired immediate confidence.

Ivy wondered why he was sailing with pirates.

The physician quickly summed up the situation with one word, "Consumption." He had nothing to offer and left.

Betty spat at his retreating back.

Later, Captain Smythe permitted the women to come on deck to pay their final respects to Mary. Her body lay on a plank, sewn up in a patched and weathered canvas shroud.

Sally said a sweet prayer, then led the women in reciting the twenty-third psalm. The captain and most of his crew surprised Ivy by joining in the recitation.

The captain gave a subtle nod. Two sailors stepped forward, lifted the plank holding Mary's enshrouded remains, and tipped it over the railing. The pitifully small bundle slipped into the tranquil silver ocean.

Rhys sniveled and wiped at his eyes. An eerie quiet and emptiness marked the atmosphere. Off in the distance, the horizon darkened. Lightning flashed from clouds to the sea and thunder rumbled a warning. Silence held sway over the cell afterward in the evening gloom.

After Mary's death, as if fearing contagion, the captain ceased having Betty brought to his chambers. All the women missed the tidbits of food.

After weeks at sea, most of the time belowdecks, the idea of seeing land—even America—tantalized like a gift held just out of reach.

Ivy yearned to tread ground and smell earth. She wanted fresh food, not swill from a rodent-infested hold or hardtack crawling with weevils. She wanted to drink fresh water. She yearned to be free of this imprisonment, yet worried about what was coming her way.

A few nights later, Ivy awoke from a restless sleep in darkness and thought it was still night. She believed Mary's cough awakened her, then remembered that Mary was gone. Silent tears came without bidding, wetting Ivy's sleeve as she rubbed her face.

The heaving ocean warned her that a storm was afoot. The waters grew heavier and swelled. The noisy wind sneaked in through every nook and cranny. It whistled, moaned, and finally roared. The ship groaned and creaked, tossed about by the wind and water.

Ivy and Fiona slipped out their rosaries and prayed, not caring if the others saw the forbidden items. As she finished her prayer and looked up, she realized no one had noticed. The English girls were too busy with their own fervent entreaties to

God. They prayed to continue living, hard as it was. All except for seasick Anne, who was too busy retching into the chamber pot.

The tumult persisted, waxing and waning for hours. During brief lulls of the turmoil, the singing chants of the sailors rang out as they united to keep the *Prometheus* afloat.

Ivy added the pirates to her prayers. No meals came their way to mark the time. In the absence of sunlight, everything in their cell faded to blacks and grays. Ivy believed an entire day passed before the sea calmed.

The hatch opened and there was Rhys. He balanced a bucket of rainwater and descended into the hold.

"Have you ever enjoyed such a fine drink, Fiona?" said Ivy. Her parched and cracked lips stung.

"Never."

The women chatted and giggled with a renewed sense of well-being. When Rhys brought the bucket of dinner, they gobbled up the miserable fare as if at a Christmas banquet. Even iron bars could not dampen the giddiness of escaping the storm.

Chapter 12

Aboard the Prometheus
Under sail off the Eastern Seaboard of British America

September 7, 1700

Like a nocturnal animal, Ivy's eyes picked out shapes in the near blackness. She recognized Anne by the light and dark pattern of her floral dress. Anne stood over Eleanor in the hammock.

"We've got to get the ship's surgeon," Anne told Eleanor. "Come over here, Ivy. I need you."

Ivy helped a doubled-over Eleanor out of the hammock. Eleanor groaned as she stretched out on the floor. Her eyes were closed, a sheen of perspiration on her face.

All six women were now fully awake. They made a racket to draw help, Betty beating a tin cup against the iron bars and the others shouting.

Faithful Rhys thundered down the ladder and was sent on his way to fetch the surgeon.

Wide-eyed, Ivy held Eleanor's hand and whispered to her, "You'll be fine, Eleanor. The baby, too." She prayed it to be the truth.

Within five minutes, clattering leather shoes on the stairs announced the arrival of Mr. Proctor, the surgeon. Rhys opened the iron lock to the cell. Ivy moved closer to Eleanor and squeezed her hand.

"We need to get her to a proper bed," said Mr. Proctor. Turning to Ivy, he dismissed her with a nod and a "Thank you, ma'am" as if she were a fine woman. Ivy let go of Eleanor's hand and stepped back. Three sailors carried the moaning woman off toward the upper deck.

Ivy leaned against Anne in the hammock. The light reaching them through the hatch changed in quality as time crawled on. A long scream around daybreak echoed into the deepest silence. Anne's fingers tightened around Ivy's.

"Do you think she's all right, Anne?"

"I don't know, Ivy," said Anne.

Betty spoke from her berth in the other hammock.

"I've heard a painful labor means a healthy child. I hope so, for Eleanor's sake."

When Rhys came to carry away the night slops, the girls clustered around expectantly.

"Rhys, how's Eleanor? How's the baby? Did you see them? Come on, tell us." All spoke at once.

Rhys grinned. "Oh, she's well and feeding the baby. She says she's going to name him Timothy after Mr. Proctor. Captain Smythe was none too pleased to find her in Proctor's bed. The surgeon barked at him right proper. Said he didn't care if she was a captive wench, she was human and deserved to be treated as such. Captain grumbled at that. Left her where she was, though."

The next morning, the fetid air on the ship carried a hint, a mere whisper, of something new. Thinking about it, Ivy suddenly realized the unique aroma wasn't new at all, but something she hadn't smelled in over two months. It was the scent of land. The earthy smell of vegetation and mud came first in subtle bursts, then lingered and became constant.

Rhys brought them a bucket of murky water to drink. He rushed over, the water sloshing over the bucket's rim.

"Almost there, ladies. Just saw our first bird. We'll be finding land soon."

The women began talking at once. They chortled and gabbed.

"What's going to happen to us now?" Sally voiced the concern on everyone's mind.

"Can we stay together? I don't want to be alone. I heard it's wild in America," said Betty.

Ivy stayed silent. Her mind raced ahead. The enormity of an attempted escape threatened to drown her. Ivy worried she would fail. The time neared when she would learn if she and Sean were strong enough and lucky enough to get away.

In the afternoon Captain Smythe brought Ivy, Fiona, Sally, Anne, and Betty up for their walk on deck. Eleanor and her baby remained secluded in the surgeon's quarters.

The *Prometheus* plowed a rolling furrow through the blue-green water. Blinking in the bright sun, Ivy felt woozy as she stood under the captain's proprietary gaze. She reached out and grabbed the ship's railing to steady herself. Billowing monotonous waves filled the seascape in every direction.

"Give the redhead an extra ration of bread today and thereafter," the captain barked at his assistant. "No one will want her if she looks half dead. I'm not dragging her sour Irish puss all the way back to England."

Ivy forced herself to stagger around the ship with her cellmates. She strained to match the others in vigor and alertness.

"We're off the coast now. Anyone with one eye can see it," Rhys announced in the evening. He passed out the tinware as if it were porcelain, and he divvied up the hardtack and dried beef as if it were a luscious spring lamb stew.

The women exchanged looks, their eyes filled with exhilaration, anxiety, and dread.

Chapter 13

Aboard the Prometheus
Under sail on the Chesapeake Bay, British America

September 11, 1700

A thrumming, thrilling energy propelled Ivy as she climbed from the hold.

"Excuse me, Anne. Didn't mean it," she said after pushing into Anne's bottom in her rush to get atop. Fiona bumped into her from below. Sally and Betty, still down in the hold, huddled at the foot of the ladder, bubbling with excitement.

"Hurry, Ivy. Land. We want to see the land," said Betty. "Don't be clumsy."

All tittered and giggled. Today when they circled the deck of the *Prometheus*, they'd be near land for the first time in months.

Light blinded Ivy when she reached the deck. She blinked and took a moment for her sight to clear.

"Oh, look," said Anne. She nudged Ivy in the ribs and pointed off to the west. A thin line of green so dark it appeared to be black lined one arc of the horizon. "Land. Can you believe it? We made it." Sea gulls wheeled and squealed overhead.

Without thinking, Ivy crossed herself, then looked around.

No one had noticed. The women all knew she was Catholic. There were more important things on their minds.

A sailor, his weathered brown face crinkled in a grin, hollered across the deck at the women.

"It's the Chesapeake Bay, my girls. We're done with the ocean for now. That's America you're looking at! Smooth sailing. Yes, indeed." The sailor hopped and skipped a few steps of a jig. His claw-like bare feet slapped the deck. His cronies guffawed.

The captive women began their trek around the ship. Rhys, at their head, gave the sailors a wide berth. An electric excitement hovered over the *Prometheus* like a fresh breeze. Rhys, though a boy, knew such energy on a ship had the power to sour and spark violence.

A few minutes after they came atop, Fiona and Ivy exchanged looks.

"What comes next, Fiona?"

"Whatever it is, you'll be fine, Ivy. You'll see. You've a good head on your shoulders. You're young, strong. You have Sean, as well. You'll be fine."

"I hope so."

Over the next few days, the ship plowed up the Chesapeake. Ivy, during one of her walks on deck, overheard the sailors referring to the Chesapeake as a river. She thought they were telling one of their fanciful tales. No river on earth was this broad. As they drew closer to the landmass, the hubbub grew. Ivy watched as the pirates lowered a small boat with three of their men in it. The fellows set to immediately and rowed toward the shore. Several hours later, down in their prison cell, the women heard huzzahs and hoorays resounding above.

Rhys clambered down into the hold.

"Oysters. They found oysters. As big as plates. The biggest oysters in the world. You wait. Captain says even you and the men prisoners will have some. Oh, and they brought fresh water."

He ran back up and brought them a pail of the water. Best of all, true to his word, Rhys delivered a bucket of briny, plump oysters an hour later, shucked and ready to slurp. Ivy joined in with the others, noisily gobbling the bounty. Rhys mentioned the captain's boast of the shellfish's restorative powers.

"I don't know about that, Rhys," said Sally. "I do know they taste marvelous—our first fresh food in ages. Thank you, little man. Thank you. And thank you for the fresh water, too. You are a marvel."

The next day, Ivy, Fiona, Sally, Betty, and Anne followed Rhys up the ladder. Standing at the opening to the hold was Eleanor. Her baby boy mewled in her arms.

"Oh, my!" shouted Sally.

Baby Timothy squalled louder.

Rhys stood back, letting the women cluster together and visit.

"We've missed you, Eleanor," said Betty.

Each of the women begged a turn to cradle the baby in their arms and stroke his soft cheeks. When Ivy held the infant, he wrapped his miniature fingers around her pointer. She chuckled.

"You should have a child of your own, Ivy. You're good with a baby," said Fiona.

Ivy smiled.

"I hope you have the chance one day, dear," whispered Eleanor. Her face glowed with the relaxed satisfaction Ivy had seen on other new mothers. Ivy murmured agreement, her eyes locked with baby Tim's.

On and on the *Prometheus* pushed up the Chesapeake Bay. Compared to the unpredictable and rough Atlantic, the estuary's waters resembled a farm pond. The women's walks on the deck increased to twice daily. The captain said he wanted them to grow strong before the ship reached harbor. The captain, according to Rhys, had warned the sailors not to molest the women. However, their hungry eyes were uncontrollable. One sailor, burly and black-haired, leered openly at Ivy every time she trod the deck. The others called him "Greenberry." Ivy kept her distance.

One morning, while walking with Rhys, dirty fists swatted Rhys to the side as if he were a bug. Rough hands grabbed Ivy from behind, and iron-like arms swiveled her about. She was face-to-face with Greenberry.

Wasting no time, while men shouted encouragement, he squeezed Ivy's breast hard, grabbed a handful of hair, yanked her head back, shoved his tongue into her mouth and probed it like a fat worm.

Ivy squirmed, gagging on his foul breath. She chomped down on his tongue with all her might.

With a roar, the pirate cast her to the deck. Blood streamed from his mouth, down his chin, and splattered on the deck.

Greenberry drew his fist back. Before he carried out his retribution, Dr Proctor and the captain grabbed the scoundrel and pulled him away.

Rhys bustled the women down to their cell and locked them in. Within minutes, the crack of a whip split the air on the deck and resounded into the hold. A roar of pain erupted with each of the twenty whistles of the lash.

"I hope he doesn't hurt me again, Fiona." Ivy pressed her fingers on her breast and felt the lingering soreness. "I'll have a bruise for sure."

Fiona returned her steady gaze. "Bruises heal, Ivy. You were good to stand up for yourself."

"Yes, you were. Proud of you, Ivy." Sally ran a loving hand over Ivy's curls. Even Betty reached out to hug her.

Ivy slept fitfully that night, chased by demons. Her own

whimpering woke her at one point. She lay on the floor, her heart pounding, with a feeling of overwhelming dread. The smell of burning peat, first faint and then stronger, filled her nostrils and calmed her. She was back in Ardmore, stirring a pot of porridge on the hearth while her mother spun wool and Honora swept the floor. Her mother's face glowed with beauty, unmarked by scars.

"Ivy," said her father, walking in the door. "Depend on God but use your own common sense. Believe in those who earn your trust and deserve it."

Ivy woke up. Dim light meandered down the ladder and highlighted the other imprisoned women's faces. She no longer feared her fellow captives. They were her friends. Her hand touched her breast, its soreness assuring the reality of Greenberry's attack. Greenberry and his ilk were her true enemies. Resolve and serenity settled over Ivy like a cloak.

The bay narrowed down. Rhys reported the water was becoming less and less salty. Soon they would drink it. Ivy peered over the ship's railing.

"Indeed, Fiona. Look. I can see a fish swimming just as if it's in a stream at home."

"It's huge, Ivy. Has to be six feet long. I've never seen a fish that big in Dungarvan or the river."

"Maybe it's a sea monster."

"Oh, Ivy. You're joking, aren't you?"

Ivy winked. The two giggled and moved along the deck, arm in arm.

Another day, Ivy and Fiona were up top for their exercise. Greenberry stayed far away and never lifted his eyes to the women. Ivy breathed in a lung full of crisp, clear air. The weather had noticeably cooled. As the girls turned back toward the bow, a black cloud approached from the north.

"Look at that!" Sally pointed. "I've never seen a cloud move so fast. Everything else is clear. It's so big and black. Maybe we should go below."

"What's that noise? It sounds like the wind in the trees," said Betty.

Band-like, swiveling, blacker than any cloud, the entity neared. Ivy and the other souls on the ship were mesmerized, frozen before the maelstrom like a deer before the hunter. Captain Smythe, statue-still, watched from the prow.

Ivy thought the captain looked like the devil himself about to be engulfed by evil. The *Prometheus* was damned, and they were all going to go up in smoke. The rustling sound grew louder. The swirling ebony ribbon spiraled down the Chesapeake and headed straight at the ship.

"Sounds like the devil grumbling," said Fiona, clutching Ivy's hand. "Oh, my lord."

Rhys moved closer to Sally. His mouth open, his eyes tracked the twisting cloud. Before anyone could react, the black swirling mass engulfed the air over the ship.

"Birds! It's a flock of birds," shouted Rhys. "Did you ever?"

Hundreds, no, thousands, of black birds, each no bigger than Ivy's hand, flew overhead in a rhythmic ribbon of twittering noise and darkness. Their thousands of flapping wings roared in her ears with one of the loudest sounds she'd ever heard. For more than a quarter of an hour, the daylight dimmed over the *Prometheus* as the migrating birds headed south.

"This is truly a wondrous place, Ivy." Fiona turned to watch the last of the flock.

Ivy believed the birds to be an omen. What sort of omen she did not know, but an omen, nevertheless.

Chapter 14

Aboard the Prometheus
Under sail on the Chesapeake Bay, Province of Maryland, British America

September 16, 1700

Silent as a cat on the prowl, Captain Smythe appeared beyond the iron bars of the women's cell. Ivy, dozing in the hammock, missed his footfall. Fiona shook her awake.

Beside Smythe was one of the older sailors, a benign-enough looking fellow the women recognized as Evans. Evans gave the girls a smile, revealing two or three blackened teeth set in an otherwise empty mouth. He doffed his ripped knit cap and bowed his head jokingly.

"Good day, my ladies," said Captain Smythe. "I'm sure Rhys has let you know you're in America now. Our time together is drawing to a close. I am certain you'll be finely treated in this British colony, Maryland. Soon we'll be landing at Baltimore County's harbor. The men there are rich and handsome and in need of your assistance. We want to make sure you're as pretty when you land as you were when you came aboard. You need to get cleaned up and made presentable for the gentlemen.

"You'll be taken two at a time up on the deck where we've made arrangements so you can clean yourselves a little. Don't worry. The sailors will not molest you. Our troublemaker Mr. Greenberry is locked up in the brig. The rest know I'll keelhaul anyone who lays a finger on one of you. Do as Mr. Evans says up top, or you'll forfeit supper. Or worse." With a sickly grin, the captain turned on his heel and left.

"You, and you." Evans pointed to Anne and Ivy. "Come with me. Don't tarry. Don't worry. You'll like this."

Anne turned her face to Ivy and raised an eyebrow. Ivy shrugged.

Mr. Evans opened the cell door, doffed his knitted cap, and stood aside as Ivy and Anne came out. The cell door clanged shut, and the two women headed up the stairs with Rhys and Evans.

Ivy felt steadier on her feet than she had, thanks to the extra pieces of hardtack she'd been given over the preceding days. Still, she became a little dizzy as she hit the sunlight.

Up on deck, the sailors stopped their work and stared.

Ivy felt her cheeks warm with a blush. She knew they had egged Greenberry on. She was so ashamed to be in such a state and humiliated by her capture. Her red curls had not been properly combed since she was stolen, though she'd often raked her fingers through them in unsuccessful attempts to keep them in order. Stains left from the ship's miserable food marked her ratty dress. Even worse, Betty had been seasick and vomited on Ivy's skirt. She'd tried to scrub the mess out without much success.

"Over here, ladies," called Captain Smythe from the poop deck. He then retreated to his quarters.

Mr. Evans grabbed an arm from each girl and walked them to the stern where the captain's quarters lay.

As she approached the stern, Ivy caught sight of a thatch of black curly hair. Sean! Her brother was mending canvas cross-legged on the deck. They exchanged a smile.

Ahead loomed a makeshift stall of old sails hung from lashed timbers. Overhead, buckets were rigged with ropes and pullies. The sailors had applied their expertise to create a makeshift shower for the women.

"Get in there and strip off every louse-infected inch of clothing you have on," said Evans, turning harsh in front of the other sailors. "Every single bit. And throw it over the top to me. Let me know when it's all off and stay inside."

Ivy's eyes met Anne's.

"We'll be okay. It's almost over, Ivy," said Anne. They took off the remnants of the clothes they'd worn when abducted. No petticoats had survived the trip—they had been sacrificed to wipe up messes and clean filth from their bodies. Their ragged dresses and chemises flew over the top of the stall, leaving them naked. Nothing remained of their life before their kidnapping except for the woolen green shawl and rosary Ivy had left behind in the cell.

Evans hallooed them. "All done?"

"Yes, Mr. Evans." Cool water splashed from above.

Rhys's sun-browned hand slid a bar of lye soap under the bottom of the canvas sheet.

"Use this and do a good job." Rhys chuckled.

"Go away, you scamp," snapped Anne. Then she laughed.

Anne and Ivy gleefully scrubbed the soap over their bony bodies. Their ribcages looked like washboards, and their hipbones protruded. Their knees looked like enormous knobs on their skinny, wasted legs. Realizing more water waited above them, they unfurled their hair and ran the wet bar of soap through it. The girls each soaped every square inch of their person they could reach and scrubbed each other's back.

"We're ready for more water," said Anne.

Another glorious deluge rinsed them, then they stood sparkling in the sun. Rhys's hand snaked under the canvas again, bearing two clean new cotton shifts. They put them on and then the cotton dresses that followed.

Ivy picked a green and white calico. The soft cotton comforted her scrubbed skin. Though the hand-me-down hung loose and fell well short of covering her ankles, Ivy adored the dress.

"After over two months in the same clothing," she told Anne, "a feedbag would be an improvement. These look quite pretty, don't you think?" Anne and Ivy stepped out of the stall.

"Here, miss," said the old sailor. Evans handed Ivy a wooden comb with a wink. "Maybe this will help." The women were pulled aside to sit on the deck and dry out. Rhys and Evans went to fetch the next pair of captives.

Ivy and Anne took turns combing out each other's hair, spreading it across their shoulders to dry in the sun while Fiona and Sally showered.

Ivy held little Timothy when his mother and Betty had their turn washing up and changing. He felt good in her arms.

Dr. Proctor had made certain Eleanor and Timothy had clean clothing and were kept tidy since the child's birth. He told Eleanor cleanliness would help them stay healthy. It apparently had.

The mighty Chesapeake had narrowed. For the first time, both sides were visible. Only a mile separated them. The sailors said the water was fresh from this point onward. They drew buckets up from the Chesapeake and drank freely. The ship turned northwest.

Ivy heard one sailor exclaim with great excitement, "We're in the Patapsco now, we are."

"What an odd name. What kind of country is this?" said

Eleanor. She held Timothy at her shoulder, rocked from foot to foot, and patted his swaddled rump.

"I guess we'll find out, dear." Sally, sitting on a pile of rope, smoothed the skirt of her raspberry-pink skirt. "Such a pretty color."

Ivy and the other women returned to the cell. During their absence, everything had been stripped except the chamber pot and petticoat privacy curtain. All else was gone, including Ivy's crucifix and shawl. The floor was swept and scrubbed. Nothing tangible remained from her life before the kidnapping. She had not one thing she could hold in her hand from home in Ireland. Nothing.

Despite her fatigue, Ivy could not sleep. Eleanor and her baby Timmy had returned to the cell. Timmy woke and whimpered but quickly quieted at his mother's breast.

MARYLAND

 Chapter 15 

Aboard the Prometheus
At the mouth of the Patapsco River, Baltimore County,
Province of Maryland

September 17, 1700

Time began to speed up, after unreeling at a desultory pace over hundreds of miles. The *Prometheus* glided to a halt after months of constant motion. Ivy's head spun with the loss of momentum. The six captive women huddled together, holding hands in their hot, stuffy cell. Rhys fairly shimmered with excitement when he brought them hardtack and gruel and—best of all—fresh water to drink. The women couldn't get enough.

"Be careful, ladies," said Rhys. "You don't want to drink too much and founder."

"Rhys, what's happening up top?" said Anne.

"Well, I'm not sure. Looks like the men are putting the ship to rights. The captain's all outfitted for doing business. I am sorry, but I don't rightly know exactly what's going on."

Fiona glanced at Ivy. "Do you think people here know this is a pirate ship?"

Ivy shrugged.

Betty grasped Sally's hand and heaved a sigh. Timmy contentedly suckled, his eyes closed in bliss, oblivious to the drama.

All day the noises of a harbor town traveled down to the women in their prison. Barrels rolled down the gangplank. Sailors cursed. Men yelled at each other. Wood bumped gently on wood as the ship rubbed against the dock.

The women huddled together and said little. Ivy worried she might be mistreated because she was Irish.

"Isn't everyone in America an Englishman, Fiona?"

"I don't know."

Sally said overhead: "Maryland's a British colony. I've heard there are all sorts of people here. Even Frenchmen and Dutch and Africans and wild naked savages. I wouldn't worry about being Irish so much as I'd worry about being a woman in a land full of randy men."

"Oh, Sally," said Betty.

"Well, 'tis true. They don't have enough women here. I just don't know if we'll have any say in what happens to us. After all, none of us came here voluntarily, so why would old Captain Smythe treat us right, now? But let's agree we'll do our best to help each other, Irish or English."

"I think you're right," said Fiona.

Ivy sat silent.

"Ivy?" Fiona prompted.

"I just want to go home with my brother. You have all treated me well and I appreciate that and love you, but I don't plan to stay. So I don't think I'll be around here to help."

"Well, Ivy, sorry we can't count on you," said Betty. "You might change your mind."

Rhys brought them fresh water, fish, and newly baked bread

for dinner which lightened the mood. He had even scrounged up butter.

"Ah, fresh bread. Can you believe it?" Anne reverently held a slab of the soft, aromatic loaf and breathed in its goodness before popping it in her mouth. Portions of all the food were the largest seen since the *Prometheus* had cast anchor in An Rinn.

Two days later, Rhys and Evans came down the ladder backlit by the morning sun. Behind them, a redheaded woman clambered down the ladder with the surefootedness of a billy goat. A brown checked dress and a white shawl draped her wiry frame. She stood back as Rhys unlocked the cell. Her amber eyes scanned the women and stopped at Timothy. The expression on her sharp-featured face relaxed as if the babe were a Christmas pudding. Swaddled in soft linen, plump-cheeked, he dozed in his mother's arms. Eleanor tightened her grasp.

Evans turned to Rhys. "Off with ye, lad."

Obediently, Rhys climbed the ladder with a parting peek at his charges.

Evans addressed the half-dozen imprisoned women. "Mizz Jane Grendon here is a midwife. She's going to make sure you are the maids you say you are. Don't give her any guff. I'm going to step aside as Captain Smythe trusts Mizz Jane to do her job. I'll be around the corner to step in if I need to. Behave, girls."

"What's happening?" Ivy whispered to Fiona.

Betty glared after Evans. Sally's lips firmed up. Miss Jane stepped into the cell. Evans locked the iron door behind her.

Impinging on the women's space, the midwife paused a few beats, inspecting the prisoners. She was unable to hide her surprise at Ivy's unusual eyes. In return, the imprisoned women noted the fine wrinkles about her eyes and mouth, the knobbiness of her knuckles, and the remarkable cleanliness of her hands and clothing.

Timothy's coos and the creaking of the wooden ship filled the conversational void.

"Mr. Evans is correct. I'm a midwife and I've delivered many a babe and attended many a woman. I'll not harm you and I'll be quick. Each of you needs to cooperate. Captain Smythe wants to know if you have been with a man or not. Be glad this is how he's learning this. You, dear," she said with a glance to Eleanor, "have clearly been with a man. I don't need to check you. Who of the rest of you will go first?"

Bold Sally stepped up. "I'll be first." Sally and Miss Jane moved to the side of the group.

"Who's next?" she asked after she had examined Sally.

"You don't need to touch me," said Betty. "I'll tell you right smart I've been with a man or two. No need to check me."

Miss Jane then beckoned Ivy. She knelt down beside her and lifted her skirt and the shift under it. Her cool hand slid up the inside of Ivy's thigh.

Ivy gasped. She felt herself drift away as she had in other times of distress, shutting down from reality. The next thing she knew, the midwife was climbing the stairs. Only the lingering aroma of lavender remained from her visit.

Fiona turned to the group. "Why'd Captain Smythe have her do that?"

"I think the captain is going to find husbands for some of us and they want to know if we're virgins. That's the only reason for that. Some men only want virgins," said Sally.

"But what if we're not?" said Betty. "What happens to us, then?"

Chapter 16

Aboard the Prometheus
Moored at the mouth of the Patapsco River, Baltimore County,
Province of Maryland

September 18, 1700

Ivy was screaming. "Ma! Daddy!" Her throat hurt, yet no sound would come. Her parents stood across the willow-lined stream, holding hands and looking down at Honora and Joey. Early morning sun sparkled on the water. All she wanted was for them to see her . . . to know she still lived.

"Ivy, wake up. Wake up," said Fiona. "You're having a bad dream. Wake up."

Ivy fought Fiona's intrusion into her dreamland. She wanted to linger with her family, to have the ineffable joy of their presence continue. She wanted them to see her. Her head felt fuzzy. When she opened her eyes, she couldn't figure out why the tree-lined riverbank was gone. Then Ivy remembered where she was. Sweat dampened her dress where she'd lain on it. Sadness weighed her down. Soon she'd be filthy again. And maybe worse.

Boots came down the steps, then veered off toward the men's

cells. Clanging metal and shuffling feet followed.

Ivy pressed herself against the iron cage, wanting to hold Sean in her eyes as long as possible. Her brother, ragged and thin, paused to smile when he reached the foot of the ladder. All too soon, he was gone, like a heat-induced shimmering apparition, a ghost.

Fruitlessly, the women strained to hear what was happening on deck. Near palpable silence reverberated through the hold.

An hour later Rhys, toting water and porridge, could only shrug when they asked where the men had gone. "I think they're finding work," he said. "They've going off with their new masters to help with the crops and such."

"What about us?" said Betty, a crease of worry between her brows. "What about us? And why do they care if we're maids or women?"

Again, Rhys shrugged. "What'd you mean, maids or women? I don't understand any of that. I'm sure everything will be fine," the boy murmured as he left with the empty tinware.

Later, in the afternoon, Evans and Rhys led the women up top. Captain Smythe, decked out in his purple coat and hat, stood like an actor against a theater backdrop of a harbor town. A smattering of crude cottages and shops clustered at the edge of the Patapsco. Men and the occasional woman strolled the hamlet. Tall lacy trees interspersed with flat open land to fill the skyline. A dog barked. A horse neighed.

Ivy sent a prayer of thanksgiving into the cloudless sky. She had survived the crossing. Sally, Eleanor, Anne, Betty, Fiona, and Ivy chattered, hugged, giggled, and laughed aloud.

Captain Smythe proudly grinned as if he had done them a great favor. After a few minutes, he clapped his ruffled hands together three times.

"Just a word, ladies. From here, you will go to a gathering

place where gentlemen await you. These men will be arranging to pay for the cost of your travel to this land, the Royal Colony of Maryland. Listen closely.

"I am a fair man, as you well know. I have promised the owner of the *Prometheus* to inform you of all your obligations and will do so now.

"In exchange for paying your passage to this place, you will be required to work for your master for a term of four years. The men also may, if they choose, pay me for your travel and welcome you as their bride."

Smythe gave a false smile to the huddling women.

"Today is one of opportunity for each of you. Once you have repaid your master for your travel, you will be rewarded with a new set of clothes, animals, and land to get you started on your own. It has been a pleasure traveling with you and I wish you all the best."

Captain Smythe plopped his feathered hat firmly on his head, gave the briefest of bows, then sauntered down the gangplank and off the *Prometheus.*

The six women were immobile.

Evans cut their trance short. "Come along, all you wenches, ahem, I mean ladies. Just follow me. We'll get you all settled in America, we will."

Fiona and Sally led off, followed by Ivy, then Eleanor with little Timmy. Anne and Betty came last. The crew of the *Prometheus* stopped their work to stare as the colorful skirts of the captives swayed down the gangplank and out into the New World.

Ivy stumbled when she stepped onto the cobblestones rimming the river wharf. Her feet had not touched the earth for many weeks. Her body, weakened and without heaving water beneath, swam in the air. Her head spun.

Like spring hatchlings, the six young women followed the old sailor past the cluster of squat clapboard shops. Perched on the stone stoop of a shop door, a disheveled woman sipped from a flask. Bare, dirty feet protruded from the hem of her red striped skirt. Her stench shoved the six passing women closer together as they walked by.

Evans led them on to a small clearing on the riverbank. Towering trees ringed it on three sides. The Patapsco River formed the fourth. Crude wooden wagons with equally rough-looking horses sheltered under the trees. A gaggle of jostling men loitered nearby. Little gray or silver hair could be seen among them. None achieved the fanciness of Captain Smythe.

Smythe, talking to a tall blond man, gave a barely perceptible signal to Evans. He slapped the man on the back. Ivy heard him say, "Well, George, I think you'll be happy with my cargo."

He sauntered away to seat himself behind a dinged-up wooden table under an ancient oak. A stack of papers, a bottle of ink, and a quill pen lay on the table. Evans lined the women up with their backs to the Patapsco River.

Timmy blurted out a squall. Rhys jiggled the babe's hand until he quieted, and winked at the women.

Off in the distance, Ivy could see the sailors rolling barrels down the ship's gangplank to the shore. She searched for her brother. She worried he was gone, and she had missed any chance to share a goodbye.

Sally nudged Ivy in the ribs. "Pay attention, Ivy. Figure out which man looks safest and do your damnedest to entice him. Smile. Flirt as if your life depended on it. Which it does."

"What?"

Fiona gave her a glance and mouthed, "Yes."

"You girls, shut up," sneered Evans, self-importance filling his voice.

A contingent of men from the crowd sauntered over. They looked the women up and down. A thin fellow of about thirty grabbed Betty's right hand. Swatting at her as she tried to pull back, he turned it over in his hands, rubbed her palm and fingertips. He repeated the maneuver with her left hand, then turned to other men.

"Look. Not one callus. Never did a lick of real work in her life I warrant. Don't have to wonder how this wench ended up on Smythe's ship."

A few of the men ran their hands up and down the girls' legs and demanded they raise their skirts to display them. Others had the girls open their mouths. They peered in and examined their teeth, as if establishing the age of a new plow horse. Boldly, the men ran their fingers through the captives' hair and felt their skulls. They felt their arms and checked their muscles. Even baby Timmy was disrobed, turned over, poked, and prodded as if he were a pork roast proffered by the village butcher.

More than one man startled when they glimpsed Ivy's mismatched eyes. Watching at Ivy's side, Sally's lips twitched in a near-snicker as one shabbily dressed fellow crossed himself at the sight.

A swarthy man with bloodshot eyes and liquor on his breath lingered. His soft lace cravat brushed against Ivy's skin as he fingered her thin legs. Tears pooled in her eyes. With a malodorous belch, he slid his hands up past her knees. A gust of cooling wind blew in off the Patapsco and fluttered her hem away from his sweaty hand. Ivy held her breath. Her chin trembled to keep the scream in.

Up stepped the fellow Ivy had seen talking earlier to the captain—George, the tall blond. His handsome face, set atop broad shoulders, towered above the fray. Agile and sober as a judge should be, he outmatched the drunk who knelt at Ivy's feet. George did not need to lay a finger on the inebriated lout, only to speak. He wielded his intimidating power like a parrying sword, thrusting forward to address the drunk, then standing back and giving Ivy breathing room.

"Beg your pardon, Mr. Lacey. I have a question, Nathan, for the lass." George's voice was as commanding as his presence.

Ivy's tormentor sneered and scuttled backward like a hermit crab.

"Miss, how many younger brothers and sisters do you have?" The good-looking man's patience was palpable, yet his relentless gaze demanded a reply.

Ivy looked to Fiona who repeated the question in Gaelic to her. Fiona added in Gaelic, "Be sweet to him, Ivy. You'll be better off with him than the others. Trust me."

"Two," Ivy said, holding up the correct number of fingers. "Joseph and Honora."

"Ah, and did you help raise them?" he said, slowly so she understood.

She nodded a yes.

Satisfied, George moved on.

Finished perusing the women, the planters retreated back to the sidelines to smoke and converse.

Captain Smythe rose. With a wave of his hand, he silenced the buzzing conversations. A brief preamble of flattery, then he quickly moved on to the business at hand.

First, the pirate reviewed the predatory terms of indenture. In exchange for payment to Captain Smythe to cover the cost of their travel and food and sundry associated expenses, any man could buy any of the women and marry her. Any man could buy one or more of the women's labor for four years. After completing her four years of service, she would be entitled to land and clothing.

"Otherwise, indentured servants, male or female, are forbidden from marrying during their indenture. Children born to indentured women will go with their mother and be subject to indenture until they are twenty-one years of age. Anyone attempting to escape will be punished. Masters are within their rights to flog runaways, brand them, put them in a metal collar or shackles. At the very least, runaways will have their indenture extended for a minimum of one year."

Of course, the wily pirate didn't mention what all the men already knew: the majority of the women would not survive the four years of service. One by one, heavy labor, disease, and childbirth would carry them off. Captain Smythe proceeded to the auction.

Evans pushed Betty to the front of the group.

Nathan Lacey, the finely dressed drunk, was the sole bidder for Betty's indenture. She became his servant for two hundred pounds of tobacco. Betty's face hardened as he led her away to stand under a nearby tree.

Next, Nathan bought soft-spoken Anne. She wept as she was led away and collapsed against Betty.

Ivy turned to whisper to Fiona. "Why would he need two women? Does he have a big farm?"

Fiona pressed her lips together and said nothing.

One by one, the men—most appeared to be farmers—bought the women and led them off. Sally's purchaser signed her bond and blurted, "We'll be wed as soon as I get my tobacco to the captain. Yes, we will, my dearie. Today's the day." Sally's smooth face gave nothing away.

Eleanor stumbled off with Timmy, stunned, in the wake of a husky yeoman.

A dimpled man whistled a spritely tune as he signed the indenture papers for Fiona.

Fiona kissed Ivy's cheek. "I love you, Ivy," she said. "Make the best of this. Keep your head up and we'll meet again." Fiona turned on her heel, flashed what Ivy knew to be an insincere smile to her new master, and lightly stepped away with him.

"Start rolling these hogsheads, men," shouted Evans to the sailors loitering in the crowd. They scurried to the wagons and rolled the four-foot barrels of tobacco down to the *Prometheus*.

Ivy remained, the last to be chosen. She wiped perspiration from her forehead and knew her hair had frizzed into a coppery explosion. A persistent fly buzzed about her head.

"Now, men, we have a fine maiden here. Very lovely. Speaks a little English—well, at least a word or two—and knows how to weave. What'll you pay?"

Nathan Lacey shouted, "One hundred pounds of tobacco. Remember, she has those be-deviled eyes. Need a discount for those."

"Oh, come on, sirs," said the captain. "A guaranteed virgin. Surely you can do better."

"Three hundred," came from the tall man—George—who had questioned Ivy.

"Five hundred," bid Lacey.

A stocky pockmarked man in the crowd shouted. "You whoremonger, Nathan. Leave the lass be. Let Stokely have her. You've plenty of women to service Baltimore."

Lacey shot a warning look toward the fellow.

"One thousand pounds of fine Orinoco tobacco, a full hogshead," rumbled forth from George Stokely.

The crowd gasped. One thousand pounds! No one had ever heard of an indentured servant being bought for such a sum. The tall blond had called Nathan Lacey's bet and raised it.

"You can have the Irish wench for that, you fool, George Stokely, and best of luck. She's cursed and you know it," said Lacey.

Laughter rippled through the crowd.

"Don't be a poor sport, Nathan," said the pockmarked man.

"Good for you, George. Always going your own way, still the independent little convict boy," said a white-haired planter, removing a clay pipe from his mouth for a few moments. He tapped the pipe against a wagon wheel.

Stokely ignored him.

"Let's do the paperwork and we can all be on our way," said Captain Smythe to hurry things along. He opened his arms and flicked his fingers, urging George Stokely to come forward, to commit to the wondrous sum of one hogshead of tobacco, a thousand pounds of cured brown leaves packed in a four-foot-high wooden barrel, the harvest of nine months of nurturing and labor.

Smythe dipped his quill into the ink bottle and hen-scratched on the vellum. George Stokely unhurriedly strolled over. He towered over the pirate. Stokely picked up the bond. For several minutes, he perused the document while Smythe squirmed in anticipation. Finished, with a brief glance at Ivy, George bent over and signed.

"Ivy O'Neill, that's her name, Captain Smythe? Where'd you find her?" George asked as if any answer would do. He beckoned Ivy to him with his hand.

The captain's lips mimicked a smile. "Yes, Ivy O'Neill. She's Irish."

Ivy's eyes sought Rhys. The boy gave an enigmatic shrug, then scampered to the *Prometheus*. Head bowed, Ivy followed in George Stokely's wake.

Chapter 17

Baltimore County, Province of Maryland

September 18, 1700

Ivy glanced about the slowly changing landscape as if looking for the door out of this exotic new world. Flat as a bannock, green and gold, the harbor town and the Patapsco lay behind them. They traveled east. With her new master beside her on a bench seat, she wobbled and bounced as his wagon rolled over a crude byway.

The horror of marrying a stranger against her will roared through her brain. She knew the loss of her virginity would likely bring pain no matter whom she married. Being bedded—or raped—by a foreign stranger would magnify her trauma.

When she was eleven, her mother took her on a walk in the sun. "Ivy, dear, your body's going to change in a year or so. You'll become a woman." Ann O'Neill shocked her daughter with the details of what to expect—a bosom, hair in new places, monthly courses, and belly cramps.

"Don't fret, girl. There're ways women care for themselves."

Her mother had pointed out the nearby feverfew bushes. Dainty white flowers dotted the yellow-green plants. "Ignore the flowers, Ivy. Pick the leaves. We'll dry them for tea." A pungent aroma rose as her mother pulled at the plants.

"When you begin having your monthly course, you drink it to relieve cramps. The tea is good for other womanly problems, too. Two or three leaves for a cup of tea is all you need. It is bitter. A drop of honey will fix that."

"Do Rory and Sean bleed?" Ivy asked. The answer disappointed her. Every prediction her mother promised came to pass.

A year or two later, Ivy had begun to find excuses to visit the Flinns' cottage. She hung on every word spouted by Kevin.

Ann again took Ivy aside. She spoke of the phenomenal power of love between a man and a woman. She went over the mechanics of lovemaking, including the unique characteristics of a woman's first experience with intercourse.

"Love is a gift a man and a woman give each other, one that can deepen over the years. You don't want to waste it on an unworthy man nor risk having a bastard child."

Ivy understood.

"You do not want the burden of birthing a fatherless child." Ann reinforced her message. "If, by a mishap, you believe you are carrying such a child, you need to come to me. I will get you help."

"Help?" Ivy had been confused.

"Not every pregnancy brings forth a baby. There are teas and roots and . . . well, you won't need to ever worry about that, Ivy. I trust you to take care with your love."

"Why is there always pain for women, Ma? Cramps, first love, childbirth? Why?"

"Maybe it's to remind us how important coupling can be, dear. I really don't know." Ann smiled. Ivy grumbled under her breath, then shot a smile at her mother. She could count on her mother.

Now, seated by Stokely, Ivy's bottom lip quivered, then firmed into a frown. Buried in the folds of her skirt, her hands clenched in her lap.

She remembered Captain Smythe's disdain for Betty, and Betty's hatred of him. Ivy wanted a respectful mate and an affectionate union. Not a forced marriage.

Eleanor's screams when birthing Timmy still rang in her ears. Her gorge rose at the thought of feeling such pain over an Englishman's child. She did not want to marry this lout beside her. She wanted Kevin.

There was much more she should know before her wedding. She had grown up assuming her mother and other women would continue to teach her what she needed to know. Yet here she was, plopped down thousands of miles from home. Separated from her mother. No one to help her.

Her eyes slid to Stokely as if to see if he had changed and become less threatening.

He had not. George Stokely terrified her with his size and dominion over her. George could inflict any damage he chose upon her with impunity. Biting off a piece of his tongue would not be enough to stop such a strapping big man. Isolated in a land which looked and smelled like no other in her experience, she was unmoored.

Ivy decided to concentrate on doing useful things. She turned her attention to the wagon's route. Memorizing the way to get back to the harbor from wherever Mr. Stokely was taking her was important. Worrying was useless.

Ivy mindlessly scratched one of the fresh mosquito bites on her arm. She felt the tingling of a dawning sunburn. George Stokely flicked a glance and an easy smile her way, then shifted his weight. For a big man, he had a grace about him. He stood five inches past six feet, by Ivy's estimate. Unlike other tall fellows, he was neither thin nor stocky. Instead, he had a muscular build with a broad chest. God had painted his face with broad brush strokes. High cheekbones, a straight nose, and a square chin all lent to his physical beauty. As a final gift, his easy smiles revealed dimples in each cheek. Ahead of them in the traces, a fat-rumped bay mare jauntily pulled the wagon. Sleek and well-muscled, she responded quickly to whatever Stokely asked of her.

Ivy glanced at his relaxed grip on the reins. Freckles dotted the backs of his square hands. Fine blond hairs on his hands and forearms caught the sunlight. His thighs bulged with muscle and were as big around as Ivy's emaciated waist.

Ivy's fingertip found the bruise on her breast and remembered Greenberry's grasp.

In the back of the wagon, a fellow still redolent of the ship's hold lay collapsed against bags of seed, like a bit of flotsam. Sally had drilled Ivy in English as they traipsed around the *Prometheus*'s deck and encouraged her to learn. Recalling Sally's explanation of jetsam being debris deliberately discarded overboard while flotsam hit the ocean by accident, Ivy decided the fellow behind her must be jetsam. Definitely. Tossed aside on purpose he was. Bony as a pile of sticks, his face obscured by lank greasy hair, he wore rags which looked like they may have been clothes many months ago in another country and another life.

Ivy recognized the entirety of the wagonload as coming from the *Prometheus*, including two packets of her mother's woven wool.

"Don't even think of running away," said Stokely, raising his voice to reach both his newly acquired servants.

Ivy stopped scratching her bites. How had Stokely read her mind?

"Running away means working another year or worse. You

could be flogged or even branded, and I'd still be within my rights." His gray eyes shot a warning her way.

Ivy looked down at her lap. A sigh escaped unbidden.

"Once you've paid me back with your labor, then I'm honor bound to help you get started on your own. A bit of land, clothing, things like that. My word is good. I just settled up with my man Edward. That's why I need you, Peter. I need your help." Stokely half turned to look back at the man behind him.

After months on the ship with the English girls, though she might struggle to speak English, Ivy understood about half of Stokely's words. But she understood all of what he meant: he owned her and the pitiful man in the back.

"Why d'you need me?" blurted Ivy in her Gaelic-accented English.

George spoke slowly and enunciated each word. "Ivy, I need help with my children and house. And I need help in the fields."

Peter roused a bit. Changing positions let loose a new cloud of bad smells. "Don't matter, my girl, why he wants us. We're here now and this man owns us. Just pray you live through your indenture. Most like us don't."

Stokely drew back into himself, like a tortoise pulling its head back into its shell, as the wagon rumbled onward.

Ivy couldn't lie, even to herself. After rolling over the ocean for months, the smells of this countryside—the greenery, soil, and fresh air—lifted her spirits. Canebrakes, reedy marshes, and still water creeks were interspersed with woodlots and flat fields. A heron the size of a child rose from fishing to soar on to the next waterway. Though far from free, Ivy's relief at being out of the iron cage and away from the captain's malevolent spirit created a joy so great she was certain she would fly up into the sky if anything else wonderful happened on this momentous day. Such a stew of joy, worry, anger, and elation.

Houses were few and far between. Most of the houses were unpainted wood. Even their chimneys were branches woven together, then daubed with mud. How can they not burn? Ivy wondered. Unlike the cottages clustered in hamlets throughout Waterford County, homes here sat in solitude at the end of long lanes.

"Don't suppose this looks much like Ireland," said George. "Never been to Ireland myself and can hardly recall England. Most homes here are set down a lane and butt up to a river. Lots of travel up and down the waterways, Ivy. The Chesapeake's our heart and soul."

Ivy tried to decipher George's words. She believed the man might expect a response, so replied, "Yes."

Peter shifted in the back of the wagon. "Anything's an improvement over the ship, sir," he said. "I'm sure the girl agrees."

As the bay mare gamely pulled them onward, the pungent smell of hogs tickled Ivy's nose. Reminiscent of her early years in Ardmore, the porcine stink reassured Ivy as she traveled through the otherwise strange land.

The mare did not wait for the flick of the reins to swing the wagon to the left. She pulled it down a rutted lane and picked up her pace. Acres of cleared land stretched to a wooded horizon. Successions of small hillocks filled the fields, each no higher than a man's knees. Topknots of big-leafed plants sprouted from each one.

"Sotweed," mumbled Peter as he roused himself.

"Orinoco tobacco," clarified its owner and planter, Stokely. "Maryland money."

The wagon rounded a low hill. A farmhouse came in view. Rays from the lowering sun glinted off glass windows and brought out the warm red of the two-story brick home. A pair of gables pierced the roof, each set with a multi-paned window.

Stone chimneys bracketed each end of the house. Ivy thought she spied a candle's flicker through one window.

"*Convict's Revenge*. My home, my land. Ivy and Peter, welcome," said Stokely. "I want you to know I am glad you're going to help me, and I will do my best to treat you right."

"'Tis a magnificent property, sir," said Peter. "I'm sure the girl joins me in saying we'll do our best to serve you well. Right, girl?"

"Yes," said Ivy. She plucked at a thread on her skirt, eyes downcast.

A brown mongrel hound bounded down the lane.

"Rascal, go home," George pointed to the house and the dog obeyed.

The opinionated mare picked up speed and voted for a trot. Stokely gently pulled her back.

"Now, Juno, we're all hungry. Not so fast, old girl," said Stokely with a chuckle. Driving the wagon behind the house, he pulled up to the stable. A miniature village of outbuildings spread behind the house. All were clapboard with the exception of a commodious brick kitchen sited a safety-minded twenty yards from the main house. Smoke belched from its chimney, carrying the aroma of roast pork. Tusked hogs snuffled at a pile of windfall apples. Hens scratched in the dirt and chased insects. Lightning bugs twinkled. A door slammed.

A boy waved his arms through the air and ran up to the wagon. A gray-headed woman trailed him, leading a toddler in a white dress. Capable hands had neatly plaited the pretty girl's dark hair and piled it with ribbons atop her head like a crown. She carried a gray kitten and looked as if she had stepped out of a painting. Rascal, the hound, affably joined the fray, tongue out. Seen up close, the long wiry hairs of his coat looked like a mud-brown explosion of sorts, going every which way but straight.

"Pa, Pa! You're back! What'd you bring me?"

Towheaded and stamped with his father's distinctive features, the boy peered at Ivy and Peter.

"Who're they?"

"Miss Ivy O'Neill, and Mister Peter Browne. They're going to help us," said Stokely. "Ivy and Peter, this is my son, Samuel. Sam, please unhitch Juno and cool her off properly. Then feed and water her, son. She's done a good day's work." Stokely jumped down and handed the reins to his son with a shoulder hug.

"Aunt Sarah and Bethany, I want to introduce you to Miss Ivy O'Neill and Mister Peter Browne," said Stokely. "Ivy, Peter, this is Miss Sarah Chichester. You may call her Miss Sarah, if you please."

The old lady paused in her perusal of the two new servants to give a smile and nod of acknowledgment.

"And Bethany, my daughter. She's three, so bears minding." Hearing her name, Bethany looked up from the struggling kitten cradled in her arms. Miss Sarah, round in every way, gave her a gentle nudge.

Ivy climbed down from the wagon and extended her hand. The child grabbed it with a giggle and dropped the kitten. Freed, the gray ball of fur streaked away.

Ivy touched a purple stain on the little girl's chest.

"Pwum. Pwum jam," said Bethany.

"Plum jam? Oh, my," said Ivy with a smile. Bethany ran to her father, who picked her up with a smacking loud, exaggerated kiss on the cheek. She laughed and snuggled into his shoulder.

Two men, laborers by their plain dress, sauntered up from the outbuildings. "Tom, Christopher, come over, please. Meet the new workers. Help unload the cart, if you would," said Stokely, still carrying his daughter. "Show them where everything goes."

Christopher, a beefy Englishman in his thirties, welcomed the newcomers with a handshake. His sidekick Tom let Christopher do all the talking.

Ivy thought Tom plain. Neither fat nor thin, tall nor short, with eyes and hair both a middling, indeterminate color, Tom's reticence and persona sent a shiver down Ivy's spine.

Ivy and the three English servants supped in the kitchen on roast pork, cornbread, and buttermilk. The fresh food, simple as it was, tasted heavenly to Ivy. Afraid her body would rebel if she ate too much after being underfed for months, she nibbled small servings, taking her time savoring and chewing every morsel.

Peter followed a different approach. He shoveled the food into his gaping maw and rarely lifted his sunken eyes from the tin plate.

Afterward, Tom, Christopher, and Peter wandered off to a clapboard outbuilding by the stable. Peter stumbled a little, his legs still at sea. Ivy hoped he would bathe or at least use a washrag.

Left alone, she sat on the kitchen's cool stone stoop and mused in the gloaming. She breathed in the cool air and with it the farm smells of animals, plants, and dirt. The beauty of the evening pierced her and underlined what she had lost. She yearned for home.

Ivy overheard Miss Sarah and George speaking in a nearby room. Perhaps they didn't realize she understood a great deal more English than she let on.

"I'm surprised you brought back a girl. A very pretty one indeed, George."

"Is she? She looked to be the youngest and most wholesome of the lot. Didn't pick her for her looks. She has helped raise a brother and sister so should know how to handle the children. You need more help around here now Bethany's getting older. She leads us all a merry chase and with the house to mind, I think it's a lot for one woman. You deserve a lightening of your load, Auntie. You do too much. I think this girl will be a help to you."

"Well, be ready, George, for tongues to wag. You know how people love to talk. You're a rich, good-looking man and she's a pretty girl. They've been waiting with bated breath for you to remarry or at least start courting. Polly Carr's been hovering around like a little honeybee at a flower. Court her. Otherwise, you'll need to mind your behavior with this servant girl and conversation out in public. Mark my words."

"I always do, Auntie. I always do. I've no interest in remarrying. Busy enough with this farm. Polly's pretty, everyone agrees. But a pretty face only goes so far. No one can replace Lydia. Such a kind, sweet soul. Nevertheless, I'll heed your recommendation." The firm closure of a door followed.

A soft tread approached Ivy from behind. A gentle hand touched the back of her shoulder.

"Ivy, come with me. I'll show you to your bed. I'm sure you're tired. There'll be plenty to do tomorrow," said Miss Sarah. She smelled of flowers. A white lace cap sat atop her gray curls. Ivy followed her, surprised at being led into the house.

Light-stepped and precise in her movements despite her chubbiness, Miss Sarah entered a central hall, then turned and climbed up a handsome staircase.

"Come along, dear. Your bed's up here." Their final destination was an airy room with a pair of windows overlooking the farmyard. A candle burned on a wooden candlestand, highlighting two lumps sharing a bed and a woven coverlet. Light snoring came from the larger lump. Ivy could see little Sam's upturned face. A blanketed pallet lay on the floor nearby.

"Ivy, you can sleep here with the children. That way, you can attend to them during the night if they need anything. I'm in the room next door. Mr. Stokely's room is across the hall. There's a basin, soap, and water too, so you can clean up a bit. We'll get you a good soak in the tub tomorrow." The elderly woman's faded blue eyes caught the candlelight. Eyes that missed nothing.

Ivy nodded in understanding.

Miss Sarah turned and quietly closed the paneled wooden door behind her.

Confused feelings overwhelmed Ivy and she wept. Exhausted, she dropped into the void of dreamless sleep.

Chapter 18

Convict's Revenge
Near the Patapsco River, Maryland

September 20, 1700

Ivy opened her eyes. The children's bed was empty. She washed her face and hands, then put on the green calico dress. She tiptoed downstairs.

Bright-eyed and pink-cheeked, Miss Sarah sipped tea by the hearth. Her blue, flowered dress lay in soft folds over her rotund body. A sparkling white cap covered most of her gray curls.

"Good morning, Ivy," said Miss Sarah. "It's a lovely day. Would you care for a cup of tea? Help yourself. I've already brewed a pot. There's porridge in the pot out in the kitchen. You can bring it in here to eat at the table."

Miss Sarah spoke slowly, as if she knew Ivy's difficulties with English. The language had begun emerging in her dreams while still on the *Prometheus*. It did not sound as strange to her ear as it had in the past. She could follow the thread of most English conversations, though she still missed many words. Her Gaelic stumbled to her tongue these days. She searched for words in Gaelic and English. Ivy knew she was losing her Gaelic and, with it, a part of home.

Ivy slurped porridge, distracted by its comforting warmth, while Miss Sarah instructed her in the workings of the *Convict's Revenge*. Fresh food lifted her spirits.

" . . . and Mr. Stokely needs you in the fields today, so I'll be taking care of the children except at mealtime. You'll be eating your meals with us so you can keep the children in order, or at least some semblance of it. They are energetic, those two," Miss Sarah said. "Tobacco! Such a finicky crop! Let's get you a hat. Otherwise, you'll be fried red as fire and no good to anyone. I see you already have a pinking up from yesterday's travels. And keep your shoes on outside."

After Ivy finished her breakfast, Miss Sarah sent her out to help the men.

"You only need to walk straight along past the stable, Ivy. Keep walking along the fence line and you can't help but find Samuel and the men."

Sun warmed her shoulders and the top of her head as she went out. Chickens scattered and a fat white gander hissed. After the collection of outbuildings, the stable, and animal pens, she came to the fields. The first small field held a hodgepodge of plants. Most were still green and held their harvest. Ivy marveled and talked to herself.

"Well, girl, what do you suppose that one is? The tall stalks all brown and tied in a bundle? Hmmm. I do see a few melons. Look at those shiny red round things."

Curious, she anticipated tasting the odd vegetables. She also noticed an orchard on the other side of the vegetables.

"Mr. Stokely is a clever man. He grows all his own food."

Ivy neared the tobacco fields and realized she had misjudged the size of the tobacco plants when she saw them from a distance. Nearly six-feet-tall plant spikes with skirts of lance-like two-foot-long leaves crowned the hillocks. Ivy could hear the murmuring of the workers, obscured by leaves as they squatted at the bases of the sotweed. She jumped up every few steps for a peek and, by following their voices, located Peter and Christopher.

The two stood together by a tobacco hill. Ivy was reminded of the allegorical illuminations in Father Declan's Bible.

Hale and hearty Christopher turned, his cheeks pink against tanned skin. "Good morning, Ivy. Glad to have you here to help." His white teeth gleamed. The early sun struck turquoise in his eyes.

Wraith-like and pale, Peter leaned on a hoe as if he were the reaper Death with a scythe. Scrubbed clean, no longer stinking, his stick-thin arms and legs swam in fresh clothing. Ivy figured another week on the *Prometheus* would have killed him.

Her thoughts turned to Sean. Where was he? Did her brother have clean clothes? Was his new master feeding him enough? Damn the pirates.

Peter looked up. "Morning, Miss Ivy. Did you enjoy your breakfast?" He flashed a skeletal grin.

"Yes, thank you." Ivy kept her English simple.

Christopher demonstrated to the newcomers how to slice the unwieldy leaves from their stalk and pointed out a ramshackle cart waiting for their harvest.

"Mind what you're doing now, you two," warned Christopher. "We don't want any four-fingered servants—or three-fingered, for that matter."

He then sauntered off to help Tom, whistling a spritely tune. Off in the distance, George Stokely's oaky baritone coupled with his son Samuel's light giggles.

"Well, what do you think, Miss Ivy, of our lot?" said Peter.

"Too early to know, Mr. Browne, but I am glad to be off the *Prometheus*. That is a fact for certain."

"Call me Peter. I left the 'Mr.' back in England. We better get started with this sotweed. How about I cut, and you carry?"

Try as they might, the pair had little strength and even less stamina. Weakened from their imprisonment on the *Prometheus*, Ivy and Peter lagged behind the pace set by Christopher, Tom, and Stokely. Their atrophied arm muscles quivered, heartbeats quickened, and breathing labored with every lift of a load and swipe of a cutting knife. Even Samuel outperformed them, flitting about among the hillocks of Orinoco tobacco with Rascal on his heels. Ivy and Peter quickly found themselves relegated to the tobacco barns while the others chopped and loaded the tobacco leaves. The small rough-hewn structures resembled roofs on stilts, with open sides and multiple crosspiece rafters.

Ivy's task was to poke an awl through each thick stem, then run hemp cording through it. After she had strung several big leaves on a cord, she handed it off to Peter. He tied the cording to the rafters, festooning the upper reaches of the barns with the bundles of leaves. Under the roof but in the open air, they would slowly age and dry.

Ivy and Peter watched with trepidation as Christopher, red-cheeked and jovial, perused their work. Ivy wondered what would happen to them if they failed at this, too.

"That's exactly what we need done. Fine work, you two. After a few months hanging and curing, that sotweed will make a good smoke. We'll pack it into the hogsheads later on this fall."

Ivy heaved a small sigh.

A broad-branched oak tree held pride of place in the midst of the tobacco hillocks. At noon, the workers lounged in its shade. Miss Sarah, Bethany, and Sam brought baskets of aromatic fried chicken and fresh corn bread. Ivy's stomach gave a loud growl. She felt a blush overtake her face. Tom stared at her. Peter stared at the food.

"Don't worry, girl. We're all hungry," said Christopher. "Let's eat."

Peter pounced on the chicken like a cat on a mouse. Ivy silently counted to three, then reached for a drumstick.

Fresh water and apples rounded out the meal. Ivy enjoyed the fresh water almost as much as the food after her months of drinking the ship's foul beverages. Her belly full, Ivy tried to follow the men's conversation. She leaned back against the oak. Her eyes soon closed. She awoke with a snort to find Sam tickling her with a bit of wild carrot. They both burst out in laughter, her first laugh in this strange new land.

By suppertime, Ivy ate her meal in a trance. Harvesting tobacco had left her arms aching and sunburned.

Sam paused from shoveling his dinner into his open mouth. "Ivy helped. Said she never saw tobacco before. Right, Ivy?"

"Chew up your food before you speak, son." George did a fake frown.

Sam swallowed. "Sorry, Pa. Anyway, it's true, isn't it, Ivy?"

"Yes, Sam. Never saw it before." She quickly went back to her meal. Wholesome and tasty, the simple boiled beef and fresh vegetables delighted her. Dessert was a poached pear.

Ivy offered to help clear the table at the meal's end, but Miss Sarah shooed her upstairs and to bed with the children.

"You'll have plenty of time in the future to help. Get some rest, my girl."

Upstairs, sleep overwhelmed Ivy like a smothering hand.

 Chapter 19 

Convict's Revenge
Near the Patapsco River, Maryland

September 21, 1700

She awoke early. Her cheek, poking from under the wool blanket, felt cool. The smell of the night's earlier rainfall still hung in the air. Soft predawn light outlined Bethany and Sam sound asleep in their bed. Ivy had decided she would do her best to be a good employee so Stokely would trust her. That way, her escape would be easier. She rose from the pallet and headed for an early start.

Dressed and with her shoes in hand, Ivy tiptoed downstairs. Stillness ruled the house, broken only by the mewing of a calico cat. Ivy bent down and scratched the cat's head. She stepped out into the morning, padded over to the kitchen, cut a square of cold cornbread, then left.

To be free to saunter in the cool morning air, to hear mourning doves cooing, and to smell the animals brought a silent prayer of thanksgiving to her lips.

Ivy walked back to where the team had left off the previous day. Her hands were blistered and sunburned, but she was still able to handle the knife she'd found in the tobacco barn. She began cutting the rain-drenched tobacco plants. *Slice, slice, slice.* She did her best to cut each plant at the same distance from the soil.

One by one, she gathered the ungainly plants and neatly stacked them in the wagon that had been left in the field. The front of her dress and her sleeves became soaked from handling the wet tobacco. Her skirt hung heavily with the dampness. She was proud to be early. It made no sense to her to miss out working in the cool part of the morning. She thought Stokely and Christopher and Tom to be foolish.

About twenty minutes after beginning, Ivy felt a little sick to her stomach. Maybe she should have eaten more breakfast.

Suddenly, she vomited. Then, she vomited again. And again. Her head swirled. Her heart thudded inside her chest like a blacksmith's hammer. Ivy walked over to the wagon, reached out to steady herself, slipped, and collapsed.

She awoke, shaded by a tree, her head still spinning. Miss Sarah's concerned face leaned over her. Tom hovered at Miss Sarah's elbow, a wet rag in his hand.

"Ivy, how d'you feel now? You poor girl—you can't harvest wet tobacco! Wet tobacco'll kill you."

"What? I don't understand," mumbled Ivy.

"The rain brings a poison out of the leaves. Even dew can bring it out. Soaks into your skin and makes you sick. Only pick dry tobacco. Don't ever do that again," Miss Sarah clucked. "You're lucky it didn't kill you. Got to be careful."

Ivy, her stomach roiling, watched the elderly woman bustle off toward the house.

"Stay right where you are, Ivy. I'm going to fetch a cup of tea."

Ivy needed to learn more about Maryland.

Ivy rested. By the afternoon, she felt well enough to help Miss Sarah get dinner ready. Sitting in the kitchen together, Ivy peeled potatoes while the older woman browned meat in an iron pot over the fire. It felt good to do chores she knew. For a fisherman's daughter, fieldwork was a puzzle.

"Miss Sarah, if you don't mind, I'd like to ask you a question."

"Of course. What do you need to know?"

"When am I getting married?"

"Well, I don't know. Are you betrothed? I believe as you're indentured, you can't marry till after you've finished your service."

"But didn't Mr. Stokely buy my indenture to have me as a wife?"

"Good lord, no, miss. George Stokely would never buy himself a wife. He's not that sort of a man. He had his own wife till Bethany was born. My niece—my sister's girl, Lydia. Mr. Stokely's been a widower for three years. I'm sure there's ladies who'd have him happily as their husband. Our neighbor Polly Carr comes to mind. But he is too busy with his work, and he still mourns his dead wife. Don't worry. George bought your indenture so as to have more help with the household."

"Oh," said Ivy, eyes on the potato she held. Miss Sarah gave a searching look at the young woman, then turned back to her joint of beef and poked it with her long fork.

"You'll be fine, Ivy. George is a good man. I can tell you're trying hard to be a help here and that's all he wants. Later you'll be able to choose for yourself who you marry or if you marry at all. That's best. You'll be able to do that."

"But, ma'am, I have already chosen my husband. Back in Ireland. A fine man. Kevin."

"Good lord, girl! What are you doing here then? Why would you leave your betrothed and come here to be indentured?" Miss Sarah put down her knife and half-peeled potato.

"Don't you know? Captain Smythe kidnapped me and my . . . others back in Dungarvan."

"Kidnapped? Are you sure? I've heard there are pirates down south, but not in Maryland. Never here. I know you're still learning our language. You can't read, can you? Maybe you and the others simply misunderstood." The knife and potato remained abandoned. Rascal barked out in the farmyard.

"Maybe 'kidnap' is the wrong word." Ivy peeled away as she talked. "One day I went to the harbor at Dungarvan. I was selling my mother's weaving to the captain. He asked me onto the ship, the *Prometheus*. I remember falling down a ladder and when I woke up I was in a cage with other women. He had caged men, too." Each spiral matched exactly the width of all others in her pile.

"Brought us here and sold us at the harbor, you know, like horses at a fair. The planters looked at our teeth, our hands, and some touched our arms and legs. Mr. Stokely bought me, and other men bought the others. Wrote on a piece of paper and passed money to the captain. Maybe I was wrong and there is another word for it. Sorry, ma'am." With a shiver, Ivy resumed peeling.

"Well, Ivy, that is quite a sad story. I don't know what to say. How about we work on our potatoes for now? Don't worry. You won't be marrying George. He's a good man, as I said, and will not mistreat you." With a perplexed expression, Miss Sarah finished her potato and reached for another one.

Despite Miss Sarah's reassurances, Ivy didn't trust George Stokely. No, sir. He was, after all, an Englishman. The most miserable parts of her young life had come at the hands of the

English, specifically English men.

Ivy cleared the dinner dishes in the evening. Every potato had been eaten, and every single bean. Only a few scraps of meat clung to the beef joint. George and Miss Sarah had settled in the parlor by the fire. Ivy could hear them as they discussed the children's day.

Rascal sat at the back door. Drool fell from his mouth in anticipation of his dinner.

"Rascal, looks like you can't wait." Ivy opened the door and threw a bit of meat to the dog. The door slammed as she returned to quietly tidy up the table.

Ivy heard Miss Sarah say her name. Before she could respond, George spoke.

"Kidnapped? What do you mean kidnapped? Are you sure, Aunt Sarah? Do you really believe I'd ever cavort with kidnappers?"

Ivy froze. She strained to hear what would come next.

"Well, of course not, George. Do you think it's true? Is the captain a pirate?"

A floorboard squeaked under George's weight. Ivy thought he must be pacing in front of the fire.

"I always thought Smythe to be ungentlemanly." His voice carried more than a hint of agitation. "Most of the ships' captains are, if truth be told. Have to be daring to take to the sea and risk a voyage on the Atlantic. No way to know if they're lying about their goods. Oh, God help us. What are we to do?"

"Maybe Ivy is just confused. Her English is still rough. Why, today she called a potato a carrot. She's learning. Slowly."

"How do you explain being held in a cage, Auntie? Unless she's lying—and I doubt she's a liar at all. Has always struck me as a good, honest girl. She's smart enough to keep her mouth shut about things she thinks I won't like. Let's say she was kidnapped. What should we do?"

“I think, dear, we keep this to ourselves and bide our time. It really is much too late in the season to expect a decent voyage back to Ireland for her, even if a ship were available. We can see how things stand in the spring, when shipping resumes. I would not want to put a young girl like Ivy on a pest-ridden ship for an autumn crossing.”

Ivy heard the rustle of a skirt as Miss Sarah settled back in her chair.

“Yes, Aunt Sarah, you have a point. The girl’s lucky to have survived one crossing, let alone two. In a cage! Next time I’ll inspect the ship’s hold before I take on any new indentures.

“We’ll give the poor thing a decent place here. I think it’s best not to discuss this further with her or anyone else for now. No point to it. Damn Smythe to hell!”

“George!”

Ivy silently slipped out into the farmyard.

They can do what they want, she thought. I don’t care what they say. Give me “a decent place.” The very idea. I’m going home to Ireland as soon as I can. I’ll not wait till spring.

She considered her master. George Stokely ran his property with a focused, hands-on manner. Rarely did he miss a day in the fields. He did not ask his servants to do anything he wouldn’t, hadn’t, or couldn’t have done himself. His size and strength underlined his financial and legal domination over his servants. Not one of the male servants looked big enough to dare him to a physical contest. Ivy knew she would not have a chance against him physically. And he was as quick as he was strong.

She needed the measure of the man who now controlled her without her permission, the man who owned her labor in a lopsided transaction. Planters owed little to their indentured servants. A few acres, clothes, and animals after years of toil. Few owners ever managed to pay even that widow’s mite.

In the short time she'd been at *Convict's Revenge*, Ivy had heard Mr. Stokely say more than once that he didn't want to depend on any man. Ivy envied him. His animals, truck garden, and fields of grain made his dream possible.

Ivy had never tasted many of his crops, including maize. She liked the ground corn flour Miss Sarah used to make fritters and bread. Sam assured her she would fall in love with the fresh corn when it ripened the following summer. Two milk cows gave all the family and their laborers needed for drinking, butter, and the white farm cheese Miss Sarah made. The children drank the buttermilk and Ivy did, too, when there was a little extra.

Ivy and Peter flourished as they settled into life in Maryland. Wholesome, abundant food and physical labor gradually sculpted the indentured servants' bodies. Time outdoors helped them recover from the months stashed in the dark belly of the *Prometheus*.

"Oh, Peter," said Ivy as they strung and hung tobacco leaves. "You're a lucky fellow. You can work and not worry about the sun. Look at you. Already all golden. You remind me of Juno. Black hair, black eyes, and the rest brown.

"Meanwhile, I have to cover every inch I can of my skin and I still burn. Just as if I touched a hot coal. I'm glad Miss Sarah gave me this hat."

"The hat's lovely, Ivy. Wish I had me a hat. Then I could sleep here in the barn and old Christopher would never know." Peter winked. "Speaking of hats, I was thinking about marriage."

"What's marriage have to do with hats, Peter?"

"Nothing. I was thinking about marrying you, though, after we serve our time with Stokely. What do you think?"

"You are so silly, Peter. You're teasing me, aren't you? Besides, I'm going to marry a man back home. I am. Someday." Ivy looked off into the distance.

"You're right. Just a joke. How are you going to marry a fellow from home, Ivy? Is he coming here?" Peter hoisted a sheaf of tobacco onto his shoulder.

"Well, I don't want to talk about it. Talking about it might spoil it. I need to keep my dream. You understand, don't you? I do like you, Peter, and want to be the best of friends with you."

"Same here, girl." Peter looped the hemp over the rafter and pulled up the tobacco.

Ivy jabbed her awl into a tobacco stem. Her mood darkened as she considered where she sat and what she was doing. Curing tobacco for a stranger. She should be married to Kevin now, washing his dishes and not George Stokely's. Cooking Kevin's porridge and not George's. Feeling her belly grow heavy with Kevin's baby. Not raising the children of a dead woman.

Inside her, rebellion—rather than a baby—blossomed and grew. Ivy did not know what to do with her hatred of her situation. But she would. Soon. She would know exactly how to change things, to get her life back.

Ivy's arms and legs, slack with disuse, had become strong and lithe again. Muddled by the travails of the sea voyage, her mind had reassembled itself to the sharp, focused instrument she'd had in Ireland. Ivy rapidly learned her tasks on *Convict's Revenge*, improved her grasp of English, and began to create detailed and specific plans for her escape.

Her day began at sunup. There was plenty of work to do in the house while waiting for the dew to evaporate from the tobacco leaves. Waking in the room she shared with the children, she rinsed her face and hands, then dressed. She tiptoed down the polished stairway, careful to avoid the squeaky third step which might wake the children. One morning, she stretched over it successfully and looked up to see a silent George. With a nod and a smile, he faded away.

Chapter 20

Convict's Revenge
Near the Patapsco River, Maryland

September 1700

Every morning Ivy saw Stokely, in his loose-limbed gait, walking east. He would return a half hour or so later. Ivy wondered where he went. Maybe there was a hamlet he visited or another farm. Curiosity overcame her. One afternoon, on her way back from the fields, she swerved to follow the path she had seen George take earlier.

Secluded from the hubbub of the farm buildings, hidden past a low ridge, she found George's destination: his wife Lydia's grave. The gray stone tablet, engraved "Lydia Stokely, Beloved Wife, 1697," protruded from manicured grass under a small pine tree. Beyond the stone, the vista held low hills in the distance and hinted of a creek with a line of undulating trees snaking through cultivated fields. Sheep pastured in a far-off field, white dots on green. Ivy thought she understood why this site had been chosen. It was serene, restful, and spoke of eternity.

Ivy swiped at her eyes with the backs of her hands, wiped them off on her skirt, and sniffled. Feeling guilty and like a spy, she hustled back to the kitchen to start cooking dinner. She felt sad. To be a wife, die in childbirth, and leave two motherless children. Her heartstrings resonated with George's vulnerability. A chip of her distrust dropped away.

That afternoon, she took pains with her preparation of dinner. She scooped up a plump hen, well past her egg-laying prime. She wrung the hen's neck. After a few feeble flops, the chicken gave up the ghost. With a silent thank you, Ivy carried the bird into the kitchen. Plucked, gutted, and broken down into pieces, the chicken soon simmered in an iron pot hanging over the cookfire, joined by an onion, leeks, carrots, and fresh thyme, sage, and parsley. Within fifteen minutes of adding the vegetables and herbs, the heady aroma of stewing chicken permeated the kitchen and wafted out into the yard.

Christopher followed his nose, stuck his head in the open kitchen window, and winked at Ivy.

"Good dinner tonight, eh? Nothing so fine as a stewing hen. Good work, Ivy."

Ivy shooed him out with a laugh. Christopher was an easy person to have around.

To complete the meal, Ivy dropped in cornmeal dumplings. She served the dish with bread and apples. Ivy wanted to please George and make up for her secretive and prying curiosity. At dinner, she unconsciously watched him eat. As if he felt her gaze, her master looked up.

"What, Ivy? Do I have gravy on my chin?" He chuckled.

"No, no. Nothing, Mr. Stokely. Just worried I may have oversalted the chicken."

"No, girl. It's quite fine. The best I've had in years." George spooned an enormous hunk of dumpling into his wide-open mouth and winked at her.

Miss Sarah dropped her spoon. The utensil skittered across

the floor.

"Oh, sorry." Miss Sarah shot a warning look at George.

"I'll get it, ma'am, and fetch you another," said Ivy.

A little while later, Ivy tucked Sam and Bethany into their beds. She ran her hands over the coverlet and smoothed it out over each child. Then she poked the edge in under the feather mattress.

"Mmm," said Sammy. "Feels good to be tucked in tight. Ivy, do you know any stories? Mother told us stories at night. I remember. Can you? Ones about princes and dragons and giants. Especially giants."

"Yes, giants," said sleepy-eyed Bethany. "Pwese."

"Well, I'll do my best. I remember stories my mother told me. Would you like to hear them? One concerned an enormous giant living in a cave by the sea."

Bethany's long black eyelashes had dropped before the giant tromped from the cave. Sammy fought his fatigue valiantly, holding on till the tale was told. Ivy washed up, said her prayers, and fell into a sound sleep. In her dreams she returned to her bed in An Rinn. Peat lent its earthy scent to the near darkness as her mother's alto voice recounted stories throughout the night. She awoke in the dawn light, refreshed and feeling loved.

Ivy, Peter, Tom, and Christopher worked six days a week bringing in the tobacco. Sam worked alongside the adults, running errands and adding cheer. George Stokely joined them in the fields at least part of every day. With years of experience working tobacco and living in Maryland, his work was done with economy and a productivity his servants could not match. He had very specific needs and relayed them easily.

Of the four servants, only Christopher was voluntarily indentured, Ivy learned. She and Christopher were unloading freshly harvested tobacco leaves at a barn.

"Yes, Ivy. I actually volunteered to take a very unpleasant journey to America. Really didn't have much choice. My parents have so many sons—six, in fact—and no girls. Not enough property to set us all up. Could've joined the military, but I'm not much of a fighting man, as you most likely have realized. So I figured I'd take a risk. Put in my years, take my bit of land and clothing when I'm done, and be off on my own."

"Why? Couldn't you stay in England?"

"Just no way to earn a living. I believe there's more opportunity here for a man to become anything he wants. Just my opinion, Ivy. Glad George Stokely bought my bond, that I am. I do my best for him. His success is my future success—one day, I hope to be a fellow planter and do business with him on an equal footing, I do."

According to Christopher, Tom came to America straight from an English jail.

"He's silent as a monk about the reason he was in jail. I can only guess, though he is a good worker. No one can fault him on that."

Ivy didn't want to know Tom's crimes, either. She admitted to herself that she was envious of Christopher's happiness with his situation.

Her workday stretched longer than the men's, though she spent less time in the fields than they did. Under Miss Sarah's direction, she prepared all the meals. She also helped the children get dressed and undressed, sat with them at meals, and looked after them when Miss Sarah asked. Miss Sarah, with a general's focus and an ambassador's diplomacy, never dithered. She knew and communicated her needs with precision coupled with kindliness. As the days in Maryland rolled on, Ivy gained confidence and skill. But there seemed to be more work than humanly possible to do.

Each night, Ivy collapsed into sleep, unbothered by the nightmares of her imprisonment. She recalled no dreams. During the day, she ruminated about Sean. Where was he? Who had bought his indenture bond? Was he healthy? She missed him—his chatter as they walked together, his red cheeks and dark hair, his soothing voice. Most of all, she missed her brother's love for her.

Ivy sat at the kitchen table with small bundles of leaves and stems arrayed before her. Miss Sarah had shown her earlier how to make a mix of herbs to flavor chicken dishes. Ivy carefully counted out an identical number of sprigs of parsley, thyme, and sage for each spray. She lined the herbs up, then tied them up with twine. She wanted each bundle to look as close as possible to the others when they later hung to dry. She told herself the reason for her fastidiousness was her desire for each bundle to deliver identical flavor. In her mind's ear, Sean chided her.

A wagon rumbled outside the kitchen and Ivy glanced up. Through the window, she saw Sam hop down. Sam, Christopher, and George were back from a trip to the landing to barter excess garden produce for bounty from the Chesapeake.

"Ivy, Ivy, come look!" yelled Sam.

Ivy set her herbs aside and hurried outside. George Stokely appeared self-satisfied as he placed two bushel baskets at her feet.

"Here's dinner, Ivy. Looking forward to it," he said, then stood back. Christopher grinned.

Ivy pulled aside the damp burlap covering the baskets and revealed a heaving, glistening mass of blue crabs, every one of them as big as her hand. Each had ten legs. Intimidating claws with orange or red tips waved about in protest of their captivity. Their spherical dark eyes rotated about haphazardly on short stalks.

Ivy looked up to see George, Christopher, and Sammy watching her. The corners of their mouths twitched with barely controlled mirth. Not to be put off, Ivy grabbed a round-bodied female crab with particularly big claws and ran after a squealing Sam.

"Did you think I'd never seen a crab? My father is a fisherman," she said. At supper, she confirmed her familiarity with seafood by putting together a fine feast.

Miss Sarah deemed the crabs too messy to eat in the dining room. Instead, everyone ate together in the small yard between the kitchen and house. Miss Sarah, as the eldest, went first. She heaped a tin plate with an impressive pile of greens, potatoes, and cornbread, then grabbed two steamed crabs from the pile.

Next came George, followed by the children helped by Ivy, and then the men servants. Ivy went last. They settled down on logs and stoops. After a brief prayer of thanksgiving by Miss Sarah, everyone dug in.

Crab shells were smashed, twisted, and cracked open in a variety of personal styles. Skinny crab legs were sucked empty of their meat. Flecks of crabmeat and juice smeared every hand and dripped down chins. Crab bits decorated Sam and Bethany's hair. Rascal sat attentively at the periphery and waited his turn with the occasional lick of his muzzle.

"Well done, Ivy," said George, sitting down with his second plateful of food.

"Yes, well done. Huzzah!" Peter clapped and the others hopped in to do the same.

Ivy hummed to herself the next morning, reliving her culinary success. She carried a shovel and a basket of messy crab shells and claws toward a distant woodlot. Bethany gamboled like a lamb beside her. The child swung an empty crab carapace and chattered as they walked. Miss Sarah, busy boiling down grape jelly, had asked Ivy to see to Bethany.

Ivy put the basket down at the edge of the wide, shallow pit. A layer of dirt covered the pile of broken crockery and other castoffs which couldn't be burned or reused.

"Peugh! This place stinks, Bethany. The crab leavings will only make it worse. Glad it's downwind of the house."

"Smells bad." Bethany pinched her nostrils with her thumb and pointer finger.

Ivy laughed and tipped the basket's contents into the pit. She took a stick and spread the shells, then grabbed the shovel. Digging into a pile of soil on the pit's edge, Ivy became absorbed in covering each bit of her refuse. *Don't want to attract wild animals*, she thought. She hummed another ditty.

Screams and cries broke into her reverie.

"Ahh, nooooo! Stop it. Stop it! Ivy! Sarah!" Bethany's screeches came from back in the woods.

Ivy stumbled as she ran to the commotion. A strange, amazing odor—a stench actually—filled her nose. Its strength increased the closer she came to Bethany. When she reached the crying child, the smell overpowered her. What had happened? Was Bethany possessed? Ivy had yet to decide her stance when it came to witches.

"Kitty. Kitty," said Bethany. "I just wanted the bwack kitty."

Ivy swooped Bethany up into her arms and dashed toward the house—terrified to look behind her, afraid of what might be chasing them. The odor from Bethany nauseated her. The inside of her nose burned with the fumes. She gagged and fought the urge to vomit.

Tom stood in the farmyard, a rake in his hand, and his jaw dropped.

"What the devil? What happened?" he said before his nose answered the question. "Oh, my God. You've let the girl get sprayed by a skunk. Stokely will not be pleased with this. No, he will not."

"What?" Ivy skidded to a stop by Tom whose nose crinkled in protest.

Miss Sarah and Christopher came in the farmyard. The hullabaloo boiled for a few minutes. Bethany wailed till she hiccupped. The adults talked over each other. Miss Sarah rose to the lead.

"Bring me the wash basin, Tom. Christopher, go get the jug of apple cider vinegar. Ivy, go fetch towels and a change of clothes for Bethany. Bring it all to the stable, to that empty back stall, the one we never use. Bethany, you come here with me, girl. Everything'll be dandy. A stinky old skunk sprayed you. What were you doing with a skunk?"

"Kitty. Bad kitty made me stink."

Ivy, under Miss Sarah's supervision, filled the basin with a mix of water and vinegar. They undressed Bethany, her chest still heaving with silent shuddering sobs, and put her in the tub. Ivy tenderly rinsed the child's hair and body.

"Thankfully, her dress took most of the musk," said Miss Sarah. "You can try rinsing it in the same tub once we're done with Bethany and then laundering it. Good chance the skunk ruined it. What happened?"

Ivy told her.

"I'm sorry I haven't told you much about Maryland, Ivy. I've lived here my whole life. Don't really know what kind of animals and plants you have in Ireland. Or in England, for that matter. I'll teach you what I do know.

"And don't be too hard on yourself, Ivy. George understands his daughter. She's quick and heedless, like her mother. Samuel's more like George. Not Bethany. She requires a firm hand and constant supervision. She's given me a merry chase more than once. That's one reason he wanted a girl to help us. To keep Bethany out of trouble."

"I'll do my best."

Bethany giggled. She splashed Ivy with vinegar water. "Your best, Ivy. Best."

The following day as they cut and strung tobacco, her fellow servants ribbed Ivy mercilessly.

"Would you like a lovely striped black kitty, Miss Ivy? Saw one back in the woods," teased Peter, reminding Ivy of Sean's frequent taunts.

"Oh, come on, Peter. You can't tell me you knew anything about skunks either. You're just lucky you didn't get sprayed."

"Well, you're not the first person to lose track of Bethany, Ivy," said Christopher. "A few weeks before Stokely bought your bond, poor Miss Sarah cried her eyes out, she did. The girl chased after the barn cats and fell asleep in the hay. Didn't find her till after supper. She's a wanderer, she is."

Christopher effortlessly tossed his load of leaves into the cart. He trudged off with his long knife to cut more sotweed, his whistled ditty floating in his wake.

Chapter 21

Convict's Revenge
Near the Patapsco River, Maryland

October 1, 1700

On a cool and overcast day, Ivy and Peter were off by themselves, slicing leaves from tobacco plants. Thrown together their first day at *Convict's Revenge* and both beginning at the same level of inexperience, they usually paired up in the field. They scorned Tom, an obvious misanthrope, by a mutual unspoken agreement. Christopher was too skilled a worker to be slowed down by such inexperienced laborers. Ivy and Peter each understood there would never be any romance between them. Instead, they were confidants, coworkers, colleagues, and most importantly, friends. At least, that's what Ivy hoped. She worried Peter still might have fantasies about wedding her.

"You know, Ivy, you were pretty the first day I saw you, but I swear you are growing more beautiful each week. Yeah, I know you'd rather be back in Ireland—but this place agrees with you. It truly does. And as a lovely girl, you need to be on your guard when it comes to men. They're going to be after you, you know. And none of us indentured servants are permitted to marry.

Unless, of course, a woman marries her bondsman. What are you going to do?" Peter's friendly face awaited an answer.

Ivy was indeed blossoming into a lush, elegant beauty. The thousands of freckles of her childhood had dissipated to a sprinkling across her nose and a few on her arms. Her curly hair had toned down from flame-red to a rich, dark scarlet which sparkled gold in the sun. Her oval face, full lips, and alabaster and peach complexion combined into a breathtaking loveliness. As if she weren't exotic enough with her green and her blue eye, at nearly six feet in height she towered over most women and many men. With age, her voice had mellowed into a facsimile of her mother's lilting alto. Ivy was impossible to ignore.

"Oh, Peter, you are a flattering one, you are. I'm not worried about men. Most of them think I'm bewitched, what with my odd eyes. If my great height doesn't put them off, my Irish accent will. Besides, I'm not looking to marry. I count on you to help me fend off any unwanted suitors. Right?"

"I'm your man, Ivy. I'll help you as much as I can."

"Peter, I do have one question for you," said Ivy.

"What would that be?"

"Do you remember an Irish man from the *Prometheus* with black curly hair?"

"Oh, certainly. Everyone remembers everyone from that hellacious trip, though I am trying to forget the whole horrible experience," said Peter.

"Oh, I understand. But about that fellow—do you happen to know who bought his indenture, or where he went?"

"Why d'you want to know?"

Ivy wasn't ready to totally trust Peter. Deep down, she didn't trust any Englishman and still found it easy to think the worst about them. And she knew Peter liked to talk. All three male servants gossiped like old crones when they thought no one was listening.

With punishment so harsh for runaways, it was clear the English wanted their servants' total allegiance. If word leaked that Sean was her brother, Stokely might try to keep them apart. He might worry they would conspire to run away—which was precisely what they wanted to do.

"He's from my hometown." Ivy hoped her half-truth would satisfy Peter. It did not.

"Sure he is. His eyes are odd like yours. Don't take me for a fool, Ivy. He's a relative, isn't he? I always figured he was your brother."

"Well, yes. I was afraid to let anyone know. Afraid they'd want to keep us apart more than we already were. Since we have different masters, you know. Maybe they'd be afraid we'd run away."

"Oh, Ivy. I wouldn't worry about that. There's really nowhere to run here. Only a fool tries to leave before finishing their indenture. Haven't you noticed? It's nigh onto a wilderness hereabouts. You're better off here than roaming around the marshes or starving as a stowaway.

"But don't worry, girl. I won't tell. Truly. You can trust me. But you have to forget any thoughts of running away, if you've been having them. Terrible idea.

"All's I know about your brother is that a big fat gouty-looking man paid for his indenture along with John from the ship. Man had a fringe of bright red hair." Peter smiled. "Red like yours, but of course, not as pretty and curly. I've no idea where they went."

Ivy glossed over the compliment.

"Hmm. Do you know where anyone else went from the ship?"

"No, Missy. I don't."

Ivy tended to the dishes after supper. As she dried them with a linen towel, she remembered her ride into Dungarvan with Sean.

Mustn't be too many fat, gouty men around here, she thought. 'Spect I can find him. Sean will be on his farm. Ivy's soliloquy soothed her like balm on a burn.

Life is too easy here. Good food, new clothes, decent people—except for Tom, of course, and I don't know what to think about George. Convict's Revenge is the devil tempting me away from my family. I can't leave Ma alone to suffer. Honora's too young to be much help. They all need me, and I want to be with them. I'm missing watching Joey grow up.

Best I leave here as soon as I can. What am I waiting for?

Ivy placed the final metal cup on the wooden shelf. She reached behind herself and untied her muslin work apron, then hung it on its hook. Ivy banked the coals in the fireplace and walked out into the farmyard.

Bethany's gray kitten jumped up on the windowsill and tracked Ivy's movements.

The evening air was warm and clear. The sun was speeding toward the horizon, though its accompanying clouds had yet to turn rosy. Chickens squawked in the coop as they settled in for the night.

Straight ahead was the door into the house. Ivy turned left, toward the lane.

A rustle came as something moved through the grass at the side of the kitchen building. It was George. She had forgotten. He usually spent time in the stables after supper.

"Ivy. All done with the meal? Out for a walk on this fine evening? Let me walk with you. We can talk about Sam and Bethany. I have a question and would like your opinion." George flicked his eyes over her and gave a small, encouraging smile. "If you don't mind, of course."

Ivy felt flustered. "No, sir. I'm happy to talk about the children with you. They are lovely little ones."

The two set off down the lane. They kept at arm's length.

Returning to the house a half hour later, George pointed to the west.

"Look, Ivy. Sun dogs."

Two small rainbow-colored suns flanked the setting sun. Cirrus clouds sketched lines in the sky above the three luminous stars.

Ivy stared in wordless wonder until the illusion died.

What was the portent of the spectacular sight?

"Come on, Ivy. Let's get home."

Chapter 22

Convict's Revenge
Near the Patapsco River, Maryland

October 2, 1700

Ivy dusted the sideboard in the dining room with care. She enjoyed running her hand over the smoothness of the polished wood. A sunbeam pierced through the glass windowpane and struck the flame mahogany, setting its rich caramel color aglow. Her new yellow calico shone in the warm light and complemented the copper curls poking out from under her white cap. Miss Sarah never complained about Ivy's slow and methodical approach to tasks. Rather, she congratulated her for her fastidiousness.

Samuel chased his shrieking sister into the room. His arms flapped like a goose chasing a cat.

"Run, Bethy, run! I'm gonna catch you."

"Slow down, children, slow down. You'll knock something over. Then we'll all be in trouble." Samuel skidded to a showy stop. Bethany flopped down on the floor.

"How would you get in trouble, Ivy? It wouldn't be your fault."

“Well, I’m supposed to be keeping you out of trouble, I am. That would be trouble and I’d be blamed. Please be careful.”

“Oh, all right. Sorry.” The two children walked out with an exaggerated slow-motion pace, swinging their arms and giggling.

Miss Sarah walked in.

“Ivy, you are so good with them. Thank you,” she said. “Today, though, I need you to go to the landing with Mr. Stokely. He’s getting a load of supplies and needs help. Sam’s going, too. You can pick out the victuals, since you cook them. The men have little skill in that area.”

Christopher helped her load the wagon with spare fruits and vegetables to trade. Ivy climbed up in the bed. Christopher watched as she took time to line up the baskets and crates he had handed her. An apple rolled out of one and Ivy put it back in the basket.

“Let no one ever say you’re messy, miss.” He chuckled.

“No one ever has, Christopher.” Ivy welcomed the trip to the landing. She needed to get her bearings in the countryside if she were to escape from Maryland. “I don’t know where we’re going. Never been to the landing.”

“Well, Ivy, it’s a small pier a few miles from here.

“The waterways are Maryland’s true roads. There’s just so much water here. Usually calm off the bay. Cheaper and easier to get around on the water. People build their houses close to a waterway and every so often, put in a pier. The landing’s our pier.”

“Why isn’t it closer? The river’s right over there.” Ivy pointed.

“We share it with several planters. We trade there. Swap our vegetables and fruits, like these, for oysters or whatever the other planters have on offer. Don’t need one for each planter’s property.”

“And we trade our tobacco there for goods from England. Tobacco’s the same as hard currency. Heard Mr. Stokely invested a big pile of tobacco in your bond."

Ivy ignored the jab. "So, Christopher, the landing's for everyday little things and the harbor's for big things?"

"Close enough. The harbor has all our shops and, now this is important—our taverns." He laughed. "Don't underestimate the power of ale.

"But most of our business happens at the landing," he went on. "It's where anyone with ears learns the news. Some are lies, some are true, but all get told. If you can, listen in today and let the rest of us servants back here know what's in the air. We go every few weeks in warm weather, less so in the winter. It's a pleasant diversion from the fields. You'll see."

Ivy liked Christopher and valued his information. Tom was not a sociable man. Given to sour moods, his expressions spoke of bad or even evil thoughts. Ivy kept her distance. She was well aware of Tom's malevolent looks. She didn't understand what she might have done to make him dislike her. Maybe he just didn't like Irish girls. Or maybe her eyes frightened him.

Peter, on the other hand, was becoming her best friend among the *Convict's Revenge* inhabitants. He, like everyone else except her, was English as could be.

She wondered if, after a time, the English would change here in America and become different from their brethren back across the ocean. Maybe a people she would not hate.

The land and climate were like nothing Ivy had ever seen before. New animals. New plants. New crops. Women were scarce. Would little Bethany grow up to be unlike girls in Britain? The strangeness of this new world must have an impact. Could it change those, like Peter, who came as adults?

Even though he was from another country, Peter reminded her of Sean. He was protective and trustworthy, though he was indeed a silly fellow. Ivy's mind roamed, mused, and pondered.

This was not the life she had imagined as she picked berries years earlier with Honora.

Juno pulled them along. Her big head nodded and her tail swished to her own favored cadence. The wagon ride went quickly. October brought the Chesapeake fine days of a not-too-warm sun and clear-as-can-be air.

George chatted off and on with Sam. They talked about horses and saddles and kites and other father-son topics.

Ivy mulled over her own thoughts. For an hour, she forgot her chores, her brother, and her captivity. She ignored the massive Englishman beside her. Stokely no longer frightened her as he had the first day, though she held a healthy respect for his power. His power, however, did not extend to her mind. She could think whatever she wished.

The countryside grew marshy. Wetlands popped up thick with bulrushes and birds. Shouts of men and the *whoomph* of cargo hitting the ground grew louder. The wagon rounded a corner and the panorama of a small ship at the landing came into view.

"We're here," shouted Sam, standing up in the moving wagon.

"Wait till we've stopped, son."

Ragtag men unloaded barrels, kegs, and baskets. Planters clotted together by wagons, the ship, and the river. Several of the laborers were Africans. Her father had told her about the African laborers at the docks in Ireland. Today was Ivy's first contact with Africans and she found them exotic. Their most vivid characteristic, to Ivy, centered in their style of movement. Their gestures and carriage spoke of a pulsing energy, liveliness, and insouciance. Naked to the waist and barefoot, all wore pants of dun-colored cloth cut off at the knee. Even from a distance, the fabric looked scratchy and uncomfortable.

Each African had embellished their appearance. The tallest

man, towering at least a full head over Stokely, wore a string of shiny brown-and-white oval shells. Ivy had never seen such shells either in Ireland or in Maryland. Another had a floppy red neckcloth. The cheeks and forehead of the youngest, surely little more than a boy, were dotted symmetrically with a pattern of raised circles.

Ivy worried the scars had come from his master and her heart went out to the boy. Intrigued, she wondered why he bore those marks and where he grew up. She startled as she realized the scarred boy was returning her stare, focused on her eyes and wild springy hair. Nonplussed, he flashed a good-natured grin.

Stokely acknowledged her curiosity. "They're Africans, Ivy. Slaves."

Her brow knitted. "Slaves? I don't understand."

"Some planters have bought slaves from Africa to labor on their land. The slaves work alongside the indentured servants. A few only use slaves."

"Why? What's the difference?"

"A slave belongs to their master for life or until they sell the slave to another master. Their children also belong to the master. They are property, same as a horse or land.

"Their masters claim they can make more money if they own their workers outright. As if humans were chattel, like a cow or a piece of furniture. The very idea is offensive. Since they believe they own these souls, they've lost any incentive to treat them right. I don't support it. Not me," said Stokely, with a nod to the Africans. "Not me. Nothing good will come of it."

"Why do they choose to be slaves? Don't they miss their home?"

"They don't choose to be slaves. They are taken, captured. They don't have a choice," said George, before he thought about what he was saying.

He shot a look at Ivy.

She did not meet his eyes. Instead, she exchanged stares with the scarred boy. Thunderstruck by Stokely's comments, she said nothing for a long while. His blindness to his use of kidnapped laborers, people like Peter and Ivy, shipped here against their will, disappointed her. She turned on her heel and walked closer to the boats.

Baskets of squash, oysters, and crabs had been lined up along the wooden pier. On the riverbank a group of farmers clustered under a tree. They jabbered in the cool shade as their servants, sweat beading their foreheads and running down their cheeks, loaded the wagons with the fruits of their labor.

Ivy scanned the planters, excited to see a middle-aged man with bright copper hair. Maybe he was the man who had bought her brother's indenture. She looked at the workers loading the wagons and there he was. Sean.

At that moment, Stokely's eyes shifted to her face. Ivy froze, not wanting to give her brother away. She wanted Sean to be her secret. She wanted Stokely to have no suspicion of her, no inkling of her escape plans.

"Do you think you can help Sam pick out a couple of baskets of oysters and crabs, Ivy? We need vegetables, too. You know better than I do what Miss Sarah likes. I leave it to you to strike a good bargain and teach Sam a bit, too."

"Yes, sir." She hopped down and rushed over to where the ship's owner was selling goods. With Sam beside her, she squatted by a bushel of oysters.

"What do you think, Sammy? Do these look good?"

Sammy shrugged his narrow shoulders. The sun shone on his blond hair. "Don't know. How can you tell?"

A man's freckled hand slid a second bushel into sight.

"Let me help you, lad."

Ivy looked up into Sean's grinning face. Tears welled in her eyes.

"Oh, yes. We'd appreciate that," she said, hiding her tears with a swipe of her arm and a sniffle. In their place, a smile covered half her face.

Sean began his lesson in oysters. "Lad, look these over and tell me what's different between the two bushels."

Oblivious to the adults' emotional undertones, Sammy dove in with questions and opinions. Sean answered each one, warming to the task. Ivy drank Sean up with her eyes. Aware of all the other people milling about, she managed to refrain from hugging her brother. Finally, they settled on the first basket. Sam skipped off to tell his father.

"Sean, we have to get away. Back to Ireland. Soon's we can find a ship. We can stow away," Ivy said in Gaelic, her voice low.

Under his breath, Sean whispered, "We need to be careful. I'll find a way to talk more. I'm kept at *Tipton's Choice* and Mr. William Tipton owns my indenture. This is where we—"

Intent on listening to her brother, Ivy startled as a booming shout rang out from the corpulent redheaded planter, Mr. William Tipton, himself.

"Hey, you! Get back to work or I'll have your hide, you lazy good-for-nothing!"

Sean's face reddened as he turned away.

Ivy's pulse jumped with the threat. She retreated to the wagon to pat Juno's nose. Ivy whispered to the patient horse.

"He's alive, Juno. He's near. Isn't that wonderful?"

Juno nudged Ivy with her velvety nose. Ivy pulled a windfall apple out for the mare.

Later, as Juno pulled them back to *Convict's Revenge*, Stokely sent a quiet look her way. "Excited about the food, Ivy? You seem to be in a rare good mood."

“Well, yes. Can’t wait to cook all this fine fare,” she lied. Her spirit would soar for days on the thrill of those few seconds with her brother. Ivy just knew she could get her life back.

Chapter 23

Convict's Revenge
Near the Patapsco River, Maryland

October 8, 1700

One afternoon after lunch, Miss Sarah bustled into the kitchen, skirts aswirl, as she often did. Ivy was working at the table, cutting a lamb shoulder into pieces for stew.

"Oh, the men will love that, won't they, Ivy? Stew is always a favorite. Did you eat stew growing up?" Miss Sarah's voice skidded to a stop, as if she wished to take her words back. "Sorry if I seem to pry, dear."

"Well, from time to time I did eat stew. My father is a fisherman. Always a fair amount of fish on our table."

Miss Sarah went on. "You know, I've lived here in Maryland all my life—one of the few women born here, along with my sister. Don't really know about life back across the sea, in Britain. Haven't ever traveled out of Maryland either, so you'll have to excuse my curiosity. I'm just a nosy soul."

"Miss Sarah, speaking of curious, did you ever marry?"

"Oh, no. I had a beau, a good man. His name was Stephen, and he was a tradesman. He died of the bloody flux before we had a chance to marry. Never found anyone else I cared to wed, though I did have more than one proposal. You see, Maryland has run short of men since the early days. All these men come over here to work. They come alone and then, look what happens. No one to marry, few chances for a family. It's changing now, though.

"I lived with my parents. When they died, I moved in here with my niece and George. Then Lydia died . . . but I am happy here. I love the children and George treats me as if I were his own mother. He is a generous man."

"Miss Sarah, why's this place called *Convict's Revenge*?"

"Oh, we'll talk about that some other time, Ivy. I don't want to keep you from your cooking."

Her curiosity piqued, Ivy planned to snoop out the name's source. Right now there was a dinner to cook. She carried the pieces of lamb to the hearth. A heated iron pot hung over a generous bed of coals. The sizzling meat sent off an indescribably appetizing aroma as she stirred it around, then swung it on its iron arm directly above the hottest section of the coals. She added a ladle of water and put the cover on the iron pot.

Miss Sarah gave an approving look, then left.

At supper every man complimented Ivy on her stew. Even sourpuss Tom shoved his bowl forward for seconds and said, "A fine stew, Miss Ivy."

The servants ate in the kitchen, all except Ivy, who helped in the house with the children. Bethany demanded the most attention. Samuel needed little instruction when it came to feeding himself. The boy was always hungry. George said he had a hollow leg.

As dinner drew to a close. Bethany, tired out by a day of play, fussed at her father over finishing her meal.

"No, don't wike it. Don't want it. Sah-wee."

"It'll make the roses bloom on your cheeks, girl. Don't you want that?"

"No." With a signal of dismissal from Stokely, Ivy gathered Bethany in her arms and took her upstairs. Returning a few minutes later, she was surprised to find Stokely still at the table with Sarah.

"Ivy, tomorrow we're going to the harbor to pick up provisions. I'd like you to come with me to help. Sarah'll watch over Bethany. We'll be leaving at daybreak, so be ready."

"Yes, sir." Ivy looked forward to the novelty of a visit to the harbor. She had been so worn out and frightened the day she was there. She only recalled a blur overlaid with anxiety.

Ivy tried mightily to engrave in her mind every crossroad and landmark between *Convict's Revenge* and the harbor without drawing George Stokely's attention. Peter, lounging in back, repeatedly interrupted their silence with silly comments and observations.

Ivy, Peter, and Stokely rumbled along behind Juno in the cool morning. Of George's half-dozen horses, Juno reigned as the chief draft horse. Ivy believed her to be one of the prettiest and most patient horses she had ever seen. Juno's daughter, Aphrodite, had yet to reach her full size and potential. A small gray dappled pony named Shadow entertained the Stokely children. The other three horses were saddlehorses, for hunting and recreation—a chestnut, a black, and a roan. George doted on all his horses. He groomed them to a fare-thee-well, fed them high-grade grain, and made certain they were all exercised.

Mist still hovered over the marshes and creeks as they passed. The squeaks and rattles of the wagon flushed gangly herons from their solitary feeding in the waters. Off they flew, with more grace than expected, their long legs an elegant rudder. A cloudless sky overhead promised good weather. Cool air freshened Ivy's skin. Though she missed Ireland's green lushness, Ivy took joy in America's version of autumn.

"Baltimore's harbor is growing into a proper village, it is," noted George. "Fine harbor on the Patapsco. Ships are thick as fleas on a hound in the warmer weather. Good for business, it is. Don't guess you saw much the one day you were there, Ivy." George Stokely was on one of his talkative streaks.

Ivy nodded to let him know she heard. He picked up the thread again.

"This was the same harbor I arrived at from England. Back then, only a handful of huts in this place. Different now. Yes, indeed."

"I'm looking forward to seeing it today, sir," said Peter. "Don't rightly recall much about the first day. Felt pretty puny, I did. Not now. Am back in full mettle, thanks to your food and help."

Ivy thought Peter laid it on a little thick, but she liked him despite his toadying. Today she liked pretty much everything. It was that kind of an autumn day. Lovely.

Her pleasure dampened as foul smells announced Baltimore Harbor's town well before it came into view. The source of the odors was obvious. Horse droppings became prevalent as they proceeded into town. The streets were awash with the contents of slop jars haphazardly emptied from second floors and open doorways. Narrow buildings crowded cheek by jowl along the roadway, crammed together as if for protection. Most of the one-room deep structures were wooden, though a few more prosperous residents of Baltimore County had managed to erect brick buildings. The Baltimoreans did their best to extract money from vagabond sailors, planters from the surrounding land, and each other. Most first floors were dedicated in one way or another to business activities, even if it were as simple as gaming. Dice rattled in cups followed by groans or cheers as they passed.

Ivy felt safe with Stokely at her side and relaxed. Peter offered little in the way of protection to her mind. She spent the brief ride through the village gathering it all in. The silhouette of a woman walking down the road ahead of the wagon caught her eye.

"Betty, Betty!" Her shout erupted before she even thought about it. Ivy jumped out of the wagon and ran to her friend from the *Prometheus*. She grabbed her arm.

Betty turned. Ivy gasped. Betty's left eye was swollen shut, black, purple, and blue. A scrape, crusted with dry blood, covered her cheek.

"Ivy. Oh, love, so good to see you, but I can't talk to you." Betty freed her arm.

"What happened to you, Betty? Can I help you? What about Anne?"

"She's gone. Gone she is. Dead. We've lost her. She didn't, wouldn't . . . Well, she tried to run away, and he beat her, and she was too weak . . . Ivy, I have to go. Lacey's in the tavern across the street and might come out. Go away, or he'll think I'm trying to bolt. Please leave me alone if you care for me. He's a bastard. Don't worry about me. Someday I'll get loose from him, the devil. If I have to throttle him dead in his sleep, I'll get away. Go. Go back. Don't make your master mad or doubt you. Go now."

Stricken, Ivy kissed Betty on the cheek, and in tears, ran back to the wagon. Snuffling, she attempted to hide her emotions.

"Sorry, sir, I'm so sorry. I thought I knew that woman, but I do not. Please forgive me for jumping down like that."

George turned to Ivy and gave her a long, silent look, one which hinted of concern.

"You don't owe me an apology. Just try to stay in the wagon. Harbors can be dangerous places for women."

Peter gaped, a puzzled look on his face.

Juno pulled them on to the shops George sought. He bought rope, a few nails for repairs, and a bucket at the first shop. At the second, he purchased sundry items Sarah had requested. After he finished, George turned to Ivy.

"If I recall, Ivy, Captain Smythe claimed you could weave. That true?"

"Well, yes, Mr. Stokely."

"What can you make?"

"My mother is a weaver. She taught me and my sister. I can weave on a loom, wool and linen yardage both. I can also handweave—sashes and belts and such. Why, sir?"

"I thought, Ivy, you might be willing to weave for me. We can always use cloth, but it takes skill and talent to make it. As you've heard me say, I like to do what I can to stay independent. If we produce our own cloth, it's one less thing to need from trade. If you would weave, we can set up a loom for the wintertime. We have a few months respite from the tobacco crop in the cold months. Life gets slow, though I know the children and helping with the house keep you busy."

"Mr. Stokely, I'm your servant. I'll do what work you need. Tell me what you want, and I'll do my best."

"Well, to my mind, Ivy, if a person doesn't like what they do, they often make a poor show of it. I can buy cloth easy enough. I figure if you know how to weave and like doing it, I can accommodate you and benefit as well. But I will not force you. Like I said, weaving seems a bit of magic, an art. I think good weaving comes from an interested weaver. What do you say?" George encouraged her with a dimpled smile.

"I'm happy to weave for you, sir. Since you asked, I do enjoy making cloth. I find it gives me ease. I find pleasure in putting the patterns together."

"Thank you, Ivy. I appreciate your willingness. Miss Sarah will be so pleased, too. She likes having options. I'm certain she'll enjoy working with you to pick out what's best. Now, let's go pick up the loom and shuttles."

Ivy beamed. From the back of the wagon, Peter flashed a smile.

The three of them went off in the wagon to a tidy white house at the edge of the settlement. It was single-storied, with windows all around, and a pathway of flat stones set in crushed oyster shell led to the front door. Tufts of yellow flowers sprouted haphazardly under the windows.

George Stokely jumped out and strode to the door. Before he could rap on the wooden door, a lanky fellow of indeterminate age opened it.

"Aye, George, good to see you. Here for the loom?"

"That's right, Isaac. Haven't changed your mind, have you? I've brought my girl with me. Ivy. She's the weaver. As well as my man, Peter." With a sweep of his arm, George indicated the pair lingering behind him.

Isaac glanced at Ivy, then Peter—and then, once again, at Ivy.

"Come in, come in. You, too, miss, and you, young man." He flashed a warm welcome to Ivy and Peter. He gestured them to join George, who had already ducked his head under the lintel and entered the house. He also unabashedly looked Ivy up and down.

Ivy felt her cheeks warm.

"Hmm, hmm," he hummed in approval.

Mr. Abner, for that was his name, kept a fastidious home as charming as he was. Everything needed in a dwelling filled the single room, which was warmed by a fire flickering in the hearth. A rabbit stew dinner bubbled in an iron pot suspended over the burning logs. Even Ivy's lingering sadness from seeing Betty could not keep her mouth from watering.

Yellow blooms, picked from the yard, graced a clay jug atop the single-beam mantle. A square of ocher, red, and yellow handwoven cloth draped a small table. A blue-and-white coverlet lay atop his bed. The household, simple as it was, reflected an artistic eye, probably his wife's. Ivy noted Mr. Abner's hair tied back in a messy queue and his mismatched clothing. A jumble of sticks and poles, which she recognized immediately as a loom, lay in the corner.

"Yes, miss, there it is. All yours if you want it. I can't weave. 'Twas my wife, Miranda, who made the cloth, you see. Made me a sweet home, she did. Miranda's been gone six months now and I doubt I'll find another weaving woman who'd marry me, women of any stripe being so scarce in these parts. I told George I'd be pleased to have all this equipment put to use. You're welcome to it. Makes me a tad sad to see it here without my wife throwing the shuttle back and forth. I even kept the last yarn she spun. You can have all of that. Need to move past my grief."

Ivy looked to George for a reply. Self-conscious under Isaac's scrutiny, her command of English had slowed, stumbled, and scrambled. George caught the cue.

"Isaac, we are very grateful to you. You are too generous. I'd like to give you something in exchange. Won't you take some vegetables or tobacco off our hands? Maybe a ham and a chicken or two?"

"No, no. Don't need a thing. I do all right and am happy as I am. 'Cept maybe a couple yards of wool from the girl here once she gets all set up. Just so's I can see the success of my gift. That would be more than enough."

"Ivy?" George prodded.

"Mr. Abner, I would be honored to weave cloth for you. Thank you so much." A pleased smile, both from the gift and her ability to come up with the appropriate thanks, flitted over Ivy's face.

"Now, George, what about a bit of a meal for you and your two workers before you travel? Don't want to leave Baltimore Harbor with an empty stomach. Never know what obstacles stand to slow you down on your journey home. That's the truth and you well know it."

Peter shot an unspoken plea to George. He had already sidled up to the fire and inhaled the aroma of simmering rabbit.

"Can't turn your kind offer down, Isaac. Never say no to supping with a friend, I say."

George and Peter dragged the table and two chairs to the bed. Ivy helped Isaac serve up the stew in his tin dishes, then perched with Peter on the edge of the bed. George and Isaac seated themselves in the chairs. What followed was the absolute quiet of congenial folks filling their bellies with tasty food. No one talked as the rabbit salved their hunger.

Isaac dipped his spoon into the last bits, but stopped short of his mouth. He peered up at Ivy and Peter. "You two are lucky, you know, to have George Stokely here hold your indenture. He's a fine man. Known him since he was a boy planting sotweed and slopping hogs for old William Tipton."

At the name "Tipton," Ivy's spoon stopped, suspended for a moment in midair, then continued on. She slurped the stew as quietly as possible and strained to learn more about the man who held her brother's indenture.

"Unlike some of the rogues here in Maryland, George is also honorable. You can trust him, you can, to treat you right. So many of the planters just plain work their laborers to death.

Tipton, for example. But George—he knows what it's like to be under another man's thumb. Don't you, George?"

George let out a sigh with a pained look.

"Oh, Isaac. I did all right. I wasn't treated so bad. Let's talk about something else. Peter and Ivy know what I expect, and they are good workers. Doesn't pay to dwell on the past. I've made my amends with William Tipton."

"Yes," said Isaac, "and you've had your revenge, a *Convict's Revenge*. Though the idea that a young lad could ever be a convict was the stupidest thing I ever heard. Glad you turned the tables on life and did well. Your property's doing all right.

"But I am sorry if I touched a sore point, George. I'm just jealous. If I had the money, why, I'd buy this pretty girl's indenture right off you, but I heard tell you paid a pretty high price. All I can say, miss, is when you've served your time, don't forget about old Isaac. I doubt I'll find another woman in the next four years, and even if I do, if I know you'll have me, I'll wait."

His weathered face held his plea and dignity as well.

Ivy shifted toward George and saw no rescue. "Thank you, sir. My English is not yet good. I don't know what to say."

"Don't worry, miss. Nothing like a beautiful girl who can weave and work. Your odd eyes don't put me off a bit. No, not at all. I know there are men who claim suchlike are the mark of the devil, but not me. Had a cat once with eyes almost the same as you. One blue, one green, but the blue was on the left not the right. Best mouser ever. Nothin' wrong with eyes not matching. Just another one of God's unknowable miracles. And back to my offer, for that is what it is . . . I'm not as old as I look. No, I'm not. And I treat a woman right."

Ivy thought of Kevin back in An Rinn—a man who understood every word she said and those she didn't say, who had been washed by the winds of the Celtic Sea as she had, who was young and vital.

Most parts of her life had careened out of her control in Dungarvan. Her captivity continued to cost her dearly. She refused to give up her dreams, especially her dream of marrying Kevin. Afraid to meet anyone's eyes, she looked at her lap.

George's face reddened under his tan.

Peter's eyes grew round. His lips struggled to keep in a guffaw. After a minute, he gained control.

"Mr. Abner, sir, any chance for a bit more stew?" said Peter. Everyone relaxed and returned to their earlier conversation.

An hour later, under Ivy's fussy supervision, the men loaded up the pieces of Miranda Abner's loom along with her tools. Isaac then climbed up into his storage loft and hauled down canvas bags of spun wool, spindles, and carding paddles. Ivy knew the three men aimed to please her and managed a grateful smile, but inside she ached to crawl away to a dark corner and have a good cry over Betty and Anne's sad fates.

As if he sensed her disquietude, Stokely drew near. He stood beside her, yet said nothing.

The drive back to *Convict's Revenge* passed without event. Ivy kept her own quiet counsel. After she cleared up the supper dishes and tucked the children into bed, she came downstairs. George and Sarah chatted by the fireplace.

"If you don't mind, I'd like to go for a walk."

"Of course, Ivy." Sarah gave her a searching look, then returned to her embroidery. With silk thread from France stitched on luminous ecru satin, the half-finished piece depicted the story of Ruth. The firelight brought out the sheen of the silk floss. A flicker of envy for Sarah's talent and freedom to express it flamed up briefly in Ivy.

"Just be sure to get back before it's dark. Easy to get lost around here once the sun's gone," added George.

Ivy drifted out through the farmyard and headed to the quiet of the woodlot. A path circled through it, a meandering narrow trail. She breathed in the refreshing cool air. Deep in the middle of the trees, Ivy made her way to a natural clearing. Like a gem set in a ring, a shallow, marshy pond glittered in its center under the open sky. Overhead a faint moon in the still-blue sky surveyed the landscape. Cattails sprang in tufts along much of its perimeter. The damp air held the scent of mud, of dying vegetation, of autumn—not unpleasant smells to Ivy.

She settled onto a stone overlooking the still water and leaned against a slender tree. Usually mosquitos infested this damp section of the woods. They were gone now. Although hard frosts had driven them into hibernation, other wildlife remained awake. Soft rattling in the bulrushes announced the advances of a fishing heron. The desultory plops of frogs into the water and the evening cries of birds intertwined to create a lonely, haunting, yet beautiful, place in time.

Her thoughts returned to the *Prometheus* and the day the women were auctioned. They were sold as surely as the Africans she had seen who were enslaved. They had no choice. Poor Anne. She'd been such a sweet, timid woman. Ivy wasn't surprised to see Betty surviving. Betty was strong. She wondered about Fiona, how she fared. And Sally, and Eleanor and Timmy.

She learned earlier, by listening to the other servants, of Tim's destiny. As a child in the indenture system, Tim would be kept by the man who bought him until he was of majority age, twenty-one years. Eleanor would legally be free after serving her four years, though as the mother of an indentured child, she would most likely stay with their master. Eleanor would not be free to live her life till she was in her forties, if she survived.

What a sorry mess. All to harvest tobacco, to reap money. Ivy gave in to her misery. Wailing, sobbing, halting, and choking on her tears, she cried until she had nothing left to give to her sadness. Then, feeling collected and again in equilibrium, Ivy prayed for her fellow captives.

She made her way back to the house in the luminous light of the ending day. Bird calls and rustles in the undergrowth kept her company until she reached the shelter of George Stokely's home. She went straight to the children's bedroom. They were asleep. Ivy washed the dried tears from her face and went to bed.

 Chapter 24 

Convict's Revenge
Near the Patapsco River, Maryland

October 11, 1700

Christopher, Peter, and Tom bent over porridge and bacon in the kitchen.

"Oh, I wager I will," said Christopher.

"How much, old man?" said Peter.

Ivy poured more tea into Tom's cup. The door opened and there was George, hale and hearty as always.

"G'morning."

"Morning, sir. Care for a cup of tea?"

"No, thanks, Ivy. Just here to ask these men to help get your loom put in order. I think today is as good a time as any to do it. Do you agree?"

"Never worked with a loom, sir, but happy to give it a try." Christopher rose and began to clear his place at the table.

Peter gaped at the pile of wooden parts in the corner. "That's a loom? I can't imagine." Christopher smacked Peter on the shoulder with a chuckle. "You silly, sorry, sad excuse of a human."

Tom smirked and scraped the last of the oats onto his spoon.

George went on. "We've only a bit of tobacco left to pick. We can take the time today to set it up, so it'll be all ready for Ivy. I'd rather have her weave than pack cured tobacco into hogshead barrels. Is this a good place for weaving? Or somewhere else on the farm? What do you think, Ivy? You're the one who'll be using it. I have little idea of how to best set it up."

"The kitchen should be fine, sir. I can keep an eye on the cooking and weave as well. The loom makes quite a clatter and I doubt you'll want to hear the noise in your home. The kitchen's fine."

Peter, Chris, and Tom took the remainder of the morning to set up the loom. Samuel's designated job was to bring each piece and to help hold things steady. Ivy oversaw the effort. Bethany sat at the table, watching as she played with her favorite doll.

By noon, the contraption sat in the corner of the kitchen, a five-foot-high, five-foot-wide, and six-foot-deep spidery collection of wooden bars and strings. Windows on the south and east illuminated the work surface.

Her fingers itched to get started.

Ivy dominated the household sphere. She was responsible for preparing meals—though Miss Sarah took the lead with the menu and often helped with the lighter aspects of preparation. Ivy maintained the household inventory of foodstuff.

The brick one-room kitchen commanded about the same footprint as the cottages Ivy knew back in Ireland, though the ceiling was higher. A storage loft tucked under the eaves lay above with a ladder for access. Homier to her than Stokely's grand house, the kitchen emerged as her favorite spot on *Convict's Revenge*. Weaving relaxed her, entertained her mind, fed her need to create. She found it hypnotic to run the shuttle back and forth. To choose a pattern, pick the colors, and make a piece of cloth with skill gave her great pleasure. Ivy sparkled with anticipation.

Isaac's bags held enough spun wool and linen for Ivy to make several yards of fabric. Having it to look at—the skeins waiting in their basket—while she peeled potatoes or stirred porridge uplifted her mood. It added familiarity to her life. Although there was no time for weaving while the tobacco needed harvesting, Ivy looked forward to getting started. Unless, of course, she managed to escape with Sean before then. That was, she promised herself, the goal.

Chapter 25

Convict's Revenge
Near the Patapsco River, Maryland

October 17, 1700

Bethany crooned to her doll at the top of the stairs. Ivy heard the creaking on the floorboards overhead from stout Miss Sarah's puttering about in her bedroom. Breakfast was done. Once she finished clearing up, she'd be back out in the tobacco fields with the rest of the servants.

As Ivy reached for the jug of cream, a shadow silently crept over her hand. She looked up.

Her scream sliced the morning calm.

A man the likes of whom Ivy had never seen stood and solemnly stared at her. His stringy bowlegs were firmly planted on the stone stoop. From top to bottom, his appearance spoke of a wild, foreign life. The apex of his head, a shaved knob, sprouted a single tuft of long black hair. Feathers erupted from its midst and enhanced its resemblance to a bird's nest. A copper earring dangled from his right earlobe, nearly grazing his bare shoulder. More than his shoulder was naked. He, and the equally flamboyant woman standing behind him, had much more in common with Adam and Eve than with Ivy when it came to clothing or the lack of it. They were dark-skinned, black-eyed, and smelled of a campfire mingled with other odors new to Ivy. Patches of deer hide and rags of cotton hid their most personal parts. Ivy had never seen such nakedness in a man.

Entranced, Ivy felt Miss Sarah reach up and softly touch her shoulder.

"They're Indians, dear. Just a couple of poor, wandering Piscataway. Probably want to trade."

Ivy stepped back. Drawn by her scream, Stokely and Christopher came into view, followed by Samuel and Peter.

George drew the Indigenous couple and their child, a girl about Samuel's age, back into the yard and beckoned Ivy and Miss Sarah to come out.

"You'll know best if you need what they're offering," said George. "I'll just watch."

The man and his wife pantomimed their wishes. They offered a basket of rough, blackish nuts and a second basket of roots.

"Black walnuts. Lovely," said Miss Sarah. "Now, don't act too interested, Ivy, or you'll drive the cost up. The nutmeats of those walnuts will serve us well for breads and cakes. We can make a lovely brown dye from the shells. We want those."

She looked the man in the eye and gave a nod.

His wife set the basket on the ground by Miss Sarah's feet.

"Puccoon," he said as he shook a small basket full of roots. "Puccoon."

"What is that, Miss Sarah?"

"It's bloodroot. Again, a dye. A wonderful red dye."

The Piscataway woman studied Miss Sarah's face as if memorizing each fine wrinkle. Ivy remembered how important selling her mother's weaving had been back in An Rinn, how her family's bellies depended on the decisions of others to buy or not buy Ma's work.

Miss Sarah nodded her agreement. Ivy saw the woman's face relax.

"Now we need to give in return. Ivy, go fetch the length of red calico up in my closet. I think they might like that. And grab two loaves of bread and a small ham from the larder. I think they may need food more than cloth right now."

Pleased with their trading, the family faded away. The trio shunned the roadway. As quietly as they had arrived, they traipsed off across the field, headed in the direction of the Patapsco.

Later, as Ivy mixed cornbread batter in the kitchen, Miss Sarah regaled her with tales of the early years in Maryland, when the Indigenous people lived in the full flowering of their culture, before they became weakened by disease and from fighting each other, and fighting the colonists. She detailed to Ivy the Piscataways' retreat from their ancestral homes, in the area where *Convict's Revenge* now stood, and how they slipped south.

"Yes, Ivy, we lived in terror of the Indians when I was a child. Lives were lost on both sides. A really sad habit then was the kidnapping of women and children to replace their own lost family. A few were returned. Not many. Some even became native. They refused to come back even when they could. The Iroquois carried their captives hundreds of miles north. Things have changed.

"Very few Piscataway remain. They seem to be straggling north, probably to Pennsylvania, to a wilder part of the country. That's probably where those three are headed. Can't say I'll miss them. No, I won't."

Her china teacup rattled as she sat it down in its saucer. Ivy noticed the cup had a hairline crack amid the pink flowers on its side. She knew Sarah would mourn her favorite cup when it finally fell apart, even if she wouldn't miss the Piscataway.

Chapter 26

Convict's Revenge
Near the Patapsco River, Maryland

October 19, 1700

Crisp air and a glorious pink and apricot sunrise combined to create a spectacular Saturday morning. Ivy slipped a blue calico dress over her shift and wandered out back into the farmyard. She was in time to see the three Stokelys and Miss Sarah driving off in the wagon. Ivy grabbed a cold biscuit from the kitchen and sat on the stone stoop. She nibbled her biscuit as she watched Peter throw feed to the chickens.

"Here, chick chick chick. Here, chick chick chick," he clucked, sounding like a hen himself.

The plump birds raced about chasing the feed, unworried about their imminent demise. Mr. Stokely kept his flock thinned of poor layers and old hens. Any day now might be the last for any one of them.

In the distance, Ivy saw Tom grooming the roan in front of the stable. As if he sensed her eyes on him, he looked up with a stare, then returned to currying the gelding.

Ivy's attention returned to Christopher, who sat on a stump

as he, too, watched Peter and, as always, smoked a pipe.

"Where'd the family go? What about the fields?" she asked. Christopher pulled the stem out of his mouth and knocked the white clay pipe against the log before he answered Ivy. The man was "slow as molasses in January," to quote Miss Sarah.

"Well, I don't rightly know where they're going. Master Stokely didn't see fit to tell me. Though what he did say was they would be back for supper and we should see to our own noon feed and take care of the animals. No field work today. Fields are almost all cut anyway," he said. "They might have gone to call on the Tiptons," he added as an afterthought.

Ivy's ears pricked up. "Tiptons? Who're they?"

"Just some neighbors over by the landing. Hardly any towns here in Maryland. Folks just float up and down from landing to landing to do their trade, so's any neighbor is dear indeed. Sometimes they visit kin. Not Stokely's—his kin, if'n he had any, were all left behind in England. But Miz Sarah has a few hereabouts. No matter to me. You got kin, Ivy?"

"Well, of course, I do. How'd Mr. Stokely get here without kin? Did they all die?"

"Don't know. I heard he came here alone just like all of us when he was only eleven, indentured, you know. Picked up by spiriters in Bedford, England, and stuffed into the hold of a ship. He was lucky. He lived through the transport and through his indenture. One of the few to make it and to get his acreage and suit of clothes.

"He's lived here in Maryland since he was eleven. Doing well here on his own land is his payback to those spiriters, it is. Bet he was a tough little son of a bitch as a young'un, excuse my rude tongue."

"Yep, that's what I heard, too," said Peter, finished with the chickens and joining the conversation. "He was a convict at eleven. Probably for nothin' more than standing on the street when one of those no-good spiriters came by looking for prey. If I ever see the pair captured me, it'll be a sorry day for them. I promise you."

"That's why he treats us all square, I think. He knows what it's like," said Christopher. "The man needs the labor to run this property. Servants for farm work can't afford the passage to America, so's they made this indenture business. Workers get passage as a swap for working a few years. Still not enough labor. Always short of workers here in the colonies. Sometimes the planters stoop low and use slaves or spirited-up prisoners and pirate booty. Even men like Stokely get caught up in it, like with you, Miss Ivy. But make no mistake. Stokely does what he has to—to survive. He can take your head off any day he wants. He's horsewhipped a man for stealing, he has."

Ivy leaned in. "How can you think it's all square, Christopher, when Peter and I were brought here against our will? I was kidnapped by smooth-tongued pirates. How's that fair? We should be on our way home right this minute. That's what I think."

Good-natured Christopher was flummoxed. "Mr. Stokely didn't kidnap you. I'll bet he thinks he's doing you a favor, in a way. He knows how the other planters treat their servants. Why, a young pretty lass like you might have all sorts of problems with the other planters. Not with Stokely, though. He's a fine man. Does he even know you were kidnapped?"

"I told Miss Sarah the other day while we were sorting out the linens. She must have let him know." A look of uncertainty crossed her face. "Maybe I'll tell him myself. But anyway, it still doesn't make any sense to me how he could risk doing the same evil that was done to him. No sense at all."

Christopher gave her a steady look. "The world is not perfect, much as we'd like it to be. George has had to find his way and make his living as best he can. Like all of us. He's practical and if he needs workers for this piece of land, he will do what it takes. Except for slaves. Refuses to invest in a slave. Can't meet all the niceties.

"The man does what he can to get along with everyone, but I believe his heart hardened somewhat when his wife died. Less concerned with the finer points of things."

"What happened to her?" asked Peter. He had followed the exchange between Ivy and Christopher with wide eyes. "I knew she had died and not just up and left. Saw her grave once."

Christopher took a deep draw on his pipe, then gave Peter a steady look over his pipestem.

"Well, she died birthing the baby girl." Christopher tipped his head toward the far side of the house. "Mrs. Stokely's buried over thataway. Mr. Stokely doesn't like us talking about her, but she was a kind, fine woman, I say."

"Poor children," said Ivy, turning back to her biscuit. Life so often offset its sweetest parts with bitterness.

In the afternoon, the four servants toiled to keep on top of the harvest. Peter and Ivy prepared green beans for drying, Tom sharpened tools, and Christopher sang as he gathered apples from the orchard.

Ivy speared the long bean pods with a needle and ran lengths of string through each one. Peter lounged nearby stabbing the legumes. He was effective, though without finesse. More than one bean had more than one hole in it. Some ended up shredded to pieces. Peter popped those in his mouth.

"You'll get sick eating all those raw beans, Peter." Ivy's green eye sparkled as the sun highlighted the left side of her face.

"Don't worry. These are tender enough," he said. "You're quiet today, Ivy. Everything all right?"

"Oh, I'm fine. I'm happy to feel the sun."

Usually this would have been a restful chore—sedentary, outdoors in the fresh air, the autumn temperature perfect. Instead, the enigma of George Stokely swirled and dominated her thoughts.

In the role of her master, George starred in Ivy's life. He alone determined what cloth she wore, what food she ate, where she went, whom she spent time with, and what she did. As her master, he gave her a life as good as that of any indentured servant, a life in many ways superior to what hers had been in An Rinn or even Ardmore. She admired him for raising affectionate and happy children, children without a mother. He took care of his dead wife's aunt, Miss Sarah, with respect. He gave the old lady responsibility, a role of importance. Ivy liked how he cared for his family.

Ivy sighed and reached for a bean. Peter glanced up. Nearby a chicken cocked its head, then dove in the dust for a beetle.

Yet George kept her in unwanted, undesired servitude. How could the man commit such a sin? For a sin it was. His own undeserved fate as a boy underscored the inequity in Ivy's mind. He, of all the masters in Maryland, had to know how her heart beat against the cage of captivity.

Ivy failed to cut this Gordian knot, to unravel the puzzle of George Stokely's behavior, the part she hated. Her only solution was to decide God would deal with George.

That night, she lay awake in bed. An owl hooted somewhere in the dark. An icy breeze brought the scent of apples to her. Winter lurked, ready to spring on the land and paralyze movement. If she were going home, she needed to leave soon. How could she survive on the run? Would she be able to steal enough food on the ship to last till Ireland? Would stealing food be a sin? How could she find the Tiptons' place and Sean? An idea tiptoed into her thoughts.

Chapter 27

Convict's Revenge
Near the Patapsco River, Maryland

October 20, 1700

Dark clouds rolled in from the west and quickly began to empty floods of rain. Ivy and the children sat on the floor with a hand-painted checkerboard. Miss Sarah, after grumbling the storm made her head pound, retreated to her bedroom.

"Crown me," crowed Sam as he shoved his acorn cap into Ivy's first row.

"Oh, you clever boy," giggled Ivy.

"Yes, cwever," said Bethany, clapping her pudgy hands.

"Why does she talk like that?" asked Sam. "It's not right."

Bethany cast a hurt look his way.

"Oh, some little ones take a while to learn some sounds. She'll be all right. My sister did the same thing," said Ivy as she gave Bethany a hug and a kiss on the cheek.

Bethany stuck her tongue out at her brother.

"You had a sister?" said Sam, his hand with another acorn cap stopping in midair.

"Yes, I still do. A sister and three brothers. Now, let's play," said Ivy, not wanting to tarry on the subject of her family.

Sam proved a tough opponent, and Ivy cut him no quarter. After losing twice, Ivy hoped she'd eke out a victory in the third game. Looking up from the board, she asked, "Sam, where'd you go yesterday? Did you have fun?"

"Well, sort of. We went to visit the Tiptons. They have two boys. Ed and John are younger than me. We got in trouble throwing rocks in the pond."

"Oh, my. Is it far to the Tiptons'? Where do they live?" Inside, Ivy felt coiled and tense, afraid Sam wouldn't know.

"Well," drawled Sam, jumping and taking one of Ivy's wood chips off the board, "You turn to the right and go down the lane by the landing. Not too far. Why?"

"Feeling curious," said Ivy. "Looks like you lose this time, my boy." She slid a chip into an unbeatable position.

Bethany giggled. "You wooze, Sammy."

Chapter 28

Convict's Revenge
Near the Patapsco River, Maryland

October 24, 1700

Ivy woke up early Sunday, wanting to savor every second of the one day she was free of field and farm work. She wasn't totally free of domestic duties, however, on Sundays. She put the meals on the table and oversaw the children. All in all, Miss Sarah treated her well. Ivy had come to enjoy spending time with Bethany and Sam. They were sweet and friendly children. They also filled a portion of the emptiness created by her family in Ireland's absence.

The male servants usually spent their time off lolling about their cabin. They smoked, napped, and bragged about what they'd do once they'd completed their service with Stokely. From time to time, they wandered off to visit other servants on nearby properties or go for a jaunt in the woods or fish in one of the waterways.

On his part, George Stokely did not ask them where they went or what they did. This did not mean he did not know, or that he would not punish infractions. The servants' activities were a frequent topic of discussion overheard by Ivy at the landing and at Stokely's hearthside. The planter community kept their collective eyes on the help.

Ivy doubted her fellow servants would be as successful as George Stokely. None of them could keep up with Stokely out in the field. He was unstoppable. Maybe Peter would succeed. He, like Ivy, was growing stronger each day with the wholesome victuals, clean water, and sound nights of sleep. She was unsure of Christopher's future. As for Tom Jenkins, Ivy refused to think about his future.

As for herself, Ivy had plans, though they felt wobbly at times. She sensed a fire hiding under George's placid, easygoing exterior. She did not want to poke the dragon. Her plan to cheat him out of the four years' service he'd paid for began to ignite little flames of guilt. He clearly needed help with his children and his farming.

Ivy decided Stokely's widower status was not her problem. Her problem was getting home.

No matter when she ran away, she would need clothes. As part of her indenture, Stokely was obligated to give her room, board, and clothing. She'd seen the rough osnabruck frocks worn by other servants at the landing. Osnabruck, a scratchy oatmeal-colored fabric, looked as cheap as it was. Miss Sarah gave Ivy the more expensive cotton, calico, in dainty floral prints. Enough for two dresses plus some white muslin for two undershifts. Miss Sarah helped her sew the dresses and shifts. She just needed to finish the hem on one shift and her clothing would be all done.

Ivy went to Miss Sarah's bedroom door and knocked.

"Ma'am, do you have a needle I can borrow please, to hem my shift?"

"Come in, Ivy," said Miss Sarah. She had already dressed. A pristine white lace cap graced her head. She doddered back into her room and closed a door in the corner.

The only place Ivy thought it might go would be the attic. She was startled to see a rosary in Miss Sarah's hand. She had not seen a rosary in Maryland. Ivy crossed herself.

"Oh, my," said Miss Sarah. "Well, you clearly know exactly what this is. Would you happen to be Catholic, dear?"

Ivy stuttered. "Well, uh . . ."

"Don't worry. I'm Catholic myself."

"Catholic? I thought English people were Protestants."

"Not all, Ivy. The English were all Roman Catholic for many years, then Protestantism came in. You'd think since each is a Christian faith, they'd love each other. They don't."

"Do they fight in Maryland?" Ivy's mind returned to the soldiers in Ardmore.

"Not openly. You know, I was born here in Maryland. A Catholic founded this colony. At first, Maryland was a haven for those of his faith. Catholics were welcome, and other faiths, too. Then things changed in England and the troubles crossed the ocean to beset us here. Right now, Catholics are out of favor. Well, to be truthful, Catholicism is officially illegal, so it's best to keep our religion to ourselves. I practice my faith in private. I'm not the only one. I expect the winds will shift again. They always do."

"Does Mr. Stokely know?"

"Oh, yes. He has no faith himself but supports my right to have one. He left his home at such a young age. Lydia made sure Samuel was baptized and I talked George into baptizing Bethany. That's all the religion the two dear children have had. I do read them the Bible as often as I can. Maybe when they're older . . . Here, let me show you my secret." Miss Sarah turned back and opened the door in the corner.

Ivy walked into the bedroom and peered past the door. It

opened onto a tiny space, no bigger than a coffin, a miniature chapel. The nook held an altar, a kneeler, a crucifix and, best of all, a small, high-set window. Fine embroidered white-on-white linens covered the altar. An open Bible sat atop the kneeler. A ray of sunshine shone on the crucifix and highlighted the Savior's features.

"It's lovely," said Ivy. "A jewel."

"Yes. I was pretty sure you were Catholic, Ivy. Don't fear. Please feel free to use my chapel anytime. Just don't tell anyone, especially not the other servants. I believe they are all Protestant and might not keep this information to themselves.

"Right now, in these days, those of our faith must take care. The Catholic Church in Maryland has been driven underground by the highest authorities. It is illegal to openly practice Catholicism. Instead, we worship, baptize, celebrate the Eucharist, and marry in our homes. From time to time, if we are fortunate, a priest will come by to lead us in our own house.

"I don't know what might happen if you or I were to worship at a church. I do know when I was in my middle years, over seven hundred Protestants took up arms here against the Catholics. That's enough for me to keep my faith private. We will persist, though, won't we?"

A memory came to Ivy. She was back in Ardmore and her father was explaining why they no longer went to church. She teared up and gave the old lady a hug.

At bedtime, she found a rosary under her pillow. The rosary, unlike the clandestine short rosary she had lost, was a full-sized one of copper with glass beads. She tucked it, a source of solace and comfort, into the pocket tied around her waist. Following Miss Sarah's invitation, she stole away to the private chapel to pray each evening after the children were asleep. At first, she prayed only for herself, Sean, and the rest of her family.

Eventually entreaties on behalf of Bethany, then Sam, Miss Sarah, her fellow servants, and finally, George Stokely, began to pepper her conversations with God.

Chapter 29

Convict's Revenge
Near the Patapsco River, Maryland

October 25, 1700

Ivy's thoughts floated pleasantly as she walked in the cool morning air. Daydreams, rather than focused ideas, filled her mind. She ran various color combinations and patterns in a stream before her internal eye, ruminating and planning her first weaving project in Maryland. Her mind play was almost as enjoyable as the actual weaving.

Ivy headed out to the most distant tobacco field, the last one to be harvested. She had been up for hours. She had put a breakfast of porridge with raisins on the table for the other servants, then served the Stokelys and Miss Sarah eggs and toast. The hens were laying eggs left and right these days. Tomorrow there would be enough to serve some to the workmen.

Fluffy white cumulus clouds set off the blue of the sky. Blue and white, one of her favorite color combinations. She reminisced about making dyes with Honora and their mother.

Loud honking drew Ivy's attention skyward. A flock of geese winged south in a wedge-shaped formation. Ivy told herself they looked like a slice of raisin pie on the move.

She skirted the fields to avoid the sun, walking along in the shadow of the woodlot. A floppy straw hat, its wide brim nearly reaching beyond her shoulders, protected her face. No matter how hot the day, Ivy wore long sleeves outdoors and stockings to protect her skin. When she last bathed in the metal tub in the cozy wash house behind the kitchen, her naked body had shown a patchwork of mismatched colors. Her sunburned areas had peeled to reveal skin more beige than white. She had an alabaster white torso, ivory arms from the sun piercing her cotton sleeves, and red, work-roughened hands. Her hands embarrassed her. There was nothing to do about them. Popping grease and splatters from the cookpot added injury to the insults of the sun. She was a servant now, a domestic, a worker. She resented losing her youth to an unwanted master rather than her own chosen husband. Her hands told the tale.

Ivy's course carried her along a curve. The only things in her sightline were the bumpy-textured fields of hillocks denuded of their tobacco topknots and the woods on her left. Peter, Christopher, and Tom had left for the field an hour earlier. She wasn't sure of George Stokely's whereabouts this morning. Knowing him, she was sure he was working full force wherever he was.

Ivy rounded a clump of trees, faltered, and drew to a stop. Her visions of blue wool and herringbone tweed dissipated like wood smoke. Less than a stone's throw away, Tom Jenkins sat upon a log at the edge of the woods. The rich aroma from a clay pipe in his mouth reached out to her. No one else was in sight.

"Morning, Miss Ivy. What a delight to see you. Come on over, if you would. I've a question for you." He put the slender-stemmed white pipe back in his mouth. He patted a spot on the log about a foot from his skinny hips. "Come on. We never get to talk."

"Well, morning, Tom. I'd love to stay, but I need to do some fieldwork. You know how Mr. Stokely is. He expects me to earn my keep."

"Come on. I won't bite. I have only one question. You answer it, then you can go and needle all the tobacco leaves you've a mind to. You're a good worker. You know you are."

Ivy had never heard Tom put so many words together at once. She did not want to hurt his feelings. Maybe she had been unfair to him. Curious as to what he wanted to ask her, she drew near, like a silver moth flitting to a bedside candle.

"Come on, girl. Sit down. Don't be afraid. I ain't gonna harm you. Just have a question."

Hesitant as a doe, Ivy took another step forward. Then she sat on the smooth log and turned to face Tom.

He carefully emptied his pipe, knocking it against the log. His leather boot slid over to the ashes and ground them into the dirt, obliterating them. No fire would reignite to mark the place. He laid his pipe on a bare patch of dirt.

Finished, he looked Ivy in the eye, his own black eyes flat and giving nothing away. He dropped his gaze to her work-roughened hands.

Ivy pulled them back and covered them with the folds of her skirt.

"Well, Tom, what did you want to ask me? I can only sit a minute, you know."

Like a cat on a mouse or a wolf on a fawn, he sprang. His right hand encircled Ivy's neck and he pulled her to him. His left hand groped her breast.

Ivy struggled against him.

"I want you, Ivy, and I'll have you. I've waited long enough, you tease. I'll have you now. I will."

His mouth covered hers and filled it with tobacco fumes. His left hand moved down. He lifted the hem of her skirt.

Ivy kicked and flailed, scratched his neck. Her knee swung up and smashed into his crotch and he pulled back. She sprang up, screamed, and tried to run.

Tom caught her by her skirt.

With a loud rip, the calico tore at the waist.

She tripped on the hem and tumbled down to the ground.

She scrambled up and extricated herself. Her eyes flicked about and searched for a stick to use as a cudgel or a rock to brain him. She reached out to a palm-sized rock, but Tom's strong grasp stopped her, and he was on her again.

The combatants panted heavily. Fueled by adrenaline, they huffed and grunted with effort.

George Stokely's voice boomed over the scrabbling noises of the struggle.

"You stop that nonsense right now, Jenkins. Stop."

Tom escalated his groping as if trying to get as much damage done as possible.

George reached into the scrum, yanked Tom's right arm away and pulled him upright within range of his own huge fists. George punched and pummeled Tom into submission. Then the towering man stood over Tom. His breath came in deep gulps.

Tom's clay pipe lay shattered at their feet. The red stripe of a long scratch marked Tom's neck.

"Shame on you, Tom. I've no use for such behavior. I think it would be best if we shake hands and agree to forget this unfortunate misstep on your part. Maybe you were confused because Ivy's kind to you. Maybe you thought you meant something more to her, but you don't. She's a decent girl. She's kind to everyone. Let me warn you: I'll do worse if you ever so much as wink at her. Do you understand? I'm bigger than you and stronger than you. And if you don't understand that, understand this: I'll sell your bond to another and have done with you. For now, I'll excuse your egregious behavior, if it's agreeable to Miss Ivy. Up to her. Now, am I clear?"

Tom sneered. His lip quivered.

Ivy looked on, round-eyed, her breathing slowing down. For the first time in her life, she managed to stay in the moment under extreme stress. She had kept her soul with her body, her feet on the ground. Amazement, gratitude, and pride tumbled together.

"Yeah, I understand your meaning, sir. No trouble from me. The girl's a tease," said Tom.

George shook his fist in Tom's face. "No, you're a fool. Now, stop it."

Tom found a stray thread on his sleeve to pick. "Yes, sir. Of course, Mr. Stokely. Let's get on with the day."

"Ivy, do you agree? Should I give Tom another chance?"

Ivy stood. Unmoored at the waist, her dress hung lopsided, the hem dragging on one side. Her breathing sounded loud to her.

"I believe I can forgive him, sir." Ivy half-stumbled as she turned to her assailant. She yanked at her skirt and pulled it out from under her foot.

"Tom, you need to know I see you as a fellow servant. I have no interest in you as a suitor and I never will, especially after this." She spoke directly to Tom, unafraid, then looked to George.

George said to Tom, "Shake my hand, then get back to the fields, Tom. I'll accompany Ivy back to the house."

Tom rose and the two men shared a firm handshake. Ivy noticed Tom's eyes darting to the woods as if he yearned to be on his way. A sweaty sheen coated Tom's face and his chest heaved from his exertion.

"Come on, Ivy. We'll go back home so you can clean up and fix your clothes."

Ivy gathered the ripped area of her skirt, tied it into a knot so it wouldn't drag in the dirt, and followed after George.

George stopped and beckoned her to catch up with him.

"Ivy, I am sorry Tom did that to you. He comes from a rough background, though there's no excuse for such misbehavior. You must let me know if he gives you any more trouble. Can you do that?"

"Yes, of course. Don't worry. I can take care of myself. I've done it before." The confession slipped out. Ivy hoped she hadn't said too much.

"I am sorry to hear that. Should never happen. Did you have trouble on the ship coming over, or back in Ireland, if I may ask?"

"On the *Prometheus*. A sailor on the ship. But I bit him proper and the captain flailed him. I will never put up with mistreatment, sir. Don't worry about me."

"I'll try not to."

Ivy next encountered Tom at dinner in the kitchen. She ladled rabbit stew into a tin bowl and chased a chunk of thigh meat until she caught it and dropped it on top. She slid the bowl to Tom. Ivy wanted no complaints of retaliation from the man. She took her seat across from him.

Peter sat at the end of the table, head down into his plate, and shoveled in his food as if it were his last meal.

"Good stew, Ivy," said Tom. Only his lips moved. His face was immobile and as expressionless as a dead man.

"Thank you, Tom. Have a slice of bread."

The kitchen's table, centered in the room with one side abutting a window, played many roles in the theater of life at *Convict's Revenge*. Ivy and Miss Sarah prepared food on its smooth wooden surface. They chattered, bustled, chopped, sorted, and kneaded in unison. The male servants clustered about it to eat their hot meals, though they also carried their tin plates outdoors to enjoy a cool breeze from time to time.

Samuel and Bethany often sat at the table to watch Ivy work while they shared their childish observations. They learned as if at a school desk as Ivy cooked, cleaned, wove, and instructed them. She described the beauty of Ardmore, shared how purple dye was made, and showed them how to make bannocks. Although the polished mahogany table in the Stokely dining room was prettier, no place on *Convict's Revenge* offered more relaxation and hospitality than the kitchen table. Even after a day which had included an assault and a beating, the four servants found it within themselves to sit together in a semblance of harmony.

"Ivy, I apologize for my behavior. I misunderstood my standing," said Tom.

Christopher and Peter looked on in unblinking attention.

Ivy didn't let on her suspicion of the apology being coerced.

"Thank you, Tom. Glad to hear it." She managed an approximation of a smile.

Christopher chimed in. "Good man."

Peter jammed a particularly enormous chunk of rabbit into his maw and destroyed it with his teeth, then swallowed. Ivy doubted he'd even heard the exchange.

Tom and Christopher, after a beat, turned their attention to their stew.

Ivy left to attend to the Stokelys' and Miss Sarah's meal.

After supper, with the children tucked into bed, Ivy mended the rip in her dress. Christopher popped his head in the kitchen as she sewed. He asked if she was all right. She nodded and mouthed, "Thank you." Just another bump in the road.

She felt herself growing up, figuring out what was important and what was chaff in the wind. Tom was chaff—misguided, and wrongheaded. The surface of their relationship flowed unchanged and, to outsiders, was as placid as a millpond. Underneath, Ivy's mistrust swam. She believed hatred, like a snaky eel, swam along, too—Tom's hatred of her.

Chapter 30

Convict's Revenge
Near the Patapsco River, Maryland

October 30, 1700

The autumn days, chock-full of harvest activities, galloped along. One Saturday, Stokely went to the landing for another bartering session. Ivy and Samuel rode along to help. Stokely rolled his wagon up alongside another. There was Sean, his back to Ivy. He lifted a splint bushel basket of red and yellow apples from a wagon. His movements were fluid and his strength palpable. Sean carried the aura of health and something else. Sean had a swagger and confidence Ivy had never seen in him back in Ireland. Adversity had fashioned her brother into an adult.

After Stokely strode off to join his fellow planters, Ivy sidled over to her brother for a few covert words.

"Sean, pretend you're talking to me about those apples."

"Why wouldn't I talk to you about these tasty fruits, Sis?" Sean grabbed a pink and yellow apple and held it out to Ivy for a mock inspection.

"Fine. We need to get home. I don't want to wait. I'll sneak out and get you soon. Bring any food you can carry and extra clothes. We can go to the harbor and stow away on a ship bound for England."

"England? We want to go to Ireland, home."

"I heard they all stop for victuals and water in Ireland. Even if they don't, we'll be closer to home than we are here," said Ivy.

"How will we eat, Ivy? It's weeks on a passage."

"We'll have to steal, brother. I think after the ship's free of the Chesapeake and at sea, you might be able to work as a sailor. Someone's always dying at sea. I'll stay hidden. You can sneak me food."

"It might work, Sis. I'd like nothing better than seeing our family and being home. I trust you."

"Then listen for my whistle. No one else knows it here."

Sean gave a nod. "Ivy, you'd better come quick as you can. The weather will be ugly in a few weeks. Now, go. Else someone will figure out we're up to something."

Ivy hurried off to find Samuel before he became embroiled in mischief. She liked the boy. She also knew better than to leave him unattended for long at the wharf. A fringe of ruffians and ne'er-do-wells lounged at the landing and sniffed around for any opportunity.

Back at *Convict's Revenge*, Ivy turned thoughts over and over as she cooked dinner. The pressure to be off, to join Sean, and go home to Ireland weighed on her. She longed to move on to the next part of her life, the grown-up part. To have her own family, her own home. To marry Kevin, not a used-up widower like Isaac Abner. To raise her own children, not George Stokely's—although her heart ached for Bethany and Samuel. George should find himself a new wife.

What had she done to be kept from living her own life? What evil? Hadn't her imprisonment on the pirate ship been punishment enough? If God would let her go home, she would be so thankful. She felt she would explode, burst like a soap bubble, and float off into the air if she stayed here. Her lack of resources and any guilt for deserting the Stokelys and Miss Sarah were not enough to stop her escape.

She had clothes, though no money and no food. Stealing was a sin. Ivy rationalized. Stokely would save money. She would not be eating his food this winter. He wouldn't begrudge her a bit of food.

Ivy did not know exactly where the Tipton land lay, but she did know how to get to the landing. Confident in her ability to find Sean, she made her decision. The next time the Stokely family went on a drive, Ivy would run away.

And that is exactly what Ivy did.

Chapter 31

Convict's Revenge
Near the Patapsco River, Maryland

October 31, 1700

Ivy awoke headachy and out-of-sorts. As if to underline her discomfort, the cool finger of a breeze wiggled through the crack between the windowpane and sill and headed straight over to her. Prodded by the cold air, she snuggled deeper under the blanket. After a minute she gathered her nerve and roused herself.

Golden leaves in the oak tree, set against an overcast sky, filled the view through the bedroom window. Ivy struggled to find the energy to dress. Her hands fumbled. She managed to get the children ready for the day and went downstairs. Over breakfast, Miss Sarah announced the family would be visiting the Willoughbys for lunch.

Ivy dropped her spoon with a clatter.

"Do I have to go, Papa?" asked Bethany with a pout. "I want to ride the pony today. With Ivy. She promised to help me."

Ivy waited for George's response. Her plans for the day did not, for once, involve the children and certainly not the gray pony.

"Another day, dear. The pony can wait. I heard the Willoughbys have a new litter of kittens, though. I'll wager they'll let you pet the kitties. Will that do?"

Bethany grinned.

"A gray kitty?"

"You'll need to wait and see, love."

Sammy gave an exasperated sigh. "You and your animals."

Half an hour after Juno pulled the Stokely family down the lane, Ivy joined Peter on the kitchen stoop. His attention was on his jackknife as he whittled the handle of a witch hazel broom. Christopher was nowhere to be seen. Tom was chopping kindling at the woodpile.

"When I finish this broom, it's yours, Ivy. A hand broom to help you keep the kitchen tidy."

"Oh, thanks, Peter. I like a whisk broom. Never seen one made."

"Christopher showed me. Took me out in the woods to where the witch hazel is. Have to make these from green wood. Just peel the bark from the bottom of the stick and pull the strings free. Makes a good, stiff brush. Wrap the lower handle, carve the top and we're done. Whittling's one of the best ways in the world to waste time that I know of."

"Haven't done it myself, Peter. Listen, I don't feel well. I'm going to go lie down. Maybe that'll help. Please wake me up in time to get dinner ready," said Ivy.

"Sure, Missy. I'll take care of it. No one will know the difference," promised Peter.

Ivy felt Tom's reptilian stare follow her from the woodpile as she left the yard.

She forced herself to walk slowly to the back door, then dashed upstairs. She gathered the few pieces of clothing she wasn't already wearing and wrapped them up in her shawl.

Downstairs, she tucked two apples into her bundle.

Ivy stepped out through the rarely used front door.

As she headed down the lane, she yearned to run, to race, to fly to Sean. She compromised and alternated short bursts of running with longer walking sessions.

The rosary from Miss Sarah was in her pocket. Ivy believed the older woman would want her to keep it. She fingered the copper and beads.

Happiness and excitement pushed her eastward, like wind in a ship's sail. Ships. She planned to steal onto a ship at the harbor. She and Sean would stow away on one bound for England. They had survived their first crossing. They'd survive another. Sean could work as a sailor, offer his skills and strength after they were asea. She would hide among the hogsheads of tobacco. Ivy looked forward to sharing her tales of Maryland with Honora.

The day was warm and still under pale gray skies. Rain surreptitiously began to fall. The first small drops plopped onto the dirt road, a ring of dust puffing with each strike.

Ivy chatted with herself. "Is that rain? Can't tell." Then, another drop and another in a crescendo until a fine drizzle came speeding down. Ivy dashed for refuge under an enormous oak tree at the side of the road.

The western horizon flashed with light under dark skies followed by rumbling thunder.

Ivy peeked around. Her shoulders relaxed when she saw a cluster of poplar trees on a nearby knoll. Any lightning should pick the tall cluster as a target.

Grasses along the roadside began to wave in unison, bowing their seed heads before the blowing wind. Black clouds heralded an early false nightfall. Within minutes, sheets of cold rain fell heavily. Ivy pressed her back against the tree trunk's rough bark. She stacked her clothes atop her head in a futile quest for protection from the storm.

With a loud crack and pungent odor, lightning felled a nearby tree.

Ivy's ears rang. Sounds seemed dampened in the aftermath. Crash after crash of explosive and simultaneous lightning and thunder struck near her. Tears mixed with the cold rain running down her cheeks.

Amid the chaos, a lightning bolt revealed a man, his face obscured by a hat, on a dark horse.

Ivy stared. She recognized water-soaked Juno's white nose blaze and stockings. George Stokely had found her. She was caught, a runaway, captured once more.

Ivy fled her body, soaring high over the storm as Stokely called her name.

"Ivy, Ivy, run over here. Please. Get out from under that tree right now! I won't harm you. Let's go! Come on, girl."

Ivy snapped. Her soul and mind and body clicked. She rushed to George.

Bending down, he whisked her up as if she were weightless and snugged her before him onto the saddle. Stokely wheeled the horse around and kicked her into a gallop.

The world blinked night to day as a monumental surge of lightning cleaved the tree which had sheltered Ivy only moments earlier.

Locked together on the horse, Ivy and George raced the downpour.

The storm roared full-throated against them, whipped the horse's mane, and beat against George's hat and coat. Firmly encircled within George's arms, Ivy tucked her chin down. Rain streamed down her forehead. It camouflaged her tears and splashed onto the soaked bundle clutched against her chest.

The foul weather cleared as quickly as it had arrived. The

tumult left behind the memento of a beautiful gloaming. Vivid scarlet and purple surrounded the setting sun. Warm against George's broad chest, Ivy breathed in the rain-freshened air.

She tried not to think about what lay ahead. What would happen to her now? What if Stokely sold her indenture to another? He would be within his rights to punish her, to brand, whip, or hurt her. He could make her work an extra year. She stayed on tenterhooks, unsure if his promise not to hurt her would prove true. Ivy wondered why the English were so much trouble.

Juno's hooves splatted down the Stokely's muddy lane. Hungry as always, the mare picked up her pace as they neared the stable. Bats winged erratically about in the failing light as they launched their nocturnal food hunt. A lamp burned in Miss Sarah's window and outlined her rotund silhouette topped by a frilly cap.

Once in the darkened stable, George put his hands to Ivy's waist and slid her off the horse. He let the big bay horse get her fill of water, then removed the saddle and began to sponge her down. Ivy helped. Once the water coming off the horse was no longer warm, George slow-walked her about the stable. Ivy walked beside them.

"Ivy, I have things I have to say to you right now before anything else happens. Please stay.

"I've got a livelihood to make, to provide for my family. I need help, laborers I can count on, more help than I now have. Indentured servants or African slaves are the only way to get extra help right now. Tobacco's a fearsome crop. Growing it takes a lot of fiddling most of the year round. You've noticed, haven't you?"

"Yes," agreed Ivy, with a wide-eyed gaze. Her soaked bundle lay at her feet. She wiped lingering rain from her eyes.

"I need help with Sam and Bethany, too. Miss Sarah is getting on in years and the housework and the children are too much for her to do alone. I love her. She deserves a bit of ease in her old age. I picked you at the wharf, not one of those other trifling girls. You seemed decent. I believed you—a family girl—you'd be able to help. You'd know how to raise children and keep a house going. And you have. My children are happier. I don't want to hurt them by taking you away or having you run away. I need a decent person like you to teach them how to be decent. That's why I paid so much for your indenture. You were the very best woman at the harbor to have around my children, to help Miss Sarah . . . and me."

Ivy looked down at her feet.

George found his voice. He continued. He spoke low and calmly as if to a skittish colt.

"I know you have a brother at the Tiptons'. I've known it since I first saw him. He might not be a redhead like you, but mismatched eyes and Irish? Not too difficult to figure out. I also know you didn't come here by choice. You certainly didn't sign on freely for that bastard Captain Smythe to carry you here. I have an idea of the hardships you faced during the crossing."

George paused. Now cooled off, Juno was led into her stall and fed. George gathered himself and spoke on, his arm resting on the stall door.

"I've done my best to be clear with you, Ivy. I'd be within my legal rights to punish you in any number of ways for running away like you did today. But I am not that kind of a person. I'm just a man who needs your help, if you are willing to provide it. But if you are unhappy here, I'll give you a choice.

"I guess I should do now what I should have done back at the wharf the day you came off the ship. Ask your opinion. If you can agree to work for the rest of the indenture, that'll give the children time to get a little older. Or I can sell your bond to someone else. But I warn you. I know of no other planter who'll treat you as well as Miss Sarah and I do. Of that, I am sure. What'll it be, Ivy? I need to know. My family needs to know. Can we count on you, or do you need to leave us?"

A bit of moonlight came through the stable door and reflected off Stokely's unwavering gray eyes.

Ivy, loath to lose her dream, blurted, "Why can't I go home? I was kidnapped, stolen. My mother and father don't even know what happened."

George sighed. "Ivy, I am so sorry you were stolen from your home. That is in the past, though I know you must still suffer from it. That was a terrible thing to happen to anyone, especially a young person like you.

"You need to be practical right now, so you don't get into any more trouble. There are no ships this time of year. You're stuck here till the spring. So do you want to stay or go to someone else? Another planter? That's the only choice I can see. That's all I have to offer."

"Would the Tiptons have me?"

George looked stricken. "As you wish. I'll look into this as a possibility. In the meantime, keep this to yourself. You will need to choose if the Tiptons say they will have you, girl."

"Thank you kindly, sir," said Ivy.

Miss Sarah had cooked dinner. Only Sam and Bethany found much appetite for the aromatic fried chicken. A heaviness pressed down on the adults at dinner and squelched conversation. Miss Sarah's birdlike eyes flitted from Ivy to George and back again.

"Apple pie, George? Ivy made it yesterday before, uh, before today," she chirped, seeking to draw the meal to a close as quickly as possible.

"No, thank you, Sarah," George said. He pushed his chair

back. "I'll go see to the other horses. Juno's all straight."

"Pie, pie! I'd like pie, Auntie," said Sam.

"Me, too! Me, too!" clamored Bethany.

Ivy exchanged a weak smile with Sarah. She fetched the cooled pie from its spot on the wide stone windowsill.

By the time she went to bed, Ivy felt totally drained. She stripped down to her chemise and lay on her rough pallet. She turned her face to the wall and quietly cried herself to sleep.

Chapter 32

Convict's Revenge
Near the Patapsco River, Maryland

November 1700

Ivy felt out of kilter in the aftermath of her botched escape. Crestfallen by her failure, George's equanimity confused her. His treatment of her remained unchanged. She wished he would yell at her and give her an excuse to hate him. After the escapade, she not only did her best to stay out of further trouble, she made a special effort to avoid George Stokely. She would duck into an outbuilding if she spied her master heading her way on the farm and tell herself he hadn't noticed.

Stokely found reasons big and small to keep his distance from Ivy. He showed up in the house for meals and little else. His horses shone like satin from the frequent currying and brushing George did in the days following the storm. Choosing the woodlot farthest from the house, George and his three men engaged in the endless task of clearing new fields. Tobacco sapped the soil's nutrients. After a few years of supporting tobacco, the land needed to lay fallow. Clearing new fields was an endless task.

The Marylanders followed the practice of the Indigenous people. To clear a field of the larger trees, they girdled them—cut a swath of bark from a tree's circumference. Damaged, the tree eventually died. Not as quick as chopping the tree down with an ax, the technique demanded less effort and worked well.

The men burned the remaining brush, added a few amendments to the soil, then shaped it into the hillocks used for the tobacco crop. To make the hillocks, laborers used a metal hoe to scrape and firm down dirt around their leg. Once the pile had reached their knee, they carefully pulled their leg out. In the spring, young tobacco plants, started from seed in nursery patches, were transplanted into these hillocks. The rule-of-thumb workload expectation allotted as many as ten thousand tobacco hillocks to one laborer's care. The crop demanded attention throughout most of the year, with only a one- or two-month break.

Ivy churned George's offer over and over in her mind. She knew she should give him a reply shortly, or he'd make his own decision.

She understood how life proceeded at *Convict's Revenge* and it was an orderly life of abundance. But at the Tiptons' she would have Sean's companionship. She knew he would watch out for her, protect her, and be a comfort. She'd certainly heard life at the Tiptons' place was not always pleasant. She pondered. Maybe she was thinking of leaving *Convict's Revenge* simply to exercise her own free will. Maybe life would be worse at the Tiptons' place. The best path forward was not clear.

Miss Sarah, an energetic soul, no longer had the stamina to do all the chores. Too short and too stiff with the indignities of age to do many of the chores even if she wanted to, she depended on Ivy. One day, while Ivy mused about her necessary decision, Miss Sarah asked her to clean up a storeroom.

"Winter will be here before we know it," said Miss Sarah. "You're such an organized, tidy young woman, my dear. I know you'll do a better job at this than the men."

Ivy glowed with the praise. "Of course."

Later that morning in a far corner, Ivy uncovered three canvas bags filled with raw wool. Apparently Miss Sarah had not found the time to prepare the wool or spin it since the spring shearing.

Miss Sarah gave Ivy a pair of wooden carding paddles. Ivy and three-year old Bethany set to work. Bethany's tiny fingers plucked out the bits of debris, twigs, and seedpods caught in the soft wool. Next, Ivy put the wool between her paddles and brushed it. The springy fibers, after a bit, mostly lined up in the same direction and formed a small roll. Ivy spun stories for Bethany while they worked. She managed to keep the young girl entertained enough to stay at her task.

"Bethany, I'd like to show you a way to say the *L* sound," said Ivy. "Would you like that?"

"I'd wuv it," prattled Bethany.

"Come over here and stand behind me."

The girl jumped up and giggled behind Ivy.

"Now, put both your hands on the front of my neck. Keep them there while I talk," said Ivy.

Bethany did as Ivy instructed. "Now, listen and feel. Lamb. Lamb. Lamb. Swam. Swam. Swam," intoned Ivy.

"The two sounds—the *L* and the *S* sounds—are different. My neck feels different when I make the *L* sound than when I do the *S*. What do you think?"

Bethany felt the vocalizations and snatched her hands away.

"Oh, Ivy. I want to do it on me. Let me try," said Bethany.

"Yes, feel how your throat moves, dearie."

The two went back and forth, practicing. Suddenly, George's face appeared at the storeroom door.

"How'd you know that, Ivy? What a wonder it is," said George. She basked in his approval and the smile she had not seen since before she ran away.

"Oh, something a woman in our village taught me so I could help my sister."

"Well, thank you. And well done, Bethany." George gave Bethany a hug and a loud smacking kiss on the top of her head.

"Daddy! Don't do that. My ribbons!"

With a final grin to Ivy, George sauntered out the door. Ivy heard him whistling through the house and out into the farmyard.

Chapter 33

Convict's Revenge
Near the Patapsco River, Maryland

November 13, 1700

"Drat!" shouted Ivy as the iron pot slipped from her hands and landed on the kitchen floor. Gooey oatmeal slopped out. "Stay back, Bethany. It's hot."

Bethany's lower lip began to protrude. The child wept, tears beading her thick dark lashes and rolling down her cheeks.

"I'm hungry, Ivy. Porridge all gone." She had begun to correctly say her *L*s much of the time, after drilling with Ivy.

With an "I'll help," Sam hopped off his chair. "There's plenty left, Bethany. You can have mine."

Tears threatened to overrun Ivy's lashes. Touched by Sam's kindness, Ivy felt rising guilt as she thought of her pending decision.

"Sam, want to ride along with me to the landing?" George asked his son after breakfast. He pointedly excluded Ivy from the outing. Her face clouded with hurt.

"Oh, yes. Can I take the reins again?"

"Of course, Sam. You're plenty old enough."

Not long after the two rumbled by the house. Ivy peered from the front window and watched them bounce away in the creaky wagon.

With Sammy gone and Ivy in a sour mood, Bethany wandered at loose ends. She whined about the troubles in her pint-sized life. The pink ribbon in her hair was the wrong color. The gray kitten was hiding. Daddy wouldn't let her ride Aphrodite.

Fed up, Ivy rallied.

"Such a pretty day out. Bethany, would you like to eat our noon meal outside, under the big tree? We won't have many more warm days like this till the spring."

"Can we, Ivy? Can we? Oh, yes!" Bethany clapped her hands in a show of enthusiasm. She jumped up and down on her toes, her dark plait bouncing.

Ivy couldn't keep the broad smile from her face.

Looking up from her potato peeling, Miss Sarah chuckled. "Sounds lovely, Ivy. I'll help you."

Together the three set up the luncheon. Ivy loaded a willow basket with a small crock of buttermilk, tin cups, and a wedge of cheese. Bethany helped her pack ginger cookies and apples into her own small basket.

Miss Sarah poked around in a chest until she found an old square of rough linen cloth. "There's only a few holes. We can use this."

They shooed a clutch of hens from the back stoop, then trundled off to the maple tree. Beneath its generous shade, Miss Sarah spread the linen. Bethany unloaded her basket. She licked the tips of each of her fingers one by one and savored the gingery sugar.

Glancing up from her own basket, Ivy burst out laughing. "Bethany, let's eat our meal and then you can have a whole cookie to enjoy. Come, girl, here's a piece of cheese."

By midafternoon, Bethany was asleep in the grass. Miss Sarah gently snored, her back against the tree trunk. Ivy, propped against a log, roused with the sound of the wagon clattering down the lane. Rascal's barks added to the din. George and Sam were home.

"Let's get up. Your father and Sam might need help with the provisions," Ivy said as she gently patted Bethany's shoulder. The three packed up their luncheon remnants, then headed back to the house, drowsy but relaxed.

Ivy watched as Juno's head bobbed around the side of the house. George followed, reins in hand. Sammy bounced with excitement beside him.

"Ivy, Ivy!" the boy called out. "Wait till you see!"

A man in a brown hat came into view, seated among the baskets and barrels of food and supplies.

"Whoa," said George as he halted Juno. The stranger pulled out a burlap bag, climbed down, and turned toward Ivy.

"Sean!" Ivy screamed. She ran full speed to her brother. They hugged, laughed, and even cried a little.

Ivy shot George a questioning look.

"Well, Ivy, we need more help here. Seems to me your family raised good workers, so I figured I'd try another one. I've bought Sean's indenture. He'll be working here from now on."

Ivy flew to George and after a quick hug, she turned back to Sean, chattering in Gaelic. George watched the siblings, a bemused expression on his face.

Miss Sarah's gaze traveled from George to Ivy and back again, then she turned on her heel and retreated to the kitchen.

Chesapeake victuals and harvesting the Tipton tobacco had slathered Sean's torso and arms with muscle. He looked older to Ivy since his tumble down the ladder into the *Prometheus*'s hold. Sure, his blue and green eyes still sparkled, and his smile twinkled, but at rest, his face fell into a serious mien. Heavy calluses thickened his palms. New small scars, the kind one gets from a life of manual labor, marked his forearms and the backs of his hands.

Those first few days of reunion, Ivy stuck close to Sean. Her gaze followed him as if he were an All Souls' Eve apparition ready to fly off into the heavens.

One afternoon, Ivy trailed after her brother to the stable.

He grabbed a rake and turned to her.

"I love you Ivy, but you're getting underfoot. Don't worry. I'm not leavin' you."

"Sorry, Sean. I've been so worried about you and missing everyone and home and all. I don't mean to be a pest."

"Well, I'm fine and happy to be here. Now, go along and tend to your work. I have to muck out the stalls."

"Sean, can I ask you a question, first?"

He stopped raking manure. Sean knew Ivy was like a terrier pup once she had an idea in her head.

"What was it like at the Tiptons'? Did they treat you poorly? Are you all right? I've heard such terrible things about that planter."

"Well," Sean went back to raking, "Tipton is of a type. He likes his power and likes to exercise it. Having servants puffs him up. He'll lay lashes on a servant at any opportunity."

"Oh, Sean! Did he whip you? I know Captain Smythe laid stripes on you back on the *Prometheus*. Did Tipton?" Ivy held her breath.

"No. I've learned to keep my head down, do the work, not to sass. I keep my opinions to myself. His reputation is terrible, so no one except indentured men and women will labor for him. He was too busy dealing with the others when I was there to worry about me.

"One Bristol fellow did run away. Not far enough or fast enough, though. Got caught right smart, in no time at all." Sean grimaced and looked down at the straw at his feet.

Ivy stretched an arm to Juno, who stood nearby, chomping her feed in her stall. She patted Juno's soft nose. "What happened to the man from Bristol?"

"Quicker'n you can say 'Jack Robinson,' Tipton grabbed up a red-hot branding iron and burned a big letter *R* on the man's cheek. Marked him forever as a runaway.

"Had to wonder how old man Tipton had the brand all ready to go. Like he'd done it before. Gave me the chills. I'm thankful to be shut of him. Stokely seems a decent man."

"I'm glad to have you near, Sean. Makes all the difference. George Stokely will not mistreat you."

The next morning Ivy sought out George as he returned from his morning visit to his wife's grave. She stopped him as he started past the kitchen door.

"Excuse me, Mr. Stokely. May I have a word, sir, please?" Ivy stood on the stoop and fidgeted with her muslin apron.

"Of course. What do you need, Ivy? Provisions? Help of some sort?"

"No, no, none of that. I wanted to thank you for bringing my brother here. I apologize for not thanking you immediately."

"Totally understandable, girl. Is that it? Anything else?" The chiseled planes of George's visage hid nothing and gave him an approachability Ivy liked.

"Yes. I wanted to give you my decision, sir."

"What decision? What have you decided?" A faint smile may or may not have begun to play about on George's face and in his voice. His gray eyes followed an iridescent dragonfly as it swooped between him and Ivy.

Eyes down, Ivy failed to see the winged beauty.

Her fidgeting intensified, her long fingers wringing her apron as if it were a wet piece of laundry.

"Well, sir, you gave me a choice the other day. You know, when I . . . when it rained and all. Whether to stay here or not. I wanted to let you know—so there would be no future misunderstanding—that I have made my decision. I will stay. Here. At *Convict's Revenge*. With you and Sean and Bethany and Sam and Miss Sarah and, well, everybody. That is my decision."

George's dimples made a showing in the discussion. "Oh, have you now? Are you sure my offer is still in play? Eh, miss?"

Ivy dropped her hands to her side. Her mouth gaped open.

George threw his head back and roared with laughter.

"Ivy, of course you can stay. We are proud to have you, girl. Don't know what we'd do without you. Now go along before bacon burns or a cake falls or a chicken explodes in the kitchen." George wagged a finger at her, then left for his morning duties. He whistled a sprightly tune as his long legs strode toward the rest of his day.

Ivy beamed and returned to her kitchen chores. Glad that's settled, she told herself, though I'm not sure what was so funny. She sang and hummed as she tidied the hearth. She forgot, for a few hours, about Kevin and her escape plot.

Life settled. Buoyed by Sean's presence, Ivy dove into the season's final harvesting work with a fresh burst of energy. Sean put in a good day's work for Stokely. Easygoing George seemed to live in perpetual sunshine. Ivy attributed his good mood to having extra manpower. She never thought it had anything to do with her. Christopher, Tom, and Peter were standoffish, at first, when faced with the Irishman, but they quickly warmed up, grateful for Sean's energetic help.

A few days later, Ivy stood at a kitchen window, washing the haphazard collection of china used for special occasions. Miss Sarah had invited two elderly lady friends over for a visit.

"My girl, it would be lovely if you could bake a cake to go with the tea. My friends look forward to sweets and you are such a good baker. We'll also need to use the good linen."

Ivy enjoyed creating an attractive table. She also had to admit she had come to appreciate Miss Sarah, Englishwoman or not. Miss Sarah made her feel good about herself, even when she made a mistake. Ivy liked to please her. She planned to gather a few wildflowers to dress up the table as soon as the washing up was done.

Ivy rinsed a blue-and-white cup from China, then rotated it in her hand and examined the delicate brush strokes. A narrow trellis paraded around the rim and hemmed in the delicate flowers that bloomed on the belly of the cup. The cup had traveled farther from its birthplace than Ivy. She fantasized about the artisan who had formed it from the clay and the artist who had painted it. So many ways to live a life.

Softly, she sang about Phelim's boat. She enjoyed the sensation of the Gaelic words in her mouth and throat.

Báidín Fheilimí d'imigh go Gabhla,
Báidín Fheilimí is Feilimí ann.
Báidín Fheilimí d'imigh go Gabhla,
Báidín Fheilimí is Feilimí ann.

With Sean at *Convict's Revenge*, Ivy spoke Gaelic aloud for the first time in months. Her native language no longer came readily to her tongue. Even her dreams were in English.

The day before she had spoken Gaelic to Sean as the servants, George, and Sam toiled to do a final clear of the vegetable patch.

Tom scowled. "What did you tell him? You know, for all I

know, you might have said bad things about me. Did you?"

"Oh, no, Tom. I was asking him to hand me a hoe."

"Well, this is a British colony. Speak English or keep your trap shut."

"Tom! Apologize to Ivy. I'll not have uncivil speech here," said George, frowning. "And Ivy and Sean, please refrain from using Gaelic in front of the others. I don't want any misunderstandings."

Ivy put her hands on her hips, incensed with the two Englishmen. Sean shot her a warning look. He slowly shook his black curls from side to side.

"They have a point, Ivy. We can speak English. We apologize."

George nodded. Tom smirked. Peter lifted his shoulders in a "Who cares?" gesture.

After dinner Sean sought out Ivy under the guise of helping her clear up the kitchen.

"I know you'd like to speak Gaelic whenever you want, Ivy. Think about this, though. We don't want to have any problems with Mr. Stokely, Ivy. Trust me. We're much better off working for him during our indenture than the Tiptons or anyone else around here. Plus, it's a chance to improve our English."

Ivy scraped leftovers into a metal pan. The hogs would be happy.

"Well, and why would I want to improve my English? Soon's I can, I'm heading home to Ireland. I plan to never speak or hear another word of English. My husband won't speak or understand English, nor my children, nor even my dog. Why d'you want to speak better English?" Ivy countered, pouring hot water into a basin. "I think we should run away in the spring, when the ships return and the weather's fine."

At that, Sean gave her an indecipherable look. "I'm not so sure, Ivy. Things were fine in Ardmore, but times change. An Rinn was not as pleasant as Ardmore. I'm sure you'll agree on that. There might not be much to go home to. I've heard terrible things while helping load wagons at the landing. The British have made Ireland a true Hades for the Irish. At least here, if we complete our indenture, we'll be free and we'll get a bit of help starting off."

"What can you mean, brother?" Ivy stacked the scraped dishes beside the wash basin.

"I heard from Christopher that Stokely, persnickety as he is, is careful to keep his word. He did give the last man who made his time the land he was promised. Our indenture bonds require our masters to provide us with land, clothing, and a few animals once we've served our time. Truly. Just, most masters don't honor them. We're lucky to be here with him. Nearly half of the indentured don't survive. Stokely treats us well and if anyone is likely to live, it's his servants."

"Oh, surely, Sean, you're not thinking of staying here?" She pictured Isaac Abner's calloused hands, his wee cottage, and narrow bed. A cloud threatened the sun.

"Well, to be honest, yes. Ivy, I am considering my future. Look, we don't even know if Ma and Daddy are still alive. Sorry, sister. It's true. We have our whole lives ahead of us and I like this land. I like the waterways. It's sunnier here. Not as rainy and gray."

Ivy's hand stilled in the sudsy dishwater. "Maybe we can get word to Ma and Daddy. I don't know, Sean. This is a lovely place and I have grown strong feelings for—"

Just then Peter poked his head in the kitchen door. Ivy was glad she and Sean had been speaking Gaelic.

"Here's a rabbit for ye," interrupted Peter, offering the soft-furred corpse to Ivy. "Nothin' tastier than a poached, I mean, a roasted rabbit." Apparently, Peter had not forgotten the errant ways of his youth in England.

Sean, with a friendly nod to Peter, acknowledged him and the rabbit.

Ivy grabbed the carcass and headed outside to butcher Peter's offering.

Chapter 34

Convict's Revenge
Near the Patapsco River, Maryland

December 10, 1700

Snow lay clean and sparkling on *Convict's Revenge*. Though the sky was dark, moonlight set the snow aglow. Only the tracks of a fox outside the henhouse and barely perceptible prints from overwintering birds dented its smooth surface.

Ivy needed to go to the kitchen to start breakfast, yet hesitated to mar the snow. Her footprints would look clumsy overlaid on the elegant tracery of the fox and bird tracks. But the men would not appreciate any delay of their meal. Breakfast was a highlight of their day. With a soft sigh, Ivy put on the heavy boots left by the door.

She drew her green wool cloak around her and pulled its hood over her hair. The porridge had been left to soften overnight on the hook over the hearth's embers. She planned to slip in a handful of currants, a favorite of Sam's. She wanted to add sausage to make sure there was enough food to hold the men over till the noontime meal.

Ivy shook the snow off her boots at the kitchen door, left

them there, and slipped on clogs. The embers still glowed. She glanced up at the attic, grateful she slept in the main house and not under the eaves like many servants.

Her thoughts drifted to her brother's surprising decision, or near-decision, to remain in America. He was older and, she'd always thought, wiser than she.

Could he be right? Maybe the rest of her family could come here. What would happen if she stayed? Who would she marry?

The sausage links sizzled in the spider skillet, nestled among the revived coals on iron legs. The inviting aroma of seasoned sausage filled the kitchen. Ivy tended to them, rolling each link over when it reached just the right brown color. Ivy liked her food to be cooked right and to look good.

Behind her, the door hinge squeaked.

"Morning, Peter." Ivy could count on Peter being first to breakfast and to spend a few minutes chewing her ear off with his rambling chatter.

"It's me, Ivy. Not Peter," answered George in his mellow baritone.

Ivy turned. George stood so near, she could smell him. His aroma was a pleasant mix of horse and clean laundry. She looked up from squatting by the hearth.

"Ivy, I want to make sure you know how thankful we are for your help here. You've made a difference for us—my children, Sarah, . . . and me." George looked around the kitchen, then brought his eyes back to Ivy. "Life became very dark when . . . Well, anyway, please know your work is appreciated."

"Thank you, sir. You are very kind." Feeling her cheeks flush, she turned away for a minute, then stood up and walked to the nearby table. "Can I do anything for you now?"

"No, thanks. I'll take my breakfast with the others." George turned and left.

Ivy returned to the sputtering sausages. Now what? Her innards were aboil, as her mother might say. She was not sure what to think and, more importantly, what to feel.

Later that morning, Ivy searched through the wooden trunk at the foot of the children's bed. Finding clean stockings for Bethany was not a straightforward job. She heard Miss Sarah clear her throat and looked up. Miss Sarah's expression was solemn.

"Ivy, I'm going to need your help, please. There's a funeral tomorrow. We need to bring our share of food for everyone. Billy Lamb's wife died in childbed two days ago. She's to be buried tomorrow."

"Oh, Miss Sarah, I'm sorry. That's dreadful. Is the baby alive?"

"Yes. Mistress Jane, the midwife, delivered the boy just fine, but then poor Mrs. Lamb hemorrhaged. She couldn't be saved. The child will never know his mother. Such a lovely woman, rest her soul. Miss Jane took great care with the delivery—she rarely loses a woman—and stayed afterward to get the baby sorted out and prepare Mrs. Lamb for burial. She sat up all night with the body and through the next day, making sure she had passed on. Don't know what we women here would do without Miss Jane."

Ivy had no desire to spend too much time thinking about Miss Jane and her own embarrassing examination back on the *Prometheus*. She diverted the talk.

"So what would you like me to do, ma'am, for the funeral?"

"Well, no time to brine a ham. If you could kill a pair of chickens and fry them up, and maybe bake a pudding . . . I can show you how to make an Indian pudding. On second thought, let's ask Tom to kill and dress the birds while we make the pudding."

Ivy found Miss Sarah always ready to teach her and especially seemed to enjoy cooking together as a team.

"The children will need their good clothes tomorrow, and of course, you'll need to come along to help serve the food and watch the children. Your dark green dress will do. Few things join everyone together as well as a burial," prattled the old lady as she sailed down the hallway and stairs ahead of Ivy.

Mrs. Lamb's funeral was a great success, if that could ever be said about a funeral. The dead woman's body had been allowed to ripen a bit, so as to make sure she was truly dead. Ivy breathed out to clear her nostrils when the coffin lid was closed.

A half-dozen neighbors and relatives carried the pine coffin out to the family burial ground. Three of the six children Elizabeth Lamb had birthed were long dead and buried there. They awaited their parents.

Ivy stayed behind with a handful of other servants, carrying in platters of ham, fried chicken, boiled potatoes, jugs of liquor, cakes, and pies. At the kitchen's hearth, a neighbor busily fried oysters, supervised by a yellow cat on the windowsill. The children, excused from the gravesite, played tag down the hill from the Lambs' home. Patches of snow lingered in the shadows under bushes and on the north side of the outbuildings. A showy male cardinal flashed red from tree to bush and finally to ground where he sorted through the brush for food. After the room aired out, Ivy's attention was split between keeping the two Stokely children in sight and setting out the food.

"Wouldn't be a bit surprised to see the table buckle under the weight of this food," said a matronly, kind-faced woman as she set a second ham down. Wooden platters of meat, smoked fish, oysters, and crabs were interspersed with clay bowls of hominy, greens, and corn. Ivy nestled her aromatic Indian pudding among the cakes and pies at the table's end.

Looking up from slicing a loaf of bread, Ivy smiled to see George Stokely walking back from the graveside, then knitted her brows. On his far side, clasping his elbow, dangled a dainty dark-haired young lady, light of step and glowing. Ivy lowered her head and sawed roughly across the bread. "Ouch!" A bead of blood rose on her left thumb where she had nicked herself with the knife.

Ivy felt grumpy the rest of the day.

She wondered about the woman. Who was she? What was she to George? Were they going to marry? Then what? Would Ivy be under the dark-haired woman's thumb? Ivy rubbed the cut on her thumb. Another drop of blood came forth. The woman looked cheap and not the sort of woman George deserved. He needed a good, decent mate to make his life right again. Bile rose in her throat.

Ivy tried to keep her mood to herself. She smiled at the neighbors when she served up pie and later helped clear off the dishes. She caught Miss Sarah studying her on the ride home. Unnerved, Ivy reached up to check her cap. The white muslin cap was straight on her head. Ivy wondered what Miss Sarah saw.

Chapter 35

Convict's Revenge
Near the Patapsco River, Maryland

MARCH 1701

Winter begrudgingly gave up its grasp. March's false spring, a few balmy days which teased early buds to swell, collapsed under heavy snows. Spring dragged its feet.

Weeks later, riotous frog song broke through the silence of winter to herald spring's tardy arrival. Hundreds of male tree frogs sang nightly from the pond in the woodlot. Piping whistles seesawed back and forth between frogs no bigger than Ivy's thumb. The amphibians carried on as if they believed loud singing with a fast tempo was the secret to enticing a mate. Each night Ivy sank into a deep sleep, lulled by the Chesapeake's tunes, music new to her ears.

Chapter 36

Convict's Revenge
Near the Patapsco River, Maryland

April 15, 1701

Drawn outside by a warm sun, Ivy tromped along the footpath. Scattered tufts of green sprouted up from the leaf-strewn woodland floor. She firmly grasped Bethany's hand in an effort to keep the girl from falling and muddying her dress. Ivy and Miss Sarah alike hated the odious chore of laundry. Sammy ran ahead unimpeded. Keeping him clean was a fool's wish. The trio was headed to the pond to see what changes spring offered.

Sammy skidded to a stop and put his finger to his lips.

"Shh . . . Look, Ivy. Look, Bethany. Up there. In the tree," he whispered. Sammy pointed high up in the canopy where the flashiest bird Ivy had ever seen perched. It resembled a blackbird wearing an orange jacket, the orange color more vivid than a daylily or even the setting sun. With a brilliant explosion of citrus and ebony feathers, the bird flew to a nearby tree, then flitted off from branch to branch in the woodlot.

"You know, Ivy, father showed me a warbler once as yellow

as a lemon. Really. Just ask him. Did you have such beautiful birds in Ireland?"

"No, I don't believe we did, Sammy. That bird was lovely."

Sam looked pleased with her agreement and raced off toward the pond.

The next morning a whiff of sausage followed Ivy as she stepped out of the kitchen. Once again, the day offered a faultless clarity of light. The air hung in perfect temperature, cool with a faint, fresh breeze. Raucous honks, calls, and twittering drifted down from high overhead. Above her, the fast-moving cloud of migrating birds briefly blotted out the sun.

Ivy pondered the magic of flight. With feathers and wings, the birds traveled between distant lands. Maybe the shiny black eye peering now at the Patapsco once looked down to the Celtic Sea. Maybe one of the tiny creatures aloft just now flew over the *Phelim* days ago as her daddy and Rory fished. Maybe Daddy or Rory had seen it. If only she had wings. She'd fly home, home to An Rinn. But here she was, trapped in Maryland and, for all intents and purposes, the property of an Englishman. Earthbound.

Within weeks the first ship of the season would pull into the Patapsco harbor and Ivy would attempt again to go home. For now, she'd let the warblers singing in the nearby bushes tell her all about their wanderings. For now, she felt calm and serene. She had her plan. She'd abide her indenture and make the best of it. Then she'd . . .

Just as the last of the flock passed over, George appeared in the doorway to the house. His rich voice rumbled her way.

"Ivy, I'm going to the landing today and need you to come along, please, to help."

"Of course, sir. What do you need?"

"There're a few things to gather up to take with us for trading. Tom has an extra brace of rabbits we can have, so get them.

There're also chickens to spare and Miss Sarah mentioned you had finished weaving a length of wool. Sam will help. The boy never wants to miss a trip to the landing. He'll mind the birds."

"Yes, sir."

"We'll leave in half an hour. No crops ripe enough to take yet, but it is Saturday. Best day for the landing . . ." Whistling a jaunty tune Ivy had first heard on the *Prometheus*, George headed off toward the stable.

Ivy knew the landing served as much more than a boat launch. At the wooden dock on the Patapsco, the planters talked business, shared news, discussed politics, made deals, commiserated over losses, and crowed about wins. They did not gossip, of course. Never gossiped. Only women gossiped. At least, that's what men thought. With a giggle, Ivy walked off to find Tom and Sammy.

An hour later sunlight reflected off Juno's butterscotch rump as she trotted along. Sammy, overseeing the crate of clucking hens in the back of the wagon, kept up a stream of commentary. He chattered away at his father and Ivy and, at times, the chickens as well. Ivy and George shared amused smiles.

The wagon rolled to a stop at the banks of the Patapsco. Sammy hopped down and began unloading the squawking spare roosters and pullets. George strolled over to the shade tree where a clot of planters jawed and smoked. Two enslaved Africans carried crates of goods from a docked boat, their musical voices ringing out. With them toiled a lone scrawny man, labeled by his *crios* sash as Irish. Ivy's mind shot home to Ireland. She remembered her mother's patient teaching.

Now, Ivy, girl, always give the crios a white border. Any color your heart desires goes in the middle but make the outside white. Just hook the loop of wool on your toe and grow it with your fingers till it's the right length. Just so.

The first thing she ever wove was a *crios* belt, and now, for the first time, a memory from home felt good and not hurtful.

Blue crabs, freshly harvested from the Chesapeake, heaved and waved their pincers from baskets at the planters' feet. Purple-tipped orange claws of the female crabs gestured right alongside the males' red tips and punctuated the crustaceans' complaints about their fate.

His bartering and other business complete, George lingered for a final few words with his peers. While Sammy pestered the workmen on the quay, Ivy sat on the riverbank and enjoyed the spring day. Movement above the river caught her eye. An enormous hawk-like bird, wings tucked in, swooped down to snag a fish from the Patapsco's placid surface. The fish writhed. It glittered and sparkled against the bird's white underside as the bird hoisted it upward. From an unseen aerie, an even larger white-headed eagle swooped in. The tussle between the predators lasted only seconds, the outcome foreordained. With a squawk of frustration, the brown bird protested as the eagle flew off with its supper.

"Poor osprey," said George, coming up to stand beside Ivy. "An impressive bird but no match for the eagle. Big and powerful wins the day, doesn't it?"

"Does it always?" said Ivy. "I'm not convinced. I think quiet and slow can win, too."

George gave her an inquisitive look. "I suspect you may be right, Ivy. For a young girl, you think old sometimes. Well, time to head back."

Sammy stood at the shoreline and skipped stones on the water's spangled surface. He begged to stay.

"I guess we can stay a little longer, son."

Ivy watched as the big man sat in the dirt and picked through the grubby pebbles. He took care to find exactly those stones most likely to skip. George explained his technique to his boy.

"Look at me, Ivy," said Sammy. "Count how many times this one smacks the water. Watch. Six times, I bet."

George and Sammy flung flat rocks till the boy was mollified, then the two loaded up the day's bounty of bartered goods.

On the way back cool air brushed Ivy's face, while the sun penetrated her muslin cap to warm the top of her head. Sam dozed on an old blanket. Juno's reins lay loose in George's hands. Juno was an easy horse. George appeared lost in reverie. Taking advantage of her idleness, Ivy sifted through her own thoughts.

Maybe Sean was right, and they were better off here than in Ireland. There were certainly more men than women in Maryland. Once she met her obligation to Stokely, she could find a man to marry. Old Isaac Abner had shared his intentions quick enough. There were good, kind men here. She glanced at George. George seemed decent. She thought he needed to remarry. Not the silly woman at the funeral.

Juno's hooves thudded softly on the dusty road. A blackbird rose up from the roadside. "Lovely day, isn't it?" said George. "A beautiful spring."

"Yes, it is." They settled back into their shared quietness as Sammy dozed.

Ivy went back to puzzling out everyone's future.

Yes, George needed to remarry. Maybe he would marry the dark-haired girl. Ivy did not like that idea. Something about the girl struck Ivy as unwholesome and less than trustworthy. George needed a woman who would be a good mother to his children and who would love him and help him. Like a younger version of Miss Sarah. Or, like Ivy.

Of course, he would never pick Ivy. Ivy was Irish and he was English, maybe born Protestant. He was also thoughtless enough to indenture a kidnapped girl. Anyway, she was a servant and much too low in life for the likes of a wealthy planter like George.

She wanted to marry Kevin, after all.

George flicked the reins on Juno's hindquarters and glanced over at Ivy. "You're thinking so much today. Planning sedition, or a new pie?" He chuckled.

"Don't know what sedition is, sir, so I guess it's the new pie." She went back to her thoughts.

What if she failed to escape? Was Isaac Abner her only choice? He was generous and sincere. Could she be happy with a husband like Isaac? Maybe one of the indentured Irishmen would marry her once they were free. Yes, she decided. If she didn't get home and marry Kevin, she'd seek a husband among the Irish in Maryland.

She gave a sigh and turned to look at Sammy.

"I need to sew him new pants. Those are too short."

George gave a quick look to his son's ankles as the child sprawled in the back. "I think you're right. Ask Miss Sarah for the cloth, Ivy. She always is prepared."

The unmistakable smell of swine announced the Tipton property's nearness. In a short while, they'd be at *Convict's Revenge*. The closer they drew, the more Ivy's thoughts turned to the chores waiting for her. All the cooking and housework piled on top of caring for tobacco loomed. A stray thought winged and wormed its way to the foreground and begged to be addressed.

She wondered why George had taken her to the landing. He and little Sammy were perfectly capable of picking out a bushel of crabs. She had chores to do for Miss Sarah—clean out the cupboard, do the mending. Without Ivy thinking about it, her eyes slid to George. Hunched over his knees, the traces in his big hands, he was the picture of relaxation and even happiness. As if he felt her gaze like a touch, George looked at her and smiled warmly.

Flustered, Ivy lowered her eyes to fiddle with her skirt.

"Home soon, Ivy. Thanks for coming."

"Happy to help, sir."

Juno picked up the pace as she always did when the wagon turned down the lane to *Convict's Revenge*. A horse of endless hunger, she aimed straight away for the bucket of oats awaiting her.

At the back of the house, George hauled Juno to a halt. Ivy jumped down to help unload the wagon. As she reached for a basket of squash, Tom squeezed in and shouldered her away.

"Oh, no, you go back to the kitchen, Miss Ivy. I'll get this for you. Happy to help any way I can."

Ivy did not like the smarmy look about him. She stepped back. Christopher loomed up.

"I'll help, too," said Christopher.

Tom's eyes narrowed. He slunk away to glare from a distance as Christopher took over the unloading.

Ivy squared away the bounty from the landing. An avid organizer, the sight of neat rows and sorted colors pleased her to no end. Since Ivy's arrival, the brick kitchen had been transformed into a cozy, welcoming space. Everyone living at *Convict's Revenge* found excuses to come to the kitchen. With the loom came the softening and colorful influence of textile pieces, balls of yarn, and spools of thread.

The young woman, confident of her responsibility for this area, kept green plants flourishing on the wide stone windowsills. She had nursed a start of wild onion and other herbs through the winter. A clay jug on the sill overlooking the table held crabapple branches. Swollen and ready to pop, the buds burgeoned with spring energy. In the winter, she had filled it with holly. Within weeks, wildflowers would festoon the jug . . . if she were still here . . . if she didn't run away.

Ivy shook out a linen apron and tied it on, settling in for an afternoon of baking. Beady crab eyes on wiggly stalks watched her somberly from their basket on the packed dirt floor. Christopher stopped by for a cup of tea. He piled a collection of small wooden mallets on the table.

"Do you think they realize what's coming their way, Ivy? Think they know these mallets will be pounding open their boiled dead bodies?"

"That's a grim thought. Don't want to think about it, Christopher." Ivy went back to kneading bread. Bethany's gray kitten somersaulted by the hearth. After pausing to see if Ivy was impressed, she scooted off to search for mice.

"Well, looking forward to dinner, Ivy." Christopher left.

At one point, Tom and Christopher's raised voices broke through her serenity. The pair's relationship had deteriorated after Tom's assault on Ivy. They sniped at each other with increasing frequency. Ivy chose to ignore their spats. She went on with her baking.

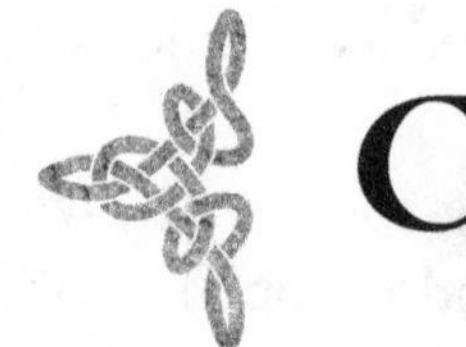

Chapter 37

Convict's Revenge
Near the Patapsco River, Maryland

April 17, 1701

Sunday's delicate dawn found Ivy awake, dressed, and puttering in the kitchen. Tom, Sean, and Christopher could sleep in. There was no fieldwork on Sundays, yet people still expected to eat every day of the week. Ivy scrubbed out tiny lingerings from the demise of the crabs. Bacon sizzled in an iron skillet. The door opened and Miss Sarah, resplendent in a freshly laundered cap and kerchief, strolled in. Despite her age, she moved with a pleasing liveliness.

"Good morning, Ivy. You certainly keep everything in order here. Very nice."

"Thanks, Miss Sarah. Christopher helped me last night."

"Oh, really? How kind. Well, I just wanted to let you know we're having company for dinner. The Carrs. If you could put together a dessert and enough food for an additional four people, I'd be ever so grateful."

Ivy glanced up and met Sarah's blue gaze.

"Of course, ma'am."

Once breakfast was over, Ivy took down a yellow earthenware bowl from its shelf. She sifted handfuls of flour into it, then added a bit of salt. Next, with two dull table knives she cut in knobs of butter and lard. Her mind roamed back to making pies with Honora and their mother. Ma always said the lard should be one-third the amount as the butter, but it had to be there.

It's what makes the flakes, Ivy. Without the lard, the pastry clumps together. And cold water, not warm, adds flakiness, too.

She knew her mother was right.

Ivy enjoyed the smell of lard. For some reason it reminded her of the scent of a new puppy. She dribbled in cold spring water and brought the dough together into two pliable balls. Putting together pie dough as Ma did relaxed Ivy. She felt close to her mother and was reminded of her love.

Ivy placed the first ball of dough on the linen and began to flatten it out with a wooden rolling pin. Sammy popped up at her elbow. He smelled of child sweat, of running and rolling in the grass.

"Who's the pie for, Ivy? We don't have pie 'cept for company."

"The Carrs."

"Oh, the Carrs. I don't like Polly. She acts so sweet with Pa, but she's mean. She pinches me. I hate her."

"Samuel! You don't want to talk about others like that," admonished Ivy. She wondered. Had Polly Carr been the dark-haired girl at the funeral?

"Now run along and behave. I'm sure Miss Polly didn't mean to hurt you. Probably she was only playing.

"I'll bake you and Bethany some rollie-pollies from the pastry scraps." Miss Sarah had taught her to make the rolled-up cylinders of dough, cinnamon, sugar, and butter. Ivy had grown up making jam tarts from the leftover pie dough. She had to confess—rollie-pollies were tasty, too.

As the pie and rollie-pollies cooled on the windowsill, Ivy cleaned up the kitchen. She hummed a ditty. Too early for berries or fresh fruit, she'd made do with dried apples and raisins. A grind of nutmeg, cinnamon, allspice, white sugar, and hard apple cider worked their magic to fill the kitchen with an intoxicating aroma.

The crunch of hooves on the yard's crushed oyster shells broke into Ivy's reverie. She looked up from her pile of potatoes. Through the window, she saw George helping the dark-haired lady from the funeral down from a wagon. She apparently was, indeed, Polly Carr. With her trailed an older couple and a pudgy adolescent boy.

Were the pair courting? Ivy burned with curiosity. Of course she was not jealous. Jealousy and envy were sins. Ivy was only concerned about any person who might impinge on her own future.

Two hours later, Ivy carried a platter of stuffed ham to the dining table and set it down in front of George. Tufts of chopped greens and onion peeked out from incisions in the pink ham. She'd never seen a stuffed ham till she came to Maryland. Miss Sarah claimed it to be a local specialty and had insisted Ivy learn to prepare the dish. Ivy looked to George for approval of her masterpiece, standing stock-still at the tableside.

George's eyes roved over the startling presentation. His lips parted. Ivy leaned forward in anticipation of a congratulatory speech which never came, stopped by Polly's interruption. The second he opened his mouth, Polly—seated to his right—grabbed his hand with a giggle. "Oh, George! Have you heard about Nicholas Durbin? He's engaged."

George turned to Polly. Her dark eyes flashed in triumph at Ivy. She had wooed his attention away.

Ivy shuffled off, shoulders hunched, cheeks ablaze. The door to the farmyard slammed.

Crossing over to the kitchen, Ivy muttered black thoughts aloud. She was tired of being a servant. Tired. Tired. Tired. Fed up completely.

After hours of peeling, paring, stirring, and rattling pots and pans, Ivy had scuttled back and forth for another hour between the kitchen and the formal dining room. Always striving for perfection, preparing a meal for guests stretched Ivy's culinary capacity. What a thankless way to live.

Her loyal brother did his best to lighten her load. Sean hovered over the pots and pans in the kitchen to keep everything at the proper temperature. He helped dish up the victuals. Mostly, he gave emotional support and, currently, a sounding board to his highly annoyed little sister.

"Oh, Sean! Aren't you weary of being at a master's beck and call? I surely am."

"Feeling tired?"

"Yes, indeed. We toil and work and do our best and then . . . Don't know what I'd do without you, Sean. I am so thankful you're here. Plus, you're very talented in the kitchen arts."

Sean hugged her, and Ivy's thunder faded away.

"You don't have to flatter me, Miss Ivy O'Neill. Happy to help my sis. Looking forward to eating after we get the Stokelys and Carrs fed." He handed her a tray of pickled vegetables and bread to take to the diners.

Mid-meal, George looked up from his plate. "Ivy, you've done a wonderful job with dinner." He flashed white teeth her way. "I don't know what we'd do without you."

Miss Carr slid her brown eyes from George to Ivy and back again. The corners of her mouth edged downward. Sammy giggled.

Bethany clapped her hands. "Yes, Ivy, yes. We love you," she said, finally able to enunciate her *Ls*.

Buoyed, Ivy floated back to the kitchen. She shared the Stokelys' praise with Sean. She convinced herself that George had not appeared interested in Miss Carr.

"Our parents would be so proud of you, Ivy. You've really grown up. You're going to make a fine wife and mother one day." Sean scraped leftovers from the dinner plates into the slop pan. Later, the hogs would feast. "Want help with the pie?"

"Don't worry, brother. I'll be sure to cut it so we get some, too." Ivy squinted her green eye and sliced the sugar pie with dramatic precision.

Sean laughed.

Ivy reveled in her newly honed ability to put together a tasty dinner. She enjoyed cooking—its orderliness, aromas, choices, and ability to bring people together.

Taking care of the Stokely children rang sweet too. Her own mother believed the world needed decent people, and a solid childhood was key.

A few days earlier, the topic had come up while darning stockings with Miss Sarah.

"Ma'am, is there anything else I should be doing with the children? Mr. Stokely doesn't say much, but I know I'm young and have no children of my own. Sure, I helped with my little sister . . . Well, what do you think?"

"I have not borne children myself, yet I have seen a great deal of life and have my opinions." She chuckled. "You know I do, Ivy. I think we each do our best and trust God for the rest. George spends more time with Sam and Bethany than most fathers, which I am sure is a help. He's told me they are happier since you've come. Just do your best, Ivy."

Chapter 38

Convict's Revenge
Near the Patapsco River, Maryland

April 18, 1701

With the warm weather, tobacco again took over *Convict's Revenge*, rolling over everyone's life with a flood of irrepressible work. The day after the Carr dinner, as clouds pregnant with rain glowered, Ivy tended feverishly to the young plants.

Nearby, Sammy, Sean, and Peter worked, each at their own pace. George often didn't come to the fields till late morning, but Christopher and Tom were also missing. She would think they were off doing a task together—except Tom and Christopher had missed breakfast. Unprecedented. Neither fellow ever forfeited the opportunity to eat. Something was afoot.

"Sean, have you seen Tom or Christopher?" Ivy pawed at a bead of sweat dripping down her cheek.

"Nope. Must have been drinking last night. Probably passed out under a tree or somewheres else. Tom can be a slackard, for sure. Christopher's rarely late, though. I'll go check once I get this to the barn."

“Well, too bad they’re not here to help. There’s so much to do. Tom’s not very pleasant, though he does get the job done. It’s hard with only the three of us and Sammy. Dratted sotweed. I’ll get you in order yet.” Ivy straightened up a wayward plant and pressed the soil firmly around the seedling’s base. Black dirt outlined the tips of her fingernails and smudged her cheek.

Ivy hummed a song from home. An apparition of Kevin rose in her thoughts and guilt bloomed. She’d rarely thought of him in recent weeks. Instead, life in Maryland absorbed her attention and stood like a veil between her and everything in Ireland. Even Kevin. To think of Kevin today felt like looking through the wrong end of a telescope. Kevin grew tinier and tinier through the lens of Ivy’s new perspective.

Men’s voices took her attention from the hillock. George and three others appeared over the rise. They muttered among themselves and strode with purpose in their step. To her surprise, the group came directly to Ivy. A glance at George’s distraught face chilled Ivy’s heart. What was wrong?

Her eyes darted about, seeking her brother. Sean was off in the distance, walking away from her, going to a tobacco barn, unaware of the men approaching Ivy.

Ivy recognized the shortest of the men as John Williams, the Sheriff of Baltimore County. She had seen the other two lounging around the tavern when George took her and Peter to the harbor.

The sheriff stopped in front of Ivy.

She sat on her haunches, hands flat on the soil, a spindly sotweed seedling sprouting up between them. Ivy’s eyes traveled up over the man’s coarse leather boots, up his britches, over his pot belly, and to his florid face.

The lawman drew in a startled breath upon seeing her eyes. He recovered his composure with a clearing of his throat, puffing up his chest like a rooster preparing to crow.

Ivy cringed below him. Evil once again was winging her way.

"Mistress Ivy O'Neill, I am here to arrest you for the murder of Christopher Jamieson." The sheriff's eyes, in turn, traveled all the way down his aquiline nose to Ivy, who sat in the dirt. Her mouth opened a bit and a soft, animal-like grunt escaped through her lips.

George stood stock-still, his face slack and unreadable.

"Come with me," said the sheriff. "I've no doubt you'll be hanging from the gallows soon enough. Mr. Cruikshank! Mr. Browne! Grab her up!"

Once again, the familiar happened. Ivy's soul rose out of her body to hover over the tobacco hillocks and peer down at the men who parsed her fate. For a few seconds, or maybe an eternity, she floated above the field. Like tiny dolls no bigger than her fingernail, four men formed a circle around an equally small girl with a straw hat and blue calico dress. Ivy. The miniature George Stokely, sheriff, and two henchmen stood as if planted in the Maryland dirt. She saw her brother Sean running toward them from the tobacco barn. His wailing and keening cries shook Ivy loose from her trance. With a swoosh, she returned to inhabit her body.

Ivy rose up on her feet to do battle with this wickedness. Her hands clenched, hidden within the folds of her skirt. "I don't know what you're talking about. I didn't kill anyone," she said with the steadiness and clarity of a woman twice her age.

Yet her words held neither power nor effect. Sheriff John Williams ignored her. He pivoted and headed toward the woodlot.

George put a warning arm up against Sean's chest to keep him at bay. "Not now, Sean. Not now," he whispered. "Later. I promise. Stay back."

Ivy shrieked as the sheriff's henchmen plucked her by her arms and, without ado, dragged her stumbling away. Her feet tangled in her skirt and her shoe dropped in the mud.

George picked it up and ran after her.

"Stop right there! At least let her have her shoes," he shouted.

The two paused, each with a furtive look toward the distant sheriff, then stepped aside. George startled Ivy by kneeling at her feet. She gasped in a little bit of air as George cradled her foot and slipped on the dirt-crusted clog.

"Hold steady, my girl. Hold steady." He rose, shouldered the deputies aside, hugged her firmly, then stepped back.

The deputies hustled her off. They pushed, pulled, and propelled Ivy in the sheriff's wake, into the shadowy woods and along a narrow footpath.

"Where are you taking me? What are you doing? Let me go." Ivy struggled mightily against their grip. At nearly six feet in height, she taxed their strength as well as their patience.

The fox-faced younger fellow dug his dirty nails into her wrist; the older man, with ox-like shoulders and little mobility to his face, merely squeezed.

"Stop it, girl. I don't want to hit you, but I'll give you a wallop if you don't stop," said the older of the pair. "We're going to the body. Prepare yourself to see your evil deed once again."

Ivy did not doubt the ox-man meant what he said.

Ivy stopped struggling, overcome with dread at what she was about to see. Behind her she heard George and Peter tromping through the brush. She turned.

"Help me, sir, please. I don't know what's happening." Her voice quavered and wobbled.

George came closer. With his voice pitched as if to calm a child or an injured animal, he said, "Just do as they ask, Ivy. Don't fight them now."

Up ahead, Ivy saw the blue of the sheriff's jacket. Coming close, her breath sucked in loudly. Christopher's mangled body lay face up at Sheriff Williamson's feet. Blood covered most of his face, turned his hair mahogany red and pooled under his head. A cloud of jewel-like blowflies noisily claimed their due. A blackened deep gash cleaved his forehead like a cracked melon, exposing patches of glistening white brain. Two feet away, its business end bloodied and clotted with gore, lay a hoe.

Ivy slid to the ground, weeping. "No, no. Oh, poor Christopher."

The sheriff's inquisitive eyes hungrily ate up Ivy's reaction.

"Ahem. We've brought you here, Ivy O'Neill, to do a test, to help determine your guilt or innocence. Even if you pass the bier test, you still could be guilty and will face a jury. Gentlemen . . ." The sheriff nodded to his deputies to proceed.

"All right, Miss O'Neill," said the older one of the pair. He grabbed her right hand and pulled her toward the body.

Ivy, too distracted to protest, followed him.

The sheriff knelt over Christopher and picked up his right hand. He carefully examined it, turning it over and back, and brushed a bit of dried leaf off it.

"Come up close, George, and bring your man. Want everyone to see this and witness it. You'll all agree this poor dead soul's hand is clean and free of blood, don't you?"

George, lips pressed tightly together, did not respond.

"Yes, sir," blurted Peter. His eyes roved wildly between Ivy and the sheriff and the dead hand. His face glistened with sweat and had paled under his suntan.

"Ivy O'Neill, you are commanded to touch the right hand of this murder victim, Christopher Jamieson. Now, do it." His voice rising at the end, the sheriff stared at Ivy. The deputy readjusted his grip until Ivy's forefinger extended from his meaty paw.

Ivy sobbed loudly as the deputy forced her to prod Christopher's hand with her finger three times, then dragged Ivy back a few feet.

The sheriff watched Christopher's hand as if waiting for a pot to boil. A yellow-throated warbler's shrill tweets broke the intensity of the moment.

"No blood to be seen. Everyone in agreement? You may be called to testify," said the sheriff.

"No blood," said George.

"None at all," said Peter.

"Don't see any blood," said Cruikshank.

"No blood," said Browne.

The witnesses were all in accord.

"What's that all about?" asked Ivy, her voice low, as she turned to George.

The sheriff rose from the body, pomposity personified.

"If there had been blood, here in Maryland, we take that as proof of a murderer's guilt. Call it the Ordeal of Touch. If a murderer touches the body, the body'll bleed. Clearly not foolproof. A lack of blood doesn't let you off the hook, miss. Enough talk. Let's get back to Baltimore Harbor. Come on, Cruikshank, Browne. Let's go."

George and Peter stayed behind to tend to Christopher's body.

The Stokely house stared with blank eyes, its doors and windows empty, as Ivy and her guardians passed by on their way to the deputies' wagon. Ivy heard Miss Sarah's distant voice coming from an upstairs window. Cruikshank and Browne shoved her into the wagon. Ivy turned to look back at the house as they drove off. She saw Sammy's face in Miss Sarah's bedroom window. He waved his hand furiously. Her hand moved in a halting reply.

Cruikshank lashed the mule with the reins in an attempt

to catch up to the sheriff. He quickly gave up. The mule had no interest in a competition. Sheriff Williams's bay gelding, a horse so massive it dwarfed him to childlike dimensions, moved with dispatch.

Chapter 39

Baltimore Harbor, Maryland
County of Baltimore Jail

April 18, 1701

At the harbor, the mules stopped in front of a squat one-story brick jailhouse. A narrow door and two barred windows fronted the street. The deputies each took one of Ivy's arms and walked her inside.

The main room held a fireplace and a smattering of plain furniture—a secretary with a few books, three chairs, a trunk, and a writing table. Ink, quill pens, and vellum lay at the ready. The men pushed Ivy to a doorway on the back wall. She gasped as she went through it, struck by the stench of alcohol-laced vomit. A single iron-barred cell faced her, nearly identical in size to that of the *Prometheus*. Two filthy men sprawled on the cell's floor and snored in a stuporous duet. To her left, an open door led through a dark shed to an exterior door.

That day, Ivy huddled in the corner of the jail cell, as far from the drunks as possible. Iron bars formed its front wall. High in the back wall squatted a window. Though too small an opening for the skinniest of prisoners to squeeze through, aromas and vermin traveled freely between its rusting bars.

Scrawlings by prior prisoners defaced the walls. Red brick peeped through the chipped plaster, joined here and there by the mahogany of bloodstains. Two iron rings at shoulder height told a harrowing tale of what might happen to anyone daring to be troublesome. The cell hummed a song of violence Ivy tried not to hear.

As the day passed, the temperature grew wintery. Faint daylight, no longer with the power to reveal color, limned the two drunks sharing the cell. The stink of sour alcohol floated out of their mouths with each belch and nauseated Ivy.

Her crust of bread eaten, she silently wept, confused by her predicament. Who killed Christopher? Why would anyone kill him?

The drunks lurched out, free, in the morning. The sheriff and the jailer—especially the jailer—did not appear to want them around. The jailer leered at Ivy. She thought he invented reasons to piddle around the cell. He swept up invisible dirt off the floor and carried in firewood for the unlit hearth.

Tall and gangly, he was exceptionally homely. He acted as if he not only knew, but also hated his ugliness. He did little to make up for his unattractiveness. Unbathed, clothes unmended, fingernails long and dirty, he would have been pitiful if he had shown one iota of compassion. Ivy doubted his ability to attract or keep a mate even if he had been in England or Ireland instead of woman-poor Maryland. His skinny neck sported a huge Adam's apple. Whenever the man talked, it bobbed and wobbled in synchrony with the register of his voice which broke, rose, and crescendoed.

Mesmerized, Ivy tried not to stare. He made her skin crawl. There was no need for the man to say how much he relished the teaspoon of power he held in the world.

"Yes, my deary, you're all mine now." He slammed the cell door shut. "Name's Smallwood. Let me know if you need anything and I'll let you know if you can have it and when. I'm a fair man. You'll see. You be good to me, and I'll be good to you." He obscenely ran the tip of his tongue along his upper lip.

Ivy shot the man a cold look. "You can go to hell, you can—and I've no doubt you will."

Smallwood, unfazed, rattled the key against the bars. "We'll just see who goes where. You just wait."

Ivy kept her face blank. She had been harassed by worse and would not let him bother her.

George arose in her thoughts. She spun his hug and touch around and around in her thoughts and examined it from every side. Upset as she had been, his behavior had thrilled her. As much as the electricity of his touch had pierced through her terror, it was his trust she savored. George had taken her side and believed her, even in the face of horrid accusations. He was her ally.

Yes, he was English, though he was different. He had been in Maryland since childhood. George was always kind to her. He was the sort she should marry, if she were English or a Marylander.

A new thought popped into her head: she had not been fair to George, nor even to Miss Sarah. She had held back. She had not thanked them for their kindnesses. But they owned her freedom. Her thoughts confused her.

Exhausted, she turned her face to the wall and collapsed into sleep. Not even the scrabbling and scurrying of the sleek rats foraging throughout the building disrupted her sleep.

In her dreams, as she had on the *Prometheus*, she returned to Ireland and her family. She was so happy, clasping each parent and brother and Honora to her chest, one by one, then strolling with them about the cathedral ruins high over Ardmore. The cool moisture-laden sea breeze refreshed her, lifting her skirt from her ankles and the hair from her nape. Once more she beheld the ancient tableau of Solomon determining the fate of the baby held out to him. Her mother was as beautiful as she had been when she first took her daughters to the ruins, her face restored to how it looked before the fire. Even her father and brothers and Father Declan joined her in the dream. Then the cathedral changed. The derelict walls transformed back to their original state, whole, solid. Worshippers filled the church. Fresh flowers, white and pure, graced the altar. From the pulpit, Father Declan gave the Word.

Ivy turned in the pew. Behind her Miss Sarah, Sammy, Bethany, and George listened attentively to Father Declan. Ivy marveled and felt peace wash over her.

When she awoke, the feeling of wholeness, well-being, and strength persisted. Unsure of exactly what the dream was saying, Ivy simply thanked God for giving it to her.

Ivy paced as she pondered her fate. Two full strides and she'd covered the cell's depth; three, she'd walked its width. Only a bucket cluttered the stone floor. Ivy made sure to use it in the early hours, before the jailer or sheriff returned.

Sheriff Williams, confident of his jail's strength, abandoned it each night. Ivy believed he spent evenings at home. Maybe he enjoyed quaffing ale in the afterglow of his wife's tasty dinners. He certainly must have allowed Smallwood to crawl back under whatever rock he called home. Prisoners were left in solitude, their only companions the rats and other creatures of the darkness.

About an hour after sunup, Ivy heard the front door creak and smelled oats. Sheriff Williams, freshly shaved with clean hands and face, approached the cell. He carried a tin bowl with a spoon in it. The sheriff put the bowl on the floor and took a crudely forged iron key from his pocket. He cleared his throat, then, in his butter-smooth voice, began his speech.

"Miss, you're my responsibility. I'm not going to let you starve, even if you are a murdering girl. I'll brook no nonsense from you. You need to stand in that corner with your back against the wall and don't make a move until I say you can. Understand?"

Ivy backed up and did as told.

"I'm going to unlock the door, put the gruel in. When you've et, just slide the empty bowl and cutlery out between the bars. Any mischief and I'll knock you down, girl or not."

As the hinges screeched, the sheriff placed the spoon and watery porridge on the floor, then retreated outside and pushed the bars back into place. After locking the door, he lingered. He held a cell bar with one hand and gestured with the other.

"It's my official obligation, Ivy O'Neill, to formally advise you of the charges being brought against you. Christopher Jamieson's body—his dead body, that is—was discovered yesterday morning in George Stokely's woodlot. I have a witness who saw you follow Christopher Jamieson into the woods on Sunday night. They have seen you and Mr. Jamieson cavorting and heard Mr. Jamieson claim to have been a special companion to you. It is believed you and he argued, and you killed him with a hoe."

"No, no, no, sir. I did no such thing! You must believe me. Let me out, sir. This is a mistake!"

"Well, it doesn't matter what I believe. My job is to keep you in jail until your trial, if there is a trial. You picked a busy time for your mischief. Jury won't meet for at least a week to decide whether or not to indict you, so get used to my jail. But I have to say, things look right evil for you. If I were you, I'd be saying all my prayers every day. You need to beg the Lord for forgiveness. You'll hang whether you pray or not. I'm sure of it.

"We don't need any murdering Irish girls here in our county. None at all. If I find out your weaselly brother was in on it, he'll swing, too. You've met your hangman already. Smallwood, the jailer. Loves nothing more than clearing the harbor of riffraff."

Ivy pressed her lips together. No one in her family had gone to jail or prison or court. Her eyes darted to the iron bars which penned her in and the stained walls which crushed her freedom. Certainly, she had overheard whispers as a child of criminals flung into dark and dingy cells to rot away. What happened after that was vague except for one story.

Kevin had entertained her on one of their walks with the tale of a man who killed his neighbor.

"You should have been there, Ivy. My brother Mike was in the tavern when old Smitty did it to Jones. Jones was sipping his ale, botherin' no one. Smitty, drunk as a lord, started in."

Kevin went on to weave his story, full of details and embellishments. He spent a full five minutes quoting the murderer's final conversation with his victim.

"And the jail, dear. A real hell-hole, if I can say that. Smelled like . . ."

Kevin detailed the odor with relish but glossed over the court and its actions. Instead, he went straight to the hanging. He told who went to the hanging, who pulled the trap, and the murderer's final words.

Ivy, desolate in her cell, wished Kevin had talked about the court. She wanted to prepare herself, arm herself, and do what she might to survive.

Pronouncement over, the sheriff watched without much

interest as Ivy dutifully finished her runny oatmeal. She slid the dish and spoon through the bars. With a grunt, the corpulent man leaned over and retrieved them. He straightened up and looked as if he were going to say something else. Ivy read his face. She recognized the moment the man changed his mind. Lips tightened, he turned and left. In his wake, a whiff of homemade soap settled among the rankness of Ivy's cell.

Chapter 40

Baltimore Harbor, Maryland
County of Baltimore Jail

April 20, 1701

"Whoa, Juno. Hold on, girl" floated into the jail through the cell window.

George! It's George. Thank God. Maybe he'll get me out of here, Ivy thought.

"Wait a moment, Stokely." Ivy heard the jailer squeak in the anteroom. "What've you got there? I have to check for contraband, even with a fine planter like yourself."

"Yeah, Smallwood. Sure you do. Feel free. Of course, this here is for you."

"Well, George Stokely, you do know the ways of the world. Appreciate this fine tobacco. Indeed I do. I know your sotweed is of the best. Everything looks to be in apple-pie order. I'll take you to your wench."

George and Smallwood came round the corner. A willow basket filled George's arms. The jailer gestured for Ivy to back up against the wall. She did so. He opened the cell, then locked George in with Ivy. Smallwood next proceeded to loiter on the other side of the iron bars, like a spectator at a bearbaiting.

"Thank you very much, Smallwood. You're so kind. I'll give a holler when I'm done speaking to my servant. Don't want to keep you from your work."

Smallwood took the hint and oozed back out of sight.

George put a finger to his lips to shush Ivy and gestured toward the front of the jailhouse.

"G'morning, Ivy. I've brought you food and a few things Miss Sarah thought you'd need," said George in a rather loud voice. He riffled through the basket and, under the cover of the noise, whispered to Ivy.

"You must be very cautious here. Don't trust Smallwood or the sheriff. Don't tell them anything. They'll turn it against you. You'll need to testify in court if you're indicted. Don't want to muddy things. I don't know who killed Christopher, but I know it wasn't you." George paused to glance up from rummaging through the basket.

"I've got my suspicions. Don't ask me to share them. Best you keep clear of any discussion. You passed the Ordeal by Touch—a ridiculous test, but some folks swear by it. They truly believe if a murderer touches the body, it bleeds. If Christopher's body had bled with your touch, you'd be done for. What rot."

Hot tears dripped down Ivy's cheeks. "Please, Mr. Stokely, please. Get me out of here. I cannot bear to be trapped. Again. Please."

"Don't cry, girl. Can't stand to see a woman cry. I'm sorry this came to you. I'll do my best to help. Sean sends his love," he whispered.

In a louder conversational tone, George went on to say, "Sit down, Ivy, and we'll sort this out. So, as your master, girl, it's my obligation to provide for you. You're under bond to me. So here's food. Don't want to overburden the good sheriff's budget.

I'm responsible for you. Don't cause him any trouble. You've done enough, don't you think?"

"Yes, sir," said Ivy, playing along. "How's Bethany, Mr. Stokely, and Sammy? Did Sammy get sick, too?"

"No, he's fine and Bethany's better. Rash all gone, fever gone. In fact, she helped Miss Sarah make this bread. Sam carved a bird for you. At least, he says it's a bird. The boy's not too far along in his carving. I've told them you had to be away for a time."

George then lowered his voice and leaned close to Ivy. His warmth and the scent of him distracted her. She felt calmer than she had all morning.

"Miss Sarah slipped your rosary into the loaf and wanted me to tell you she's praying for you, and she and the children are fine. Stay strong, Ivy."

The two sat on the floor, the basket between them. George set a clean square of linen on the filthy surface as carefully as if it were a dining table. He laid out two apples, a small loaf of whole meal bread, cheese, and a chicken leg.

Before eating anything, Ivy pried the rosary out of the bottom of the loaf and stuffed it into her pocket. She reached for the cheese, then stopped.

"What's the matter, girl? Food not to your liking?"

"I'm so filthy from this place, sir." She was glad she had taken her weekly bath on Sunday.

"Ah, well . . . The sheriff has his rules. No bath for prisoners till right before court. Doesn't want to worry about his prisoners escaping and running naked through town. Don't worry about me. This isn't the first time I've sat in a jail cell or smelled piss and vomit. But I bet I can wheedle a basin out of our friend Smallwood."

George stood up and walked over to the bars. In a pleasant tone he asked—as if requesting the salt be passed at the table—

"Smallwood, do you have a minute?"

Smallwood willingly brought a small basin and cloth.

"Thank you, Smallwood. She'll need a basin every day, please. Don't be worried. It's a small thing. I'm sure the sheriff won't mind, and you'll be rewarded on earth, if not in heaven, for your troubles."

After cleaning her hands and face, Ivy set to eating with gusto while George watched. His jovial smile failed to reach his gray eyes or wrinkled brow. George looked worried.

Ivy leaned back against the cool wall.

"Ivy, don't let imprisonment gnaw at your soul. I know how it can happen."

"What? How so?"

"As I'm sure you've heard, I came to the Chesapeake as a wee little thing, only eleven. I came as you came—unwillingly—though I had been plucked not from an errand but from the bowels of Bristol's prison."

"Prison? As a child?"

"Oh, yes. I became a street urchin after my ma's death. Didn't do very well at begging—lasted less than a week. Picked up and thrown into a cell like this, only one full of other children. Filthy and starving, we were."

"What about your family? Your father? Didn't he miss you?" Ivy offered George an apple. He refused.

"Well, I know I had a father, but never knew him, if you know what I mean. I had an older brother, too, who left for America years before Ma died."

"Oh, I am so sorry, sir."

"Well, I believe I was lucky. The authorities tired of feeding us—what little they did—and thought it would be more profitable to sell us into indenture. I came on a ship and have known nothing else since. I love the Chesapeake. A man can do well, no matter his background, with hard work. I've done better here than I ever would have in England. But, back to you. Don't be embarrassed by your circumstances. Spend your energy making a plan for freedom."

"I see what you're saying. My heart still breaks at the thought of you as a boy suffering in a jail and on a ship. If you could stand it at eleven, I should be able to do so now. Thank you, sir. I've had my fill. I'll eat the apples later. Please give my thanks to Miss Sarah and my love to your children."

"Goodbye, Ivy. Either me or someone else from *Convict's Revenge* will be by every day."

Ivy grabbed his hand like a drowning sailor grasping a lifeline. "Thank you, Mr. Stokely. My English is not good enough to tell you how grateful I am."

George gave her a quick hug, then left.

Ivy heard his footsteps outside, followed by Juno's whickered greeting. The wagon wheels noisily rolled away over the cobblestones. She sobbed.

After George's departure, the scratching of a twig broom nattered through the silence, overlaid with Smallwood's open-mouthed breathing. The jailer spoke to Ivy before he came into view.

"Well, well, well. Patronage from George Stokely. Says he's going to get an attorney for you. Quite the generous planter.

"You might think you're a lucky woman. You might think old George's popularity will get you out of this pickle. Well, you should know, here in Maryland, we take all our crimes very serious-like. Man or woman, makes no difference. We punish anyone breaking the law." The smirk on Smallwood's face preceded him as he approached Ivy.

She examined a hangnail and did not respond. Smallwood needed no encouragement.

"We don't mind hanging women here in Maryland. Hanged old witch Rebecca Fowler for her deal with the devil. That was a few years back. My uncle Johnny took me to the hanging. I was a little boy. Would have been bad enough if she only practiced magic. You can almost get away with that. No, what caused her problem was she made a pact with the devil himself. Can't do that in Maryland, nor in England, either, I hear."

From her peripheral vision, Ivy saw the scaremonger look up from his broom. She examined another fingernail.

"Don't know, as I was only a lad and too young for the details . . . don't know if she were examined by a woman's jury or not. Would expect so. They like to check if a lady happens to have a third teat to feed the devil's spawn or the like and check everything else for any signs of devilry. Usually have a midwife or two on a woman's jury just for such things. But I was so young when Mistress Fowler climbed the gallows. 'Deed I was.

"Did you know the gallows had thirteen steps? Not sure why, but I counted them as the old witch climbed up to the hangman. My pa said it needed thirteen to break her neck. But . . ."

Ivy flicked her mismatched eyes up at the jailer.

He swallowed as if reminded of—and put off by—her unique appearance.

"Well, don't say I didn't warn you, Miss Ivy O'Neill. We take our crimes to heart here and hang a woman as quick as a man. Still can see Rebecca drop. Yes, I can. You see, the hangman didn't line the knot up right with her spine and—" The sound of the outer door opening and the sheriff's heavy boots stopped Smallwood's oration.

Chapter 41

Baltimore Harbor, Maryland
County of Baltimore Jail

April 26, 1701

George kept his promise. Every day Ivy had a visitor, usually George. He whispered encouragement and explained her legal situation. A jury of local free men were being called to meet in a week or so. They would decide whether there was enough evidence to indict Ivy. If she was indicted for Christopher Jamieson's murder, there would be a trial with a judge presiding. The judge and jury would hear the facts and make a decision. The penalty for murder could be death by hanging.

"Marylanders are an independent lot, Ivy. They make up their own minds and in their own way. Sometimes they acquit people who surely appear to be murderers. And if found guilty, the one thing every convicted murderer must do is ascend the gallows and make a public confession. At least one woman, after standing before the whole of her neighbors and confessing, was reprieved. Such a cruel thing to do. She thought her time had come. She tiptoed down from the gallows, alive."

George stopped.

"Oh, I'm sorry, girl. I pray you escape indictment. Although it is good to know that even at the last minute, God can save you from death."

"I understand." Ivy lowered her eyes and plucked at her skirt. She considered all George had said. She reached into her skirt's slit and slipped her fingers into the pocket suspended from her waist. She fingered her rosary, lips moving.

George leaned against the scarred wall in companionable quiet.

"You're lucky, Ivy," said George as she half-heartedly ate one afternoon. A bird sang with deafening abandon at the window. "The Governor agreed to let a county jury decide your fate. Much better than having you carried off to the Provincial Court in St. Mary's. I know the people hereabouts and, for the most part, they are a fair group."

"Whatever you say, Mr. Stokely. I have little knowledge of courts and judges and juries and such."

"Another thing, Ivy. I've arranged for an attorney to act on your behalf."

"Attorney? Why? You are going to too much trouble."

"Oh, girl, you have to be prepared. Once the indictment comes down, if it does—and I hope it doesn't—the jury will want to hold the trial immediately. They won't want to travel home and back again. We have to be ready."

"I don't have any money."

"You're my responsibility, Ivy. I'm taking care of this. Besides, we need you back at *Convict's Revenge*. No one else can bake a pie like you can." George winked. "Come on. Buck up. We need you."

"Tell me about the attorney, can you, please?"

"You already know her. The midwife, Mistress Jane Grendon."

"What? Her? A woman? Oh . . ."

"Look, Ivy, women can serve as attorneys here and they do. The midwife has been called to court more than once to testify and to serve on juries. I don't want to fill your head with unpleasantness, but sometimes the court has women juries to deal with certain crimes."

He paused. Ivy looked off into space, processing the information.

"Oh, I see . . ." She understood. George was referring to womanly crimes such as abortion, infanticide, and adultery.

"Most importantly, the midwife's a person of rare wisdom and love for women and children. She'll do well by you, Ivy. I trust her. You can trust her too." George helped himself to a few raisins.

The next day the midwife Jane Grendon came by. The sheriff sent nosy Smallwood out on a fool's errand. The sheriff himself brought the midwife into the nether region of the jail and sat a wooden chair for her outside the cell.

"I'll let you two have privacy to talk. Don't worry about me. I'm not a gossip, as you know, Jane, and have no interest in whatever defense you're cooking up for this girl. You can stay all day, as far as I'm concerned." With a nod to the midwife, Williams faded away.

Ivy put aside any lingering embarrassment and welcomed the woman.

Jane Grendon's amber dress set off her auburn hair. Ivy looked down at her own stained gown and grubby fingers. Jane's clever eyes caught the slight flush to Ivy's cheeks.

"Mistress Ivy O'Neill, good to see you. Don't worry about the state of your clothes and such. No one expects an incarcerated woman to look her best. Let's concentrate on what's important—getting your life spared."

"Yes, ma'am."

"Please call me Jane. I love to hear my own name."

"Yes, Jane. You can call me Ivy."

A look of amusement flashed over the older woman's face. "Well, I've spent time with your master, Mr. Stokely, and heard how things have gone since you've come to Maryland. He's a good man, as is his word.

"I remember you from the *Prometheus* and Elizabeth Lamb's funeral, too. Not often do I run across such remarkable eyes. It sounds like you're a good worker and the type of person we need here in the colony.

"Before we get started, here's a flagon of water and a pear. Nutrition's important to keep your spirits up." She handed them through the bars. Ivy was struck by the beauty and gracefulness of her hands.

Jane settled in her chair and waited patiently as Ivy ate and drank. Only when Ivy was finished did the midwife proceed.

"Now, I need you to tell me what you know about this business, please, Ivy."

The two women sat close with only the iron bars between them, their red heads nearly touching as they spoke. Ivy, after assuring the midwife of her innocence, described her relationship with Christopher as well as Peter. Last, she discussed Tom Jenkins and his assault.

"I see. I don't know who the witness is who claimed to see you attack Christopher. We should be prepared for it to be Tom. Let's talk about that."

The midwife seemed to understand the smallest details of Ivy's life without Ivy explaining them. Her soothing voice emanated solace and her words, empathy. Ivy's heart warmed and she felt her attorney understood her. The only other woman coming close to instilling such feelings in her had been Miss Sarah. However, even Miss Sarah couldn't match the midwife's ability to envelop Ivy in a sense of her own agency, her ability to sail her own ship, to pilot her own life. It was nothing short of wonderful.

"I'll be back once or twice before the jury meets. I'll verify our information and help you understand what will happen if we go to court. And I'll help you prepare for both a possible conviction and for life after you're released from jail, if we are fortunate enough for that to happen. Your freedom is our goal. I will do everything in my power to bring it to fruition, young lady. Everything."

Chapter 42

Baltimore Harbor, Maryland
County of Baltimore Jail

April 30, 1701

The incarceration of an eighteen-year-old woman was complicating the County of Baltimore's primitive penal system. Peter gossiped when he came to deliver Ivy's daily meal. George somehow discovered the sheriff had allowed two drunks to be housed with Ivy her first night in jail. George, according to wagging tongues, informed the sheriff of his extreme displeasure. With a whisper, Peter shared what he'd overheard.

"George said, 'Any repeat of that or anything like it and I will see you unseated at the next election. I may well run for sheriff myself.' Wouldn't that be amazing, Ivy? George Stokely as sheriff. Anyway, Sheriff John Williams vowed to keep you safe. How's that, my dear? George does take care of things, he does. Somehow he manages to always get things done and stay popular at the same time. Wish I had his knack. Maybe I'll learn his secrets by the time I'm done with my indenture." Peter gave a self-satisfied chuckle and grinned.

"Mmhmm," agreed Ivy, her mind elsewhere, realizing why

she'd had no cellmates after the first night of her incarceration.

"I hear there are people around who think the sheriff feasts off the misfortunes of others. You know, drums up excuses for his position, Ivy. Apparently he claims to protect the harbor from all sorts of dangers which may or may not exist. What do you think?"

"Uh, sorry, Peter. My mind wandered." She lowered her voice. "I'm worried about Sean. How is he?"

Peter took the hint and whispered in his conspiratorial manner. "He's worried about you, but Stokely says he needs to stay away from the harbor right now. He's better off out of sight, out of mind. Don't want Williams trying to drag him into this. Sean sends his love, he does. He's a hard worker and busy, now Christopher's dead."

Ivy nodded.

"I love him too. I wish I could see him. Please tell him, Peter. Poor Sean. I feel so sorry."

The next day, George brought Miss Sarah with him. Her encouragement buoyed Ivy.

"Your appetite appears healthy, dear," said Miss Sarah, a note of surprise in her voice.

Ivy looked up from the cold pork chop she had gnawed to the bone.

"I know I need to keep my strength up, ma'am. And anyways, I don't like to leave food around."

"Rats," said George. Miss Sarah drew in her breath.

One morning, Ivy dozed in the corner of her cell after eating the oatmeal brought by Sheriff Williams. Unlike Smallwood, Williams toed the line without a hint of impropriety about him. She sensed an anxiety in the sheriff, a need to control, to do the right thing, to always be right. She believed that need could work to her advantage. The young woman did her best to keep on good terms with the powerful man.

Ivy thought the sheriff might have been a friend under other circumstances. Smallwood, never. She knew she was only safe from Smallwood because George bribed and intimidated him.

With the warm days, the volume of noise floating in through the window grew. Never as quiet as Stokely's peaceful farm, business in town picked up.

Frustrated, Ivy heard the sailors through her window. The first ships of the season had docked.

Ivy covered her chest and arms with a wool shawl from Miss Sarah. Despite her best efforts to spend her days awake in contemplation, prayer, or pacing, she often retreated into fugue-like dreams.

The specter of the nearby gallows refused to be tamped down. The spidery structure rose in her mind like a black sea monster emerging from the ocean and filling the horizon. Even prayer failed to keep her free of terror, so she'd nod off to dream of happier times. Where in the past, these reveries were of Ardmore or even An Rinn, now Ivy often dreamed of *Convict's Revenge*, Miss Sarah, the children, and . . . George. Especially George. George laughing, George whistling, George pulling her up onto Juno and taking her back to *Convict's Revenge*.

Footsteps in the front room roused her.

Ivy opened her eyes and saw a scarecrow of a man with Smallwood. At his Gaelic greeting, she shrieked.

He called her by name and sounded like Kevin. Kevin, the man she had hoped to marry back in Ireland. The neighbor boy all grown up. This fellow had Kevin's black eyes and brown hair. He looked like an aged, ravaged version of her Irish sweetheart.

"Kevin, is it really you, or am I dreaming?" Ivy replied in Gaelic.

Smallwood, unlike during George's visits, stubbornly stayed.

His brow wrinkled.

"Miss O'Neill, this man says he knows you. I can see he does, so out of the goodness of my heart, I'll let you two speak a minute or two, then he has to go. He can't come into the cell. If the sheriff finds out, we'll both be in trouble."

"Thanks, Mr. Smallwood. I am grateful."

Smallwood smirked at the recognition.

Kevin started to reach through the bars. Quick as a snake, Smallwood grabbed Kevin's hand.

"No. None of that. Tell him, Ivy. Only a bit of palaver and then he's back to the dock. His master's waiting for him."

Curious, Smallwood's eyes roved back and forth between Ivy and Kevin as they spoke in Gaelic. Thinking back to George's advice and her own ability to hide her bilingualism, Ivy kept her comments as bland and unrevealing as possible.

"Kevin, how did you get here? Why are you here?" She shot a warning glance at Smallwood and whispered, "Be careful. Many here understand our language."

Kevin blinked in acknowledgment.

"Well, Ivy, I came here freely under a bond of indenture. I heard this was a place where a man can own land, prosper, and do well if he's willing to work. And I am.

"I came to find you and marry you. Back in Dungarvan, when your horse and wagon were found, well, town folks figured you and Sean were taken, spirited away. I hoped and prayed you'd be here. Seems the ship's captain let slip to a harlot that he was headed to the Chesapeake. Baltimore's the only harbor of worth. You know I'm not rich. I didn't have enough money to pay my way. The indenture takes care of that."

"Kevin, I am touched. I know the trip here is hard. I didn't have a choice. You did. I'm sorry you went through all that."

"Oh, Ivy, I didn't know you'd get yourself in such trouble.

Everyone in town and in the countryside talks of nothing else. How you murdered another servant, with a hoe. Oh, Ivy. Why'd you do it? You always had murder in your heart, since the first day you came to An Rinn. Even as a child you always swore to do vengeance on the British. I hoped and prayed you'd come to reason as you grew up. Become a better Christian. I've prayed and prayed for your soul, for you to let your hate go." A bit of drool slipped from his mouth. He wiped at it with his ragged cuff.

"What, Kevin? You think I did it?" Ivy stepped back from the bars. Her hands, hanging down at her side, clenched into tight fists. Her mouth hung open.

"Look at you. You're in jail." Kevin's arm swung about to encompass the shabby space. His voice carried more than a hint of a whine. "For the sake of loving Jesus, girl. You killed a man. You can't deny it. Why else would you be in jail? Why'd you do it, Ivy? You've ruined everything. What if they hang you? They say you're to go to trial and likely to be executed. You always were a headstrong, straight ahead, impetuous girl . . ." Kevin's gaunt face, flooded from his pounding heart, shone red and shiny.

"Mind your tongue, Kevin. You don't know what you're talking about. How dare you assume I'm guilty! I no more killed that man than flew to the moon last night."

"Well, I only know what I hear, and knowing you and your temper . . . you need to understand. If, by a miracle, you are freed, I'll still have you. I will. I'll wait for you. I'll forgive you your sins and marry you once my bond is served. I pray every night for your soul and your release." Kevin's chest heaved and he hung his head.

Ivy stared wordlessly. Unshed tears glistened in her eyes. A heavy weight descended on her.

" . . . and Ivy, I am sorry. I do have bad news to share as well. I am so sorry. Your poor mother died a few weeks after you and

Sean disappeared. Father Declan said her heart broke. Wasn't a month later, your dad married Widow Clancy. Said he needed a wife, and the widow needed a husband to help her raise her two daughters. I know this is hard to hear . . ."

"Get out," screamed Ivy, recovering her voice. "Go away." Switching to English, she looked at Smallwood. "Take him away and don't bring him back."

Kevin, red-faced and choked on tears, nearly knocked Smallwood down in his rush to leave.

Breathless, her heart hollowed out, Ivy slumped to the floor. There were no tears to shed. Instead, a dry blankness took over.

Was that really Kevin, or a changeling? Had the fairies exchanged her beloved Kevin for one of their own enchanted selves?

Ivy tossed her head and sighed. Father Declan had taught her years ago that fairies were imaginary, a poor attempt to make sense in a difficult world. He taught her to follow Christianity and set aside any pagan beliefs. For the most part, Ivy did.

The priest was probably right. The ghost-like man who had berated her was Kevin. The scrawny fellow was no mystical changeling. He was Kevin, all grown up into a disloyal excuse of a person. Ivy's indignation and anger crowded out any sympathy for him. Like a bridge swept away in a flood, Ivy's affection for her sweetheart floated away.

Hammered down by the grief and guilt swirling inside her, Ivy didn't sleep or eat. Stunned at first, then sad, her feelings rapidly evolved to fury.

She blamed Captain Smythe for her predicament. She mourned for her mother. She grappled with her displacement. Her father's new wife would not want his grown daughter lingering around the cottage, eating their food, taking up room. She had nowhere to claim as a refuge back in Ireland. She was moorless. Free, in a tragic, miserable way.

Ivy imagined her very heart was hardening deep in her chest, that it had melted in the inferno of her anger and was becoming a hard black piece of obsidian, replacing what had once lovingly throbbed with life. She felt her soul sliding toward an abyss of hate. She wondered if she'd be able to stop before tipping over the edge. She recognized danger yet didn't know if she had the strength to resist it.

Torn with grief, she knew one thing—she would do what she could to be free from this prison.

Chapter 43

Baltimore Harbor, Maryland
County of Baltimore Jail

May 3, 1701

Ivy overheard Smallwood, ever ready with a spoon to stir the pot, tattle to George about the Irishman's visit and claim to not have any idea what Kevin told Ivy. After he spread out the food from home, George kindly asked if there was something she needed. The smell of cold fried fish nauseated Ivy.

"Nothing you can do, sir. Nothing. Thank you, though."

A perplexed expression came over George's face. After a few more prods and pokes, George became quiet. He pulled out a small knife and whittled on a chunk of pine, softly whistling a melodic tune. Ivy sat lost in thought, then forced herself to eat the fish.

The third day after Kevin's visit, Ivy stirred up her courage. Portions of her misery were being refashioned into reasonableness. She understood her father needed a helpmate. How could he fish and take care of Joey? She began to forgive him.

That day Ivy told George about Kevin—at least, the part where Kevin was from her hometown in Ireland and had brought news of her mother's death. She didn't even know herself how she felt about Kevin's offhanded marriage proposal. Since she could not legally marry till she fulfilled her indenture, there was no need to bring the matter up.

"Ivy, I'm so sorry. The world is never the same after we lose our mother. All I can say is your grief will be more bearable as time passes." He grasped her hand, his warm eyes grave. "Please try to get your rest and eat. You'll need all your strength. It's good you walk around the cell and keep your blood moving. Tomorrow the jury meets to decide to indict you or not."

"I'll try. I am so sorry for all the trouble I've caused you and your family. I know you need help back home."

"We'll be fine. You've been so kind to us. It's time to turn the tables. We'll do what we can to help you. Just listen to Jane, Ivy, and follow her lead. She is your best hope now."

And you are my best friend, thought Ivy.

The next morning the sheriff came as usual with breakfast. He said nothing about the jury.

"Red sky this morning. Probably going to squall. We do need the rain."

Ivy believed him. The air hung heavy and gave her a dull headache.

An hour later, Smallwood breezed in. Ivy noticed his frenetic movements as he hurried down the hallway. The jailer's ferret-like eyes and pointy nose appeared more animal-like than usual. Smallwood carried things back and forth from the shed out back, humming a ditty. His eyes darted to Ivy, then skittered away. Mr. Smallwood appeared as excited and nervous as an untried stallion in spring.

Ivy gasped aloud as she realized her looming fate was the likely cause of his mood. The jailer appeared to anticipate her indictment with glee. She imagined he looked forward to frogmarching her up the thirteen steps of the gallows. She realized he wanted to feel the rope in his hands. He wanted to hang her.

Ivy prayed to be spared.

By midafternoon the prophesied storm tiptoed in with a musical soft drizzle. Unpleasant thoughts of the gallows outside on the green swirled and eddied in Ivy's mind. They interrupted her attempts to doze. Her head ached in dull discomfort. As if he knew, Smallwood rattled the dustpan and jostled several loads of wood into the bin, keeping her awake.

Jane Grendon's alto voice broke through Ivy's discomfort. "Good afternoon, Mr. Smallwood. I'm here to see Miss O'Neill. Privately, if you please."

"Right you are, Mistress Grendon. I'll take you back soon as I stir up these coals."

Smallwood's chirpy voice stabbed into Ivy like cold steel. Did that mean bad news if the toady was so cheerful? Jane's grave expression as she approached Ivy's cell confirmed Ivy's fear.

Jane stepped up close to the bars and reached through for Ivy's hand. Her cheeks were damp, but whether from the rain or tears would stay the midwife's secret.

"Ivy, dear, I am so sorry to bring you this news. The jury did decide to indict you for Mr. Jamieson's murder." Jane paused, giving Ivy a moment to absorb this.

Ivy felt the blood rush from her face and felt dizzy.

"Remember, though, an indictment is not a conviction. An indictment means we now go to trial. And Ivy, that will be tomorrow."

Ivy's chin quivered with the effort to maintain control. Failing, her face crumpled. She erupted and wailed aloud.

Jane's eyes welled with sympathetic tears. She kept Ivy's hand in hers, and gently massaged it with her thumb.

With a shuddering sob and loud sniff, Ivy swiped at her wet cheeks, then looked straight at Jane. "How can they think I did this? There can't be any evidence. I don't understand."

"It's a serious matter and the jury doesn't want to risk freeing a murderer. Simple as that. Someone put together a convincing enough story to frighten the jurors into an indictment. We'll do our best to share the facts. I am confident, Ivy."

"Confident of what, please?"

"Well, girl, that if you tell the truth and let your true nature be seen, reasonable people—which I believe the jurors are—will see the truth. You couldn't be a murderer even if you wanted to. I believe in you."

Jane drew a chair close to the bars and proceeded to instruct Ivy in the details of the upcoming trial. She coached her to answer questions honestly and in a brief, straightforward way.

Ivy settled down quickly and listened to every word.

"Ivy, answer the questions only if you know the answer. If you don't, say so. Be honest. Be brief. Tell the truth. Don't laugh or smile—ever—and keep your hands quiet in your lap. Don't lose your temper or let the prosecutor bait you. He will try. Of that, I'm sure. Keep it simple.

"You didn't do this crime. Your hope to be found not guilty rests on your convincing the judge and jury of this. You are a decent woman, and I have confidence in you. Keep steady, dear. We'll get through this.

"Tomorrow morning George will bring Miss Sarah by with fresh clothes for you. The sheriff doesn't want to be accused of undermining your case, so he's agreed to this. You can bathe in the morning, too. Miss Sarah will help you."

"Oh, I am indeed grateful, ma'am. I'm so ashamed of the state I'm in."

"I'll take my leave now, Ivy. Do your best to rest tonight and have faith. You are a decent, God-loving woman. You'll do well in court. I'm proud to be your attorney. Good day."

Ivy reached through the bars and clasped hands with Jane. "Oh, I am so glad you're helping me. I'll try. I will."

As the afternoon rolled on into evening, rain blew in the cell's window and puddled on the floor. Ivy huddled in a corner, prayed her rosary, and tried to keep out of the drops flying by. In the way of storms, the downpour ceased suddenly. Clear white light streamed through the window and crossed the cell. The ray slid through the bars and lit the opposite wall. Outside, a raven cawed, and horse hooves splashed in the wet street. Tomorrow Ivy would go on trial before a court presided over by, according to Jane, a no-nonsense judge.

Though she faced being sentenced to hang from the gallows, Ivy found a modicum of peace. Her hours alone in meditation and prayer in the weeks since her incarceration were a balm to her pain.

Chapter 44

Baltimore Harbor, Maryland
County of Baltimore Jail

May 10, 1701

Sheriff Williams arrived the morning of the trial with, as usual, a bowl of porridge. His wife had thought to add currants. The sheriff, his eyes evasive and his expression one of embarrassment, watched Ivy eat.

Miss Sarah bustled in carrying a basket of fresh clothing, towels, and soap.

"Come along, Ivy," said Sarah, as she nodded toward a shed attached to the back door. "George helped me set up a tub, dear, before he went off on an errand. You can bathe and I'll help you with your hair. Looks like it's been a while."

An hour later, Ivy returned to the cell in her favorite blue calico dress. Being clean and having her mop of curls under control gave her confidence. She felt intact and ready to fight for her life.

Sheriff Williams came to stand outside her cell. As he was wont to do before any pronouncement, he drew himself up, puffed out his chest, and cleared his throat with a brief "Ahem."

"Miss O'Neill, today you'll be tried. It's all up to the jury and judge. If you are found not guilty, you'll be free to go immediately, and you won't need to come back here. If you're found guilty, you'll be brought here to await your punishment. I do not know if you committed the crime. I am a neutral party. If you are found not guilty, I want you to know there will be no hard feelings on my part. It's clear to me George Stokely is quite fond of you, and I expect you'll continue to work for him in that case." His eyes sharpened and searched her face.

Ivy felt her face warm. She said nothing.

The sheriff picked up the thread of his speechifying. "George is well thought of, and I want no trouble from him. So I hope you understand. I have been doing my job as sheriff—no more, no less. I've explained this to Smallwood as well. You know Smallwood. He's extremely proud of his position and depends on me for his placement. He's agreed to not hold your incarceration against you if you should, by some miracle, be freed. May God bless you today, no matter the decision. I have watched you here. I see you were brought up right, though you are a young, inexperienced girl. That's it. We'll be going soon enough to court. Be ready." Ending, the sheriff raised his chin and peered down his long nose. An answer was expected.

Ivy shifted, her fresh clothes comfortable against her skin. "Thank you for allowing me to bathe and have clean clothes, sir. Please thank your wife for the food she prepared for me."

The sheriff softly cleared his throat. His eyebrows lifted. More was needed.

"Sir, I understand all you have told me. I have no questions. I am ready."

Satisfied, or at least knowing he would get no other response from his prisoner and ward, the sheriff left.

A rivulet of cold sweat dribbled down Ivy's back.

Smallwood appeared within minutes, and unlike the sheriff, was unrepentant and unbowed by his time tending to Ivy. "Today's the day, my fine Irish girl. Court today, and you'll swing tomorrow, I'm sure. Let's go. They're waiting." Smallwood moved with the barely controlled excitement of a hunting spaniel waiting to be unleashed.

Ivy walked out into a drizzling rain. Smallwood grabbed her elbow. Ivy winced, and the jailer squeezed harder. He hurried her across the small green between the jailhouse and a log building.

The bad weather had dampened most of the harbor layabouts. Only a few men and boys plastered themselves against the log building in a vain effort to stay under the overhang of the eaves. Few women were about, though Ivy caught sight of movement across the street and was sure she saw a woman or two peering from shop windows.

A stocky, square-faced female in a soiled dress stood inside the doorway of an alehouse. As Ivy neared her, the woman leered and, in a gravelly voice, crowed, "There she is, the murdering wench. Just look at her. Those damned eyes say all you need to know. Thought she'd get away with it. We'll watch her on the gallows tomorrow, we will."

From inside the alehouse, a man's voice boomed, "Shut up, Molly, you stupid trollop. You've not room to talk."

A faint smile played on Smallwood's lips as he caught Ivy's eyes. She would have liked to kill him and smack the woman in the mouth. Smallwood's eyes flew away as if he'd read her thoughts and was scorched by her hatred.

He shoved Ivy into the log courthouse. "Take a seat, O'Neill. Don't move until I say you can, or the judge beckons you."

With Ivy's appearance in the doorway, quiet dropped over the courtroom. Gawkers overflowed crude wooden benches which creaked and tipped under their weight. Realizing the crowd probably included many who had watched her be auctioned and humiliated in the autumn, Ivy took a deep breath and elongated herself to her full height of six feet. Her family would have been proud.

In the blur of faces, her eyes found George's. The hat, twirling in his hands, dangling between his knees, stilled. She held his eyes for a moment . . . or forever. Whatever the length of time, the interlude enveloped Ivy with a sense of safety, of having the world be as it should be, of being loved. Although George wasn't on horseback or carrying her away from a tempest as on the day she had tried to flee, he was present. He was on her side, and he was her friend.

Ivy stepped into the room. An empty spot awaited her, front and center, beside her attorney on the first row of benches. Jane, her face expressionless, pointed a forefinger to the bench. As she approached her seat, the hive-like buzz resumed. She recognized others in the room. A few rows back, Kevin sat and, as if struck by lightning, stared at Ivy. His face was taut and body still. Gaunt from his voyage, his clothes were freshly laundered even if ill-fitting. He nodded his head at Ivy, an acknowledgment she did not return.

Farther down the front bench, Tom Jenkins glowered. He emitted enmity as a dying fire gives off heat. He had gone to the trouble to wash, comb his hair, and put on clean clothes, though the dirt on his shoes betrayed his status as a field laborer.

Ivy shared a brief glance with George who sat directly behind her, then turned and sat down. She remembered Jane's instructions and kept her posture erect, her hands folded in her lap, and her feet crossed at the ankles. Ivy smelled George's distinctive, yet familiar, scent of cured tobacco and the soap Miss Sarah made. The aroma floated lightly over the room's reek of wet wool, wet leather, dirt, and other men. She closed her eyes and willed George's strength and support to come to her.

The courtroom, though rough, carried an air of authority. Gray light from the rainy day seeped through the windows and set the whitewashed walls aglow.

Lined up against the far wall sat the jury. Ivy scanned the twelve men. She was surprised to realize she knew at least half of them.

Isaac Abner grinned back and started to give a wave but stopped himself and looked down. Ivy worried. Had she been grateful enough when he gave her Miranda's loom? Had she offended him by not encouraging his proposal? She believed he was a generous man. She prayed Isaac was also merciful.

She recognized two men from her first day in Maryland—the farmer who had purchased Sally and the cheerful dimpled man who had bought Fiona's bond. Billy Lamb, Elizabeth's widower, thinner than at her funeral, sat next to Polly Carr's father. Sean and George's prior master, William Tipton, sat front and center on the jury. His red hair glowed in the low light of the courtroom.

Ivy twisted her hands together. She had history with so many of these jurors. She wasn't sure if that was good news or bad. She took a deep breath.

Reaching into the pocket through the gash in her skirt she found her rosary. Ivy opened her eyes and looked out the window to the gray day as she silently prayed her rosary. She prayed for God to help her not fail herself, to do the right thing.

Smallwood, his gait as offbeat as his appearance, strode to the front of the room and, in his role as bailiff, announced, "Oyez! Oyez! Oyez! Court is called to order! The Honorable Judge

Jeremiah Warfield will preside. All rise."

With the scuffle of boots and the rattle of wooden benches, the crowd rose to their feet.

A door in the far side of the room opened. A man with a crude white wig atop his head took a moment to gather in everyone's attention. He stepped up on the elevated platform at the front of the room and sat behind a carved mahogany table.

Judge Warfield's dignity reminded Ivy of a priest at an altar, ready to serve communion. His youth surprised her as he appeared only a decade or so older than she. Of course, Maryland was a land for the young and vital. The judge, of middling height and middling build, moved with grace. He exuded intelligence. She hoped he was also wise, like Solomon in the carving back in Ardmore. Her life depended on it.

Like a cat waiting for a mouse to stick his head out of a hole, the berobed black-eyed judge stared boldly at Ivy as if he had every right in the world. As if she should fear his being down into her very core.

Ivy took the man's measure and returned his gaze with a neutral expression. The judge was a working man. Brown, from outdoor labor. She realized men of leisure were few and far between in Maryland.

I'm a human, too, just as much as him. He can look all he wants. I'll not waver.

Judge Warfield broke first. Picking up a piece of paper from the table in front of him, he read the charge against Ivy aloud.

The judge picked up his gavel.

After a single loud rap, he said, "The Court of Baltimore County is in session.

"You, Ivy O'Neill, are charged with the crime of homicide, of murder, specifically the murder of Mr. Christopher Jamieson, one indentured servant working under bond to Mr. George

Stokely of the *Convict's Revenge* plantation on the Patapsco River, here in the County of Baltimore, the British Crown Colony of Maryland, on the evening of Sunday, April 17, 1701, or early Monday, April 18, 1701.

"This is a capital offense. If found guilty, the penalty is hanging till dead. You may confess now or plead not guilty."

The judge paused, lowered the paper to the table, and fixed his gaze on Ivy.

"How do you plead, Ivy O'Neill?"

Smallwood started to reach out to Ivy, to prod her, but she was already on her feet.

"Not guilty, Your Honor." Ivy spoke evenly and clearly to the judge and, as she finished, turned to the jury as well.

"Given that, we will proceed. You may sit down. If you are convicted, you'll have the opportunity to explain your evil actions at your hanging, miss. Mr. Daniel Johnson, a deputy of the Attorney General, is serving as prosecutor. I have been notified Mistress Jane Grendon is representing the accused. The proceedings today will include sworn testimony by witnesses. A written record will be taken by the court reporter and preserved. The jury will then decide on a verdict of guilty or not guilty. I expect everyone in this courtroom to behave with decorum and broach no outbursts or talking out of turn. Now, Mr. Johnson, if you please."

Well-groomed and polished as an apple, a stocky man glided into place before the judge. Daniel Johnson sparkled with charisma, his physical beauty set off by a tailored blue jacket, waistcoat, and breeches.

"For my first witness, I call Thomas Jenkins."

Tom rose and approached the witness chair set between the judge and jury. His brown pants had a large blue patch on one hip. Tom's bandy-legged walk screamed of a poverty-ridden childhood. The judge gestured. Tom sat in the chair. After being sworn in by Smallwood, he proceeded to answer Prosecutor Johnson's questions.

"Tell us what you have to say against the prisoner, Mr. Jenkins."

"Yes, sir. Well, she's a lowbred Irish servant girl, she is. A papist, I'm sure. Been working for Mr. Stokely at *Convict's Revenge* where I have worked since the autumn. She enticed Mr. Jamieson, lured him with pies and biscuits and such. Every day, she'd call after him when he finished work and invite him into the kitchen. Who could turn that down? They'd sit and talk while she cooked up supper. Sip tea. She fed him special food and pretty soon, they were courting. Old Chris was a strong man and she'd get him to lighten her load in the field. He'd carry her tobacco to the barns and ease her burden every chance he had. Yes, he did.

"Well, what I know is that Mr. Jamieson and Miss O'Neill were courting. They went walking together in the woods on a regular basis and I observed them embracing and kissing on more than one occasion. She's a regular witch in my opinion. She is."

Like the tide running in over a dry beach, soft chattering spread through the onlookers in the court room. Ivy sat unmoving, frozen in an unnatural quietude.

"Thank you, Mr. Jenkins. I have no more questions."

Ivy remembered to breathe. Her shoulders dropped an inch or two.

Jane Grendon approached Tom. The only sound in the courtroom was the soft swish of her skirt on the stone floor.

"Mr. Jenkins, tell me how you determined the woman with Christopher was Ivy O'Neill."

"She had her green cloak on."

"Does it have a hood?"

"Yes, of course."

"So you didn't see her face. Am I correct?"

Tom hesitated. His lips compressed and turned down. "Well, it was her. I know it."

Jane turned to the onlookers and gestured to a young man in the third row.

"Come forward, please." He carried a bundle of green cloth in his arms. Jane pulled off the top bundle, a green cloak.

"Is this it?"

"Yes, I think so," said Tom.

"Or is this it?" Jane unfurled a second green cloak, of a barely perceptible lighter green color.

"Look, it was her. I've seen her a thousand times," said Tom, his voice raised.

The judge shot a scowl toward Jenkins, who immediately froze.

"Thank you, Mr. Jenkins. I have just a few more questions," said Jane.

"Is it true you assaulted Ivy O'Neill earlier this year in an attempt to be intimate with her against her will?"

Tom erupted. "She wanted it. She teased me for days and then, when the master caught us, tried to act as if she didn't. She knew she'd get in trouble. I don't have to force myself on any female."

Ivy struggled to keep her body still and relaxed as Tom lied. She felt her skin grow hot and knew her face was likely colored. She worked hard to keep her mouth closed and relaxed. Her fingers tightened on her rosary, and she began to pray silently.

Tom rattled on, as unable to stop as a rock rolling down a hill. "The night Christopher died, that girl walked out with him. Yes, she did. I heard some yells, too. She's the one. Had a lover's spat and killed him."

"I have no more questions for you, Mr. Jenkins. Thank you."

The prosecutor slid back into his spot before the judge, unruffled by Tom Jenkins's outbursts. "I'd like to question Nathan Lacey."

From the back of the room, Lacey made his way forward. Ivy had not seen the oily character since he had been outbid for her indenture at the harbor by George Stokely. Nausea rose in her gorge.

"Please tell us what you have to say against the prisoner."

"I came across this wench at the wharf last fall. She was one of a gaggle of lowbred females brought over as sporting women on the *Prometheus*. Any man here can have one of her fellow trollops any day of the week. She's just lucky enough to have become a one-man concubine."

George rose with a shout. He scrambled over the bench and knocked Ivy forward in the process. His big fist, clenched, was pulled back and ready to fly at Lacey.

Daniel Johnson smoothly reached up for George's wrist. "Sir, this is neither the time nor the place."

The judge banged his gavel on the table. "Back to your seat, Mr. Stokely, or I'll have Smallwood take you away. Get control of yourself."

George, beet-red, lips pursed, gave Ivy—now in tears—an anguished look. Under the judge's stern attention, the room settled back into a semblance of order.

"No more questions."

Jane came forward.

"Mr. Lacey, did you attempt to buy Ivy O'Neill's indenture?"

"I'm not sure. Maybe . . . It was months ago." He raised his chin in defiance.

"Do you happen to remember seeing me at the harbor that day?"

"Maybe."

"Are you possibly able to stretch your memory and recall my statement about Miss O'Neill?"

"No, absolutely not."

The judge leaned forward. "I'd like to know, Miss Grendon. Tell me."

"Your Honor, I examined all the women in my capacity as a midwife. Miss O'Neill was a maid with no evidence of any intimate experience with men. I have no reason, either, to believe that her status has changed. I am sure she will agree to another examination if that becomes necessary."

Oh, my God, thought Ivy.

"That won't be necessary." The judge looked down and shuffled papers for a moment.

The hint of a twinkle came to Jane's eyes. "I have no other questions for Mr. Lacey."

The prosecutor called Kevin Flinn forward and jumped to the point.

"Mr. Flinn, did you, while visiting Miss Ivy O'Neill in jail, ask her 'Why did you do it?' in regard to Christopher Jamieson's death, and tell her you forgave her for what she did?"

"Uh, uh, yes, sir, I did, but I didn't mean—"

"Thank you, Mr. Flinn. That will be all."

"I have a few questions, Your Honor," said Jane to the judge.

"Proceed."

"Now, Mr. Flinn, please tell us when and where you met Miss O'Neill."

"Back in Ireland, in An Rinn, my hometown. I think she was about six or seven years old."

"Why didn't you know her when she was younger?"

"She's not from An Rinn. She and her family are from Ardmore. The soldiers came and burned them out."

"Burned them out?"

"Yes. The soldiers burned down their cottage and many others, too. Killed her baby brother. Her mother was burned terrible, scarred all over her face."

Ivy heard Miss Sarah gasp behind her.

Kevin looked at Ivy. "Sorry, Ivy, to mention it."

"Confine yourself to the questions, young man," said the judge, shifting in his seat and thrusting his face toward Kevin.

"Please tell us how you came to be in Maryland," said Jane.

"I came to find Ivy and fetch her home and marry her, I did."

"Please explain."

"Well, she and her brother Sean were kidnapped to America last summer, they were."

"Kidnapped? Don't you mean they left under an agreement to be indentured? Didn't they just emigrate?"

"No. They were stolen. Not the only ones. They took the horse and wagon into Dungarvan to sell some woolen goods and all and never came home. Their father went after them and only found the empty wagon. Someone stole the horse."

"That sounds like quite a tale, sir. How would you know to come here for them?"

"The *Prometheus* had set sail the day they disappeared. The captain, Smith or Jones or something like that, had been with one of the town's women at the alehouse. He bragged about setting sail to the Chesapeake. Not too many big harbors on the Chesapeake. So I indentured myself. Figured I'd pay off my time, and then marry Ivy and we could go home to Ireland. But she went and killed Mr. Jamieson. But I'll still marry her, if she lives and will have me."

Ivy heard George shift his seat on the bench.

The prosecution rested and the trial moved on to the defense witnesses.

George took the stand first. He testified as to Ivy's indenture to him, the quality of her work, and her wholesome decency.

Jane proceeded.

"Mr. Stokely, did you ever witness any trouble between Thomas Jenkins and Ivy O'Neill?"

"Yes, he assaulted her a month or so ago."

"Please tell us about that."

"I heard Ivy screaming in the fields as I walked out one morning. Tom had her pinned against a downed log and was pulling her skirt up. Ivy managed to get free, fell, and fought him. He was relentless, even once I ran up. After things settled, I sent Ivy back to the house, as her clothing was ripped. Tom apologized. I let him know there was to be nothing like that ever again."

"Was Ivy raped?"

"No. I asked. She said he hadn't completed his action."

"Did Christopher Jamieson learn of this?"

"I believe so. After the assault, I overheard heated discussions between Christopher and Tom."

"Was Christopher courting Ivy?"

"Not to my knowledge."

"Thank you. Just one more question, sir. Please tell us what you know about Ivy O'Neill's whereabouts on the night Christopher died."

"My daughter, Bethany, became sick at dinner with a fever and so forth. Ivy and Miss Chichester spent the evening attending to her. Ivy sleeps in the children's room and was there all night. I myself was up until at least three in the morning when Bethany's fever broke. I can't rest when my children ail."

"Thank you."

Daniel Johnson had no questions for George or for the next witness, Sarah Chichester.

Miss Sarah confirmed George's testimony and added that she and Ivy both spent the entire night with the children. She had spelled Ivy for a few hours so the young girl could rest before making breakfast and going to the fields.

Ivy's head jerked up as the next witness was called—Polly Carr. What did she know? Ivy wondered.

Every male chin in Ivy's view rose at the sound of swishing silk. Like sunflowers turning with the sun, the men's faces followed Polly Carr's swaying stroll to the witness chair. Polly seated herself, fluffed out her green dress, adjusted the lace on her sleeves, then looked up. Her glance gathered in the room before alighting on Jane Grendon. Polly's glossy black hair gleamed in the sunlight flooding the room. The rain had moved on to other places, taking the clouds with it.

"Please tell us what you know about Christopher Jamieson, Miss Carr," said Jane.

"Quite a lot, actually, indirectly and a bit directly." Ever coy, Polly smiled. "Christopher courted my maidservant Sybil and proposed marriage. Sybil talks frequently about Christopher. She found him to be a decent man, kind and friendly. She knew he was fond of Ivy, but believed it was more a brother to sister affection. I can understand that, as Ivy is a mere kitchen girl. Sweet, but unpolished. Sybil and Christopher planned to marry once he completed his indenture."

"Do you know anything the court should know about this murder?"

"I do know Sybil has a green cloak—the only cloak she owns."

“Green. Same color as the cloak worn by the woman Mr. Jenkins saw cavorting with the murdered man, Christopher Jamieson. Right?” Jane said.

“If you say so, ma’am.”

The crowd in the courtroom stirred as one. Gasps, mutterings, and whispers filled the background.

“Silence,” said the judge.

“Anything else, Miss Carr?” said Ivy’s attorney.

“Only one thing. Christopher was very upset with Tom’s ill treatment of Ivy, and the two men no longer got along. They squabbled like chickens over the least little thing.”

Daniel Johnson, seated at a small desk in the corner, icily perused his notes. He shook his head to Jane’s questioning look. He had nothing to ask of Polly.

“I’d ask Peter Browne to come forward, please,” said Jane.

Peter came forward, a bounce in his step, and shot a dark glance toward Tom.

After he established his identity and his job, Jane asked if Christopher had been romancing Ivy.

“Oh, no. No one was or is romancing Miss O’Neill. We think of her as a little sister. She’s a lovely girl.”

“Did you notice any recent changes in Christopher and Tom’s relationship?”

“Yes. They fought all the time. Not fist fights. Just sniping and saying ugly things back and forth. I don’t know why, so don’t ask me. Didn’t know about Tom’s attack on Ivy till today. Everyone kept mum.”

“Changing direction, Peter. I have something to show you and I want to know what you know about this object.”

“Of course. Anything for you, Jane. I mean, yes, ma’am, Miss Grendon.”

Jane tipped her head toward the young man in the back who

had brought the cloaks forward. He brought a canvas-wrapped bundle, about a foot long and half a foot wide, and handed it to Jane.

She unwrapped a black iron implement attached to a broken-off wooden staff.

"Peter, what is this?"

"Well, it's a broken hoe, of course. The one found with Christopher's body. You can still see the blood and gore on it."

"Look at it carefully."

"Can't read anyways, ma'am. Hmmm." Peter turned the hoe over. "This is Tom Jenkins's grubbing hoe. The one he always uses and won't let anyone else touch."

"Thank you, Peter. I have no more questions for you, but maybe Mr. Johnson does."

"I do indeed. How would you know one hoe from another? They're just hoes, all alike."

"No sir, they're not. I know you are a learned man, but those of us who work the fields learn one tool from another. There's grubbing hoes to break up new land, hilling hoes to make our tobacco hills, weeding hoes, well, to weed. Makes a difference. It does.

"The other hoes back at *Convict's Revenge* are all repaired or have chipped edges. This one is rock-solid . . . had a sharp edge and really does a good job. Tom insists it's only for him to use. He's like that. Very particular. We let him use it. He's a real bear if he doesn't get his way. Easier to let him have his favorite hoe. Not worth fightin' over."

"How do you know it's Tom's and not someone else's?"

"I jest told you. Tom's is the only one with a clean edge. But of course, it's also the only one with a peculiar maker's mark." Peter took the hoe and turned it over, then held it out to Daniel Johnson.

"Right here, sir. See that impress of a little heart? That's the maker's mark. Only one hoe at *Convict's Revenge* has the heart for its maker's mark. Also has these two letters here. Probably from the merchant. Can't read or I'd call out what they are, but they are the ones on Tom's hoe. Only one hoe."

"Thank you, Peter."

The judge looked expectantly from Jane Grendon and back to Daniel Johnson. Picking up on the cue, they agreed the testimony phase of the case was over.

As if the curtain rose on a play's final act, each pair of eyes stared at the bewigged judge seated on the platform. The room was quiet as a church at midnight. A cat squalled outside, then hissed. A faint cloud of annoyance at the one-upmanship of the feline crossed over the judge's face. He soon recovered from the interruption.

"Sheriff, please ensure that no one leaves the room until the verdict is reached."

The sheriff and Smallwood left their seats and stood blocking the only door out.

The judge continued, "Does the prosecutor have any comments at this time?"

"No, Your Honor." The prosecutor looked like a guest anxious to leave a dull party. He discreetly lined the edges up on the stack of papers before him.

"Attorney for the defense, Miss Grendon?"

"Yes, Your Honor. I do."

Jane Grendon rose and stepped forward and approached the jury.

"You have heard the testimony today and you must consider it as you decide on Ivy O'Neill's fate. You don't need to decide who killed Christopher Jamieson, only whether or not you believe Ivy O'Neill did so. I will point out other, more likely killers have been identified by the witnesses.

"As for Ivy, she is only guilty of vulnerability—of being young, a servant, an Irish girl, and raised a Roman Catholic. As such, she is an easy one to blame for deeds done by others as she has little ability to defend herself. I ask you to look honestly at the evidence, at the type of person Ivy is. The only word against my client comes from a man of proven low character, a man who treated others shabbily, a man of ill temper. Look at Tom Jenkins, then look at Ivy O'Neill. Who do you believe the more likely assassin? Despite being kidnapped and brought here against her will, she has found it in her heart to work hard for George Stokely and his family, to raise his children lovingly and with kindness, to ease the burden of the elderly Miss Chichester.

"As for her religion, a child has no agency over where or how they are raised. Maryland was created as a sanctuary of religious tolerance. Though Catholicism was once acceptable and now is not legal, I'll wager we can wait a bit and see the wind spin in another direction.

"Miss O'Neill has the character and strength we need in our land. We must look beyond arbitrary classifications, such as the sex we're born with, and treat each other with respect."

Jane Grendon paused to look at the jurors one by one. Each returned her gaze with rapt attention.

"Most of you know me as a midwife, beyond my duty here as an attorney. I've delivered your own babies. I can tell you we all start out the same. We need to make life here better than what we left behind on the other side of the Atlantic. We need to cherish people like Miss O'Neill who are willing to give their energy and lives to making our world here a good place. I implore you to see the truth and free Ivy O'Neill. Thank you."

The judge adjusted his robes and directed his attention to the jury.

"You will remain here and make your decision. Please keep your comments low. Mr. Abner, I am appointing you to deliver the decision. We will wait."

The jury jostled and moved the benches till they created a closed circle. Hums and whispers and the occasional word or two floated out of the scrum. The onlookers, kept in the courtroom by the sheriff and bailiff, spoke softly among themselves. Ivy sat in silence. She prayed her rosary. A bead of sweat ran down her neck. Her chemise stuck to her thighs.

A short time later, the jury moved their benches back to their original position. The room became quiet.

"Do you have a verdict?" said the judge.

Isaac Abner stood up.

"Yes, Your Honor, we do," he said.

"Please share the verdict."

"We have found Ivy O'Neill not guilty of murder. Ivy O'Neill is innocent."

Strong arms pulled Ivy to her feet and embraced her, friendly arms, warm and loving, George's. Other hands patted her. Voices murmured their happiness. Ivy turned and Miss Sarah patted her shoulder and gently put one of Ivy's errant copper curls in place.

"So happy for you, dear," said the beaming woman with a loud sniffle. Jane fairly crackled with happiness.

The judge cut off the crowd's commotion with a "Silence."

"Sheriff, please arrest Thomas Jenkins for the murder of Christopher Jamieson," said Judge Warfield.

Quick as a wharf rat, Tom popped up and raced to the door. He tried to shoulder Smallwood aside.

"Oh, no you don't!" shouted the sheriff. Between the

sheriff's rough hands and the grasping paws of bystanders, Tom was snared. After an ineffectual wriggle or two, he settled down. Like a fox with a hen, Smallwood took his latest prey back to the jail. A broad smile plastered the jailer's face.

Judge Warfield stood and beckoned the sheriff and Daniel Johnson over. Head bowed and eyes in motion, the sheriff listened. He nodded in agreement, and left. Daniel looked resigned to whatever was agreed upon. Warfield resumed his place behind the mahogany table.

"Quiet," said the judge. "We have decided to proceed with the case against Thomas Jenkins, having heard sufficient testimony to ask the jury here today for an indictment. If indicted, we will carry on with the case. We have several good hours of daylight left. No reason to pull a jury away from the fields on another day. Gentlemen, proceed. Witnesses Mr. Stokely, Miss Chichester, Mr. Browne, Miss Carr, and Mr. Flinn are free to leave, as they have given sufficient testimony in this matter if Jenkins is indicted. Miss O'Neill is also free to go."

Later, Ivy thought she may have sprouted wings and flown from the courtroom. Whatever the case, she could never recall leaving the log building. All was a blur up until she found herself waiting at the wagon for the others. George appeared as she petted Juno's neck.

"Mr. Stokely, do you have an apple tucked away for her?" asked Ivy.

"Call me George, Ivy. Call me George." He dug a yellow apple from his pocket and gave it to her.

George settled Miss Sarah in the back of the wagon in a nest of pillows and blankets. She took his hand and mouthed a thank you with a meaningful glance at Ivy. Peter hopped in back and opened a parasol to shade Miss Sarah. With Ivy and George on the bench seat, the happy group hurried back to

Convict's Revenge.

"Uh, George, what about Sean?" said Ivy as they left the town behind them.

"I've spoken with Sean each time I saw you, Ivy. He's known what was happening every step of the way. It would've been risky having him seen around Baltimore Harbor town before today. Folks might have come to a wrong suspicion. Trust me, though. He can't wait to see you." George beamed.

"And Bethany and Samuel? Do they know? What do you want me to say to them?"

"I've been truthful with them, Ivy. Only way to be. Told them the sheriff had you in jail, but it was a mistake and I thought you'd be home soon. They'll be so happy to have you back."

"What if I hadn't been freed?"

"Couldn't think that, miss. Couldn't let the thought cross my mind nor theirs. Right, Aunt Sarah?"

"Absolutely. Had to trust God things would turn out right—and they did."

Her conversation with George, Peter, and Miss Sarah refreshed Ivy on the trip back to *Convict's Revenge*. Her incarceration had warped her sense of time. The minutes and quarter-hours and seconds lagged, crawled, and lollygagged. Yet, the milestones and scenery went by quickly. Hours later or maybe just five seconds after leaving Baltimore Harbor, Juno turned down the lane. As on every jaunt, the mare picked up speed as she headed home.

In front of the stable, Sean was leading Sammy and Bethany on their pony.

"Ivy! Ivy!" The children gave extravagant waves.

Ivy jumped into Sean's embrace before the wagon had come to a full stop. Red curls mingled with black. The siblings' tears of joy and murmurs of reunion brought answering sniffles from

George and Miss Sarah.

Ivy turned to the children.

"You two! You look grand, you do."

George took the pony's lead and watched Ivy as she bounded away, hand-in-hand with Sean. Silver laughter and musical Gaelic floated in their wake. Miss Sarah watched approvingly.

"You did a good thing, George." She hugged him. Her short arms encircled him only halfway. George bussed her cheek.

Tom did not return.

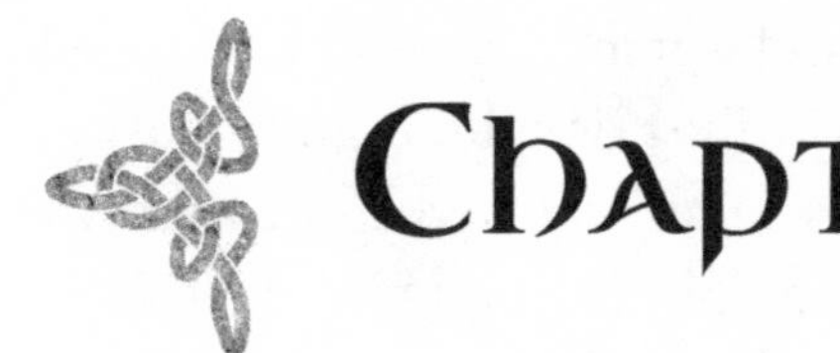

Chapter 45

Convict's Revenge
Near the Patapsco River, Maryland

May 11, 1701

In the morning, George came to the kitchen, dropped a leather pouch on the table, and asked Ivy to pack it with food.

"Ivy, I need to go to Baltimore Harbor to check on Tom. I'll be gone all day."

George hummed as he paced around the kitchen. Ivy wrapped a small loaf of bread in a muslin square. He stopped in front of her, danced a brief jig step, and dimpled into a smile.

"I am so glad to have you here, Ivy."

Cheeks warm with embarrassment, she studied the bread.

Ten minutes later, George trotted off on his flashy bay gelding.

Not till the following morning did Ivy learn Tom had been hanged for murdering Christopher. George was brief in relaying this to Ivy, but after dinner she overheard Miss Sarah and George talking.

"Did he confess, George? You know, at the gallows when it was his time to speak?"

"No, I'm afraid the scoundrel failed to grant us that relief.

Actually, he ranted on about being innocent and cried like a wee baby. The sheriff had to step in and quiet him."

"Do you think he was telling the truth—that he didn't kill Christopher?"

"I don't know, Sarah. I don't know. But I have the feeling that no matter what, Tom Jenkins earned his hanging—whether for murdering Christopher or other evils. He was a bad man."

"I'll pray for his soul, George. That's best."

Ivy looked down at the dish in her hands. She smeared off the tear which had dropped onto it.

After learning Tom's fate, Ivy spent a long time in Miss Sarah's chapel. Although he had treated her poorly, she could not dislodge a stubborn kernel of guilt. She struggled to delineate her part in the course of life which had ended with two deaths. Tom joined Christopher as regular topics of her searching conversations with God. She wondered if she would ever be free of this particular burden.

"You are not responsible for another's sin, Ivy." Sean's reassurance when she brought it up with him was a balm. "If we ever find a priest, you can confess to him. That will help."

Ivy believed him.

She saw little of George over the following few days. Caught up with bringing the kitchen to rights and tidying the house, she was busy. Bethany followed her around like a sticky shadow, big-eyed and solemn.

"Don't worry, Ivy. She'll settle down," said Miss Sarah.

Ivy, seated at the wooden table in the kitchen, plucked the fat hen's feathers and set them aside. Sammy needed a new pillow and would be comforted by her feathers long after he'd eaten the hen for dinner.

"You have given so much, old girl," Ivy said as she pulled the final feather. "Eggs to eat, peeps to raise, meat, and now even your feathers. You did get shelter and food. Was it a fair exchange?"

Peter, his step as springy as ever, came through the door.

"Ah, talking to yourself, Ivy? Talk to me. Tell me what's for dinner."

"This old hen, Peter. Stewed with dumplings, a few carrots, and fresh greens."

"You are a wonder. Did I tell you how happy everyone is to have you back?"

Ivy smiled as she gathered the feathers into a cloth bag.

"Where's Mr. Stokely been, Peter?"

"He's going to the other planters, trying to get help to put out the new plants. Good thing he's so well-liked. What with Christopher and Tom dead, we're in tight quarters, at least until the next ship comes with more workers. Should come shortly. Speaking of work, I need to get out to the fields. Looking forward to reacquaintin' myself with that old biddy there later tonight."

Ivy reached into a nearby crock and pulled out a raisin cookie. She handed it to him.

"Did I say you are a wonder, miss? Very grateful." With a chomp of the cookie, Peter was gone.

Ivy picked up a butcher knife and carried the bird to the yard to gut it. Under her breath, she hummed Phelim's boat song to herself. Her hands were deep in the bird's cavity, tugging, when George appeared, picked up on her song, and began whistling along.

"Oh." Ivy stopped. "Do you need anything? A drink of water, maybe, or cool tea?"

"Don't stop, Ivy. It's a lovely song." He sat on a nearby stump. A fine sheen of perspiration coated his forehead. "I do want to talk something over with you. I'll wait till you're done with that hen."

George wiped his arm across his handsome face. "I'll get my

own drink and be right back."

Ivy finished dressing the meat, cleaned up, then went back into the kitchen where George awaited her.

"Yes, what do you need? I'm sorry I haven't been in the fields much today. Been trying to catch up on the house."

"That's not what I want to discuss with you, Ivy. We need to talk about your future."

"My future? What do you mean?"

"Ivy, I've been thinking about you. You're a young woman and you've had more trouble in your short life than most. I don't want to be one more problem. I want you to have power over your own life—starting where you are right now, as we'll never be able to go backward—to make your own choices."

Ivy's brows knit. "I don't know what you mean. What choices? Like whether I work in the field or in the kitchen? I already make those decisions, for the most part. Haven't I done a good job for you? I am so sorry if I should have been in the field today. Without Tom and Christopher, I know—"

"Stop, Ivy." George reached across the table and cradled her hands between his. "I want you to be able to choose your future. I don't want to hold you here in a continuation of your kidnapping. I have benefited from your tragedy and I feel bad about it. I wasn't thinking. I spend all my energy on my business and never spent enough time thinking about your terrible situation—grabbed away and brought here against your will. I'm so accustomed to having men show up at the wharf ready to work and I was so worried about my needs, Miss Sarah, and the children. I didn't stop and think about you the way I should have. I did come here against my will, but once I reached Maryland, I just wanted to stay and do my bond and become a planter. I guess I assumed the same for you—that you had accepted Maryland as your home."

"What are you talking about, George? I don't understand."

"Ivy, I only want you to work for me by choice, to live here at *Convict's Revenge* if you want to. I am saying, if you want to return to Ireland, I'll not stand in your way. I'll release you from your bond and pay your passage home."

"Home? To Ireland?" Ivy's eyes glistened. She looked out the kitchen window. Off in the distance, a door closed.

"Yes, if you wish. You don't have to say right this minute. You can think about it. But, girl, if you stay, I am only allowing you to work for me as a free woman. I am nullifying your bond and your indenture. I'll pay you wages as a free woman. You'll be free to leave at any time and to marry at any time. I know you have a suitor."

"Kevin only thinks he is a suitor. We have no agreement."

George looked up quickly from their clasped hands.

"Well, you'd be free to marry anyone. I understand Isaac Abner has taken a liking to you, and he's a decent man. One thing there's no shortage of yet in Maryland is men looking for a wife."

"I don't know what to say . . ." A tear rolled down her cheek.

"I'm not finished, girl. I've spoken today with your brother. I made the same offer to Sean. I'm releasing him from his bond, if he wishes. He can stay here and work, work for someone else, or I'll pay his way home. It's the least I can do."

Ivy, sniffling and snorting, blurted out, "You are the kindest man I've ever known. I do love you for this, George."

George colored and withdrew his hands. "Well, take your time. Think about this. Talk it over with your brother. If you work for me for a wage for three years, I'll give you land and set you up just as I would have with the bond. Married or single, I'll help you, Ivy."

George patted Ivy's shoulder and walked off. Ivy had a good

cry, then left to find Sean.

Ivy's thoughts careened in her head, darting and smacking against each other as she hurried to the fields. Ahead, Sean squatted among the erupting tobacco seedlings. Tenderly, he pulled a baby weed out. His glossy black curls hung down, hiding his face.

"Sean. I talked with Stokely. What are we going to do?"

Sean stood up, rubbing the dirt off onto his pants.

"Whatever we want. Whatever we want to do, Ivy. Isn't it grand?"

"My head still spins. I don't know. What do you think?"

"Come on over into the shade, Ivy. I can take a few minutes' break." The siblings walked over to the woodland's fringe and found a large, downed log and sat. Though Sean was short and his hair dark while Ivy was tall and redheaded, their gestures and speech mirrored each other's.

"Ivy, Stokely has outdone himself. I always knew he was a decent man, though this is spectacular. I know one thing. I'll stay in Maryland. Lots of opportunity here and none whatsoever back home in Ireland, sad to say."

"Really? You know you'll stay? What if I want to go home?"

"Then you should. But I'll stay here. Sorry, Ivy. There's not enough to convince me to make another hellacious trip over the sea. Don't want to risk my neck again on such a voyage. Neither should you. Too many people die, one way or the other." Sean waited for Ivy's reply.

"I've had my heart set on returning, though I confess in my time here I've come to enjoy the land. I like the people here, too." Ivy rubbed her hands against her knees. A bird sang.

"I know you were hoping to have a family in Ireland with Kevin, but now he's here. You don't need to go to Ireland to have a family. Though I have to say, sis, I've lost respect for

Kevin. He treated you poorly. Anyway, Maryland's not short of marriageable men. You don't need Kevin."

Ivy nodded. "Kevin showed his true colors, Sean. Don't worry. I'm done with him.

"Will you stay here, Sean? Or work somewhere else? George says if you stay three years he'll fit you out. What do you think?"

"I'm sticking with George. He says I don't have to commit to a time period. If I'm still here in three years, he'll give me one hundred acres and some equipment and a horse. Can't turn up my nose at that offer. George treats us right." Sean paused and caught his sister's eye. "You should stay, too. That's what I think."

"I think you're right, Sean. I want to stay. I do. Let's tell George." And they did.

Chapter 46

Convict's Revenge
Near the Patapsco River, Maryland

June 12, 1701

Life at *Convict's Revenge* settled down. Spring, always a busy time for any farmer, sped by. George brought on three new workers, indentured. However, he spoke with them to ensure they were voluntarily bonding themselves out. He'd switched Peter to a paid employee like Sean and Ivy. Whether he'd do the same with the new workers remained to be seen.

George and Ivy found excuses—none too tiny or too silly—to be together, to help one another, to talk, to share ideas. From time to time, they went off on rambles. At first, George took pains to announce his need to discuss the children, or plan the provisions, or find out what she needed for weaving. Eventually he dropped the explanations. All at *Convict's Revenge* took note and held their breath in optimistic anticipation.

On a Sunday night in June, George came into the kitchen after dinner. Ivy glanced up from the crockery on the table.

"Yes, George? What can I do for you?"

He dimpled a twinkling smile her way. "I'd like to go for

a stroll with you, miss. Leave those things for now. It's a lovely time of day for a conversation."

"Why not talk here? I'm happy to walk with you, but there's all this work to do . . ." Ivy placed a salt-glazed bowl on the windowsill.

"Let's walk. Please." He held out his hand and grasped hers, drawing her toward him.

"Of course. It is lovely out. I'm always happy to wander with you, George."

She had become emboldened since the trial and no longer hesitated to accept George. They walked out. The flock of hens scattered before them. A spotted hog lifted her head in curiosity.

George was correct about the evening's beauty. The faintest of cool breezes caressed Ivy's face. Daylight slowly faded. George took Ivy's hand and led her to the woodland's meandering path. Pine scented the air. A flashy orange-and-black bird winged through the canopy. The gloaming was in full glory by the time they reached the pond. He picked her up and set her atop a large smooth stone bench then sat beside her. A crystalline quarter moon shone suspended in the opening over the pond. Lightning bugs, one by one, began to set their lanterns afire. A frog kerplunked into the water and broke the silence. George, beside her, smiled.

"Ivy, dear, I have a question for you." He reached in his pocket. He opened his broad hand. A ring reflected the light from the moon.

Acknowledgments

Writing is a team sport, and I was fortunate to have a team as talented as they are kind to help me with this book.

Deepest thanks to the Hellenic Writers Group of Washington, D.C. and to Patty Apostolides, its founder and Executive Director. Your critiques, encouragement, patience, and enthusiasm encouraged me to bring this book to fruition.

My beta readers, Dixiane Hallaj, Molly O'Dell, Sheila Ralph, and Beth Smith each added seasoning with their perspectives and tips.

Tahlia Newland gave early and pivotal insight.

Thanks to John DeDakis for his spot-on editorial expertise and willingness to pitch in.

I also owe a tremendous debt to those who bring history to us and keep it alive—researchers, academics, archives, and historical associations such as the Maryland State Archives, Monica C. Wikowski, Ph.D., and the Virginia Department of Historic Resources.

I could not find a more patient pair of listeners and critics than my husband and son—you mean the world to me.

Of course, all errors are unintentional and owned by me.

Enjoyed this book? Please tell others.

Reviews from readers like you help not only other readers find books they enjoy, but they also help everyone involved in bringing a story like Ivy's to life. Don't be shy. Post a review online. Mention the book on social media. Pass your paperback or hard copy on to a friend. Buy a copy for your sister. Your support and enthusiasm mean so much. Thanking you in advance, I look forward to bringing you future books and stories.

To sign up for my mailing list and learn more about the research behind *The Indenture of Ivy O'Neill*, visit my website: https://www.dianehelentjaris.com.

CPSIA information can be obtained
at www.ICGtesting.com
Printed in the USA
BVHW041118250522
637927BV00030B/279/J

9 781922 329318